Ex-National Hunt Champion Jockey John Francome is now a frequent broadcaster on racing for Channel 4 and is fast establishing himself as one of the front runners in the racing thriller stakes.

His previous bestsellers, *Break Neck*, *Outsider*, *Rough Ride*, *Stud Poker*, *Stone Cold* and, with James MacGregor, *Blood Stock*, *Declared Dead*, *Eavesdropper* and *Riding High*, have been enthusiastically praised:

'The racing feel is authentic and it's a pacy, entertaining read' *The Times*

'Francome knows how to write a good racing thriller' *Daily Express*

'Pacy racing and racy pacing ... Francome has found his stride as a solo novelist' *Horse and Hound*

Dead Ringer

John Francome

headline

First published in 1995
by HEADLINE BOOK PUBLISHING

First published in paperback in 1996
by HEADLINE BOOK PUBLISHING

11 12 13 14 15 16 17 18 19 20

ISBN 0 7472 4941 5

Typeset by Keyboard Services, Luton, Beds

Printed and bound in Great Britain by
Mackays of Chatham plc, Chatham, Kent

HEADLINE BOOK PUBLISHING
A division of Hodder Headline PLC
338 Euston Road
London NW1 3BH

Dead Ringer

Chapter One

'Do you think he's really who he says he is?'

The disbelief in Joe Peters's voice was mixed with more than a little envy. His pride wouldn't let him believe that David Tredington, supposedly so inexperienced, could be such a good jockey. Since he had arrived from Ireland less than two months before, David Tredington's name was one that had crept into racing conversations with increasing regularity as his tally of winners had mounted. As far as many of the professionals like Joe Peters were concerned, he looked too tidy, was too sure of himself, and knew too many moves for the amateur he claimed to be. As if that weren't enough to stir the bubbling cauldron of jealousy which was the jockeys' changing-room, David Tredington was also disarmingly good-looking and potentially very rich.

Joe shot a glance at the young man who sat beside him watching the race. 'Come on, Jason, you should know. What do you think?'

Jason Dolton pondered the question as if giving it thought for the first time – which Joe knew couldn't be the case.

Keeping his eyes fixed on the small closed-circuit TV screen in the corner of Fontwell Park weighing-room, Jason watched as the six runners in the Handicap Chase splashed over the water jump.

David Tredington had only one horse behind him. He'd been pushing hard for a circuit and a half of the tiny Sussex course, and although victory seemed, at best, unlikely, it was obvious to anyone watching that defeat was never going to be accepted until certain.

'I don't know, Joey.' Jason Dolton spoke slowly. His expression betrayed none of his feelings. 'But whoever he is, he can certainly ride.'

As the remaining half-dozen runners turned for home through the lashing rain, David Tredington felt he must be blowing harder than his horse. The ache in his legs from pushing it, together with his annoyance at its lack of effort, produced a sudden but not uncommon desire to pick up his whip and deal the lazy grey a couple of telling cracks across its generous quarters; but instinct, the rarest and most important quality in a racing brain, told him to wait. If Groats, his recalcitrant mount, was going to be beaten into any effort at all, it would only be for a short distance. Better to ask for it after the last fence than before the final open ditch which they were approaching.

David could barely see through goggles smeared with mud kicked up by the horses in front. He was contemplating whether or not he should quickly pull the back of his mittened hand across them and face the risk of making visibility even worse, when a lump of wet Sussex earth made the decision for him.

Smoothly, he slipped his whip into his left hand as it rocked with the motion of Groats's big head, and wiped away enough of the mud to restore his vision. His hand was barely back on the rein when, through the sound of sloshing hoofs and jockeys' urgings, came the familiar clatter of horn against wood as the horse directly in front galloped into the guard-rail. The animal hadn't got its back end high enough to fall but, as it crashed through the birch, it was turned sideways by the impact.

For an instant David felt sure he would slam straight into it but, even as the thought was being transmitted to his hands, Groats bobbed his head and moved his feet nimbly to the right, aiming for a narrow gap between the wing of the fence and the awkwardly angled head of the horse in front. David jerked both knees up into the relative safety of the slope of Groats's shoulders a split second before they barged into the other horse's head, shoving it back on course. Its jockey was still recovering from the first collision when the second almost fired him into David's lap. He made a desperate attempt to save himself from falling beneath the trampling feet of both horses, but David pushed him sharply away as he grabbed hopelessly at his slippery breeches. David hated doing it, but there was never a real choice in that situation; your own welfare always came first.

The excitement caused by the collision had somehow affected Groats with a rush of adrenaline. He showed a sudden willingness to take an interest in what was going on. By the time he had jumped one more fence and was approaching the last, he'd recovered the earlier lost ground and was less than two lengths from the leader.

With his horse running at last, David didn't risk the chance of Groats losing his enthusiasm. The prospect of a long uphill slog to the winning post had sullened braver horses than this one. He drew his whip and slapped his horse hard down the flanks to drive him at the final obstacle. For the first time, David sensed that the plodding grey was on his side.

Groats launched himself over and beyond the fence. He landed running, head down and ears laid flat against his neck. David was still pushing hard, squeezing with his legs, urging Groats through the sticky mud. As they rounded the left-hand curve to the post, the horse seemed to sense that it could win. He made one more effort. Twenty yards from the post, he strained his head into the lead, and stayed there, until victory was theirs.

Groats had eased his big frame back to a walk within ten strides of passing the line. His muddied head hung low from this rare exertion. David patted him gratefully on the neck while his own breath came in hard gasps. As they turned back towards the winners' enclosure, David pulled his goggles from his face. He stared down the course and felt some relief as he spotted the colours of the fallen jockey, now walking towards a Land Rover. He had done what any other jockey would have; he knew that. He also knew, because of his success, it would be resented.

David wished his father had been there to see them win. Sir Mark Tredington had bred Groats at his own Great Barford stud, and nothing gave him more pleasure than seeing home-bred horses win, especially now, with his son on board.

To David, Sir Mark's enjoyment from winning was as important as his own. To provide it was a way of repaying the kindness and affection with which his father had welcomed him back to the fold. He had arrived at Barford Manor eight weeks before, like the Prodigal Son returning, unannounced and totally unexpected, after having been away for more than fifteen years.

As Sir Mark hadn't come to the races that day, Sam Hunter, one of his two trainers, came out on to the course to lead Groats to the winner's slot in front of the weighing-room. David's slightly rotund, older cousin George was waiting there, grinning beneath his soggy brown trilby, and waving a bookies' ticket.

'Bloody well done!' he bellowed, slapping David on the back as he dismounted.

Pulling off the saddle, David smiled, still grateful for his cousin's genial reaction to his arrival in England and subsequent success on the race-course. He doubted that he would have reacted in such a gentlemanly way if the roles had been reversed. But then, he wasn't a gentleman, yet.

After he had weighed in and changed, David walked outside and stood under the veranda. The winter dusk was descending fast. The rain had eased to a drizzle that played a diminishing pattern against the light from the building opposite.

George appeared by his side and took him by the elbow. 'Come on, cousin. Time for a drink.'

The pair ran across the saturated lawn under the cover of George's umbrella to the timber-framed members' bar. George pushed his way through a damp, huddled mêlée of racegoers and effusively ordered a bottle of champagne.

David guessed that George had good reason to be grateful on this occasion. It had been Groats's first run for some time and, although everyone at Sam Hunter's yard and Great Barford knew he ran better when fresh, nobody had told the bookies, and he'd started at the generous odds of twelve-to-one.

On the other hand, since David had arrived at Great Barford, George had seen wiped out at a stroke his chances of inheriting most of the Great Barford estate – the baronetcy, the beautiful Queen Anne house, the four thousand acres that surrounded it, the historic stud, and who-knew-what investments in property, industry and international trade – an inheritance worth, it was rumoured, at least ten million.

You'd have to be a saint, David had thought, not to feel a little peeved at having all that snatched from under your nose.

And yet George had welcomed him with as much warmth as Sir Mark. The reception given to David by one of his sisters had been altogether cooler.

'David, that was a brilliant piece of riding!' George was saying. His big red face beamed with admiration. 'I thought you'd had it when that horse almost fell across you at the last ditch, but then you got the old sod going again. Where do you get your energy from?'

David shrugged modestly. 'Well, you'd get fit if you'd ridden some of the nags I have in the little races round Mayo,' he said with the West of Ireland lilt he'd brought with him to Barford Manor.

A few more people – some complete strangers, some

who had befriended him since he had started winning races in England – came over to congratulate him on his modest victory. He accepted their praise with diffident charm, a smile and a nod.

George stood by, sharing his cousin's glory. 'Do you need a lift home?' he asked when they had been left alone for a moment.

'It's OK. I've got the Range Rover.'

George nodded absently. 'It's a pity I had to come from London or we could all have come together. Are you going back home along the M27, then up through Salisbury?'

David nodded.

'Let's meet up for a half-way pint, then,' George said. 'There's a decent pub in Mere.'

'Sure. I'll see you there, but I'll be a while. I want a word with Sam before he leaves.'

George gestured his willing acceptance of this. 'No problem.'

David found Sam Hunter checking his two runners before they started their long journey home.

Sam was driving the lorry himself, and wouldn't reach his yard until an hour or so after David. For a while they discussed a mare David was going to look at there. As David left, Sam asked, 'How are you getting back?'

'In the Range Rover. I brought Mickey with me.'

'Mickey?' Sam asked. 'Who's he?'

'He's that lad who works in the stud; comes up with me sometimes when I ride work. He was that keen to come to the races, I asked Dad...' he hesitated, '...if he

7

could come. He's just seventeen, a slip of a man and racing mad. It won't be long before he starts getting a few rides himself. He has a talent, that's for sure. I'll be sending him along to you when he's ready. Anyway, I'd better have a look for him before he gets into bad company.'

Mickey was outside the jockeys' changing-room, gazing with fascination at the familiar faces of the better-known riders as if they were film-stars. He turned to David with a mischievous grin across his boyish face. 'You ought to pick on jockeys your own standard. Then let's see how good you are.'

David laughed at his cheek and squeezed the young lad's left earlobe between his thumb and forefinger. 'I was just thinking what a nice easy ride he'd be for you to start your career on. He'd make you give up smoking soon enough.' David gave the ear a sharp twist.

'Well done!' Mickey squealed in submission.

'Come on. Let's get going.'

David collected his gear from the weighing-room and they walked together to the jockeys' car-park. They climbed into a brand-new metallic maroon Range Rover, and set off towards Chichester and the M27.

Sir Mark had asked David to stop off in Somerset to make a judgement on a well-bred mare that one of Sam Hunter's owners wanted to sell. It wasn't much of a detour on the long drive back to Devon, and David had only had the one ride; it was a small favour. Besides, he was pleased that his own judgement should be trusted.

Mickey subjected him, as he always did, to a barrage

of eager questions. 'Tell me when you thought you were going to win. Why didn't you hit him earlier?' the boy urged.

David responded with equal enthusiasm. He liked Mickey – he was totally uncomplicated, judged people on what he saw, not what he heard from others. He had been brought up to make the most of life by parents who doted on him and yet as an only child he hadn't been spoiled. He and David had spent hours chatting as they got on with the jobs around the yard.

'If I have to get blisters to get rides, then that's fine,' Mickey had once said. 'Of course, if I had a rich dad like yours, I'd have been champion jockey twice by now.'

The banter continued as they headed for the motor-way; as they talked, David enjoyed the experience of driving the Range Rover, the smell of the leather upholstery, the four-speaker CD system, the phone and all the other gadgets which were new to him. In Mayo, his only motor had been a rusty Toyota pick-up which didn't even have a radio.

He was feeling thoroughly contented, savouring his eighth win since he'd taken out his English jockey's licence. Judging from what he'd seen of the other half-dozen horses his father had put at his disposal, there'd be plenty more to come before the season closed.

He thought, too, about the profound changes in his life that his decision to come to England had brought about.

When his son had turned up at Barford Manor in early September, Sir Mark Tredington, a life-long agnostic, had almost been prepared to believe in a good and merciful God.

David had disappeared when he was twelve, shortly after Sir Mark's wife, Henrietta, had died from a vicious fall whilst out hunting. The boy had been desperately fond of his mother, and the letter which had arrived, post-marked Bristol, had spelt out his deep unhappiness: he was finding it too hard to cope with his mother's death and his father's constant absences. It seemed he had simply decided to run away from home, for good.

Despite the intensive search that had been mounted, no trace of the boy had been found. Police had combed every inch of the estate, dragged every river-bed and lake, and searched every cave along the coast, but they had come back with not so much as a single sighting.

It had taken Sir Mark a long time to come to terms with the loss of his wife and his only son. Those few who knew him well agreed that he had never really accepted either; the dull ache of loneliness had never disappeared. It had just become more bearable as time passed.

For the past seven generations, the Tredington family had handed down their inheritance on a strict basis of primogeniture. That was what had kept the estate intact, and Sir Mark, though no rabid traditionalist, didn't want to break with this particular custom. Without David, his next natural heir was George, the son of his younger brother, Peregrine – a soldier, and one of the most senior officers killed by the Argentinians in the South Atlantic War.

George was a few years older than David, a podgy, awkward sixteen-year-old when his cousin had run away. Although his features bore a discernible likeness to David's, he lacked his lissomeness and precocious self-confidence.

But as hopes of David's return faded, George had grown increasingly aware of his new status, and he had taken the role seriously. He'd left his public school with results as good as his moderate ability allowed, and joined a merchant bank in the City where he had found his métier. He had an instinctive eye for a risk, and now, at the age of thirty-two, was well on the way to a directorship. The slightly disgruntled boy had become a secure and self-confident man, prospering and preparing for his eventual ownership of the Great Barford estate.

Sir Mark also had two daughters, Lucy and Victoria, who were fond of each other, but different in both character and looks.

Lucy, the elder by two years, was twenty-six, a committed artist with three years at the RCA behind her and two solo shows to her credit. She had had the good fortune to take after her mother; almost five feet ten tall, with a taut, well-kept body. Her dark curly hair, cut loosely around her oval face, fell to below her shoulders. Her brown eyes were perhaps a shade too close together, suggesting a sharpness of character, but overall she was a beauty. She still loved spending time at Barford, but now lived and worked in a small mews house in Chelsea.

Victoria loved horses and the country, which was as well. The glitz of London life could never have been a happy setting for her. Where Lucy's looks were guaranteed to attract attention, Victoria's plainness brought only the occasional curious stare. She was four inches shorter than her sister, stoutly made, with biceps that bulged from heaving feed-buckets. She had a square jaw and straight brown hair cut short. She refused to wear make-up, or a dress or a skirt on any but the most special occasions, normally, it was jeans, jumper and jodhpur boots.

To her family's thinly disguised disappointment, she had got married young, two years before, to a professional jockey a few years older than her. Jason Dolton was the son of an underpaid Somerset farm-worker. With no justification, he had grown up thinking that life owed him a living. He was a bad loser, and ungrateful on the rare occasions that success came his way. His short ginger hair, and a mouth that was little more than a red pencil line across his face, alerted observant strangers to the chippy character they were about to encounter. He was never going to ride more than a few dozen winners a season, and had a reputation for being easily persuaded to change his tactics for a race.

Everyone except Victoria assumed that he had married her for the four-hundred-acre farm which her father was rumoured to have settled on her. In fact, Sir Mark had always intimated that his daughters would receive a farm each; when George inherited he could incorporate Braycombe into the whole estate to make up for them. Now that David had come back, though, it looked as if this wouldn't happen.

The sisters took this change of fortune in their stride; Jason Dolton was less accepting. He viewed David not only as an unwelcome and privileged rival on the race-course, but also as the cause of his being deprived of a farm he'd long considered as a dowry. Ingenuously, Victoria couldn't see why her husband resented David so vehemently, and tried to make up for it by being extra kind to her brother, which only increased Jason's resentment.

Although, since his return, the sisters had warmed to his charm and uncanny skill on a horse, their brother's return had not provided for them the life-line that it had for their father.

There remained between the girls and David a void, an emotional gap stretching back more than fifteen important years that could never be retrieved. Their brother, likable and charming as he was, had once betrayed them and lost their trust. He wouldn't recover it lightly; certainly not from the more self-sufficient Lucy.

The rain was driving harder as the Range Rover swept smoothly towards the motorway.

David glanced at Mickey, asleep now in the passenger seat, and grinned through the windscreen and hard-working wipers as his headlamps pierced the gloomy night. He had a vision of the reception waiting for him back at Barford – exuberance from Sir Mark and Victoria; quiet approval from Lucy; and grudging, ungenerous congratulations from Susan Butley, Sir Mark's secretary, who, while not exactly part of the family, was a resident influence in their lives.

Although she had started life from the other end of the social scale from the Tredingtons, Susan Butley possessed an aloofness and self-confidence normally associated with girls from privileged backgrounds. David had been instantly attracted by the strength of her personality and good looks. Her father, Ivor, had been a respected head-groom at Barford, although he had left under a cloud soon after his wife and child walked out on him fourteen years before. But it wasn't out of guilt or pity that the Tredingtons had absorbed Susan into their lives as a necessary counter-balance to their own mildness. Her intelligence and organisational skills were obvious, and she was fiercely committed to Barford. Perhaps that was why she had been the only person besides Jason Dolton who had been unwilling to accept David.

'A bloody cuckoo – that's what you are,' she had said to him privately, soon after he had arrived. When he had asked her to explain, she'd turned her back on him and walked away. The hostility he had encountered in her during those first days at Barford hadn't diminished in the weeks since. She made it plain that she didn't trust him or his motives in turning up in the way he had.

It was a not uncommon irony that, of all the people who had come into David's life recently, she interested him most; that for a very brief interlude, before she knew who he was, there was no doubt that she had not found him altogether unattractive.

The M27 motorway on the edge of Portsmouth was bathed in orange light. David relaxed a little as he pulled out into the fast lane to pass a pair of trucks lumbering abreast of each other.

The Range Rover swished under the first exit at a steady ninety, as if it were sucking up the road beneath. David held the wheel lightly, tapping his fingers to the beat of the music. He leaned across to turn up the stereo against the noise of the wind. As his eyes came back to the road, he almost dismissed as imaginary the solid object which seemed to part company from the overhead bridge at the Fareham junction.

A survival reaction less than a microsecond from his brain had both hands yanking the steering wheel to the left before he was even conscious that it was no illusion. In the same instant, he jammed his right foot on to the brake pedal. The tyres screeched as they strained at the wheel-rims; their rubber burned through the surface water into the tarmac.

David yelled, staring with wide-eyed horror as whatever it was crashed down and bounced straight across his path. The Range Rover's front off-side wheel smashed into the bulky object and sent the vehicle into a violent whirligig spin, pirouetting across the carriageway in front of the lorries they had just passed, heading uncontrollably towards the inner concrete piers of the bridge.

David froze with fear. On a bolting horse he'd have thought of a dozen different ways to deal with the crisis; in a careering Range Rover, he had fewer options.

The vast slab of a wall spun into view a matter of yards away now. The car was hurtling crazily towards it. And David knew there was nothing, absolutely *nothing* he could do.

He had only one trick left up his sleeve. 'Please Lord,' he begged instinctively, 'forgive me and save us.'

He didn't have time to specify if it was his body or his soul he wanted saved.

The Range Rover hit the wall at a forty-degree angle, smashing the near-side front wing on the unforgiving concrete, the car shrieking and scraping thirty feet until it met a substantial protruding buttress.

The left-hand side of the vehicle buckled savagely.

The front near-side pillar became a jagged spear – and a weapon which lanced the chest of his terrified passenger.

Beside him, David heard an anguished howl as the bucking vehicle rocketed out from under the bridge, slewed across the hard shoulder, mounted the shallow banking, tipped over on to its roof, slithered along the shingle at the edge of the road, mounted the bank again, rolled back on to its wheels and, mercifully, came to a juddering halt on the hard shoulder.

The engine had cut out and petrol vapour filled the crunched and shrunken metal box where David still sat, momentarily blacked out and still strapped in.

The silence which followed was broken by the hiss of steam from a ruptured radiator and the clatter of smashed, dislodged parts falling to the ground.

David blinked his eyes open, listening, disoriented, disbelieving.

After a moment, he raised his head until it touched the caved-in roof, moved his neck, his torso, his legs and knew that, if nothing else, he was alive.

In the eerie orange glow of the motorway lights he looked at the 'slip of a man' beside him.

Mickey sat rigid-still on a nest of shattered glass; pale, open-eyed, red-breasted, impaled to the back of his seat.

For several moments more, David couldn't move as he

tried to absorb the blunt, horrifying fact of the boy's death.

There was no sleep for David that night in the accident and emergency wing of Portsmouth hospital, only a few snatched moments of unconsciousness between conversations with ambulance-men, doctors and policemen – conversations in which he was restricted to monosyllables and gestures of the head, because he could barely hear or understand what was being said; everything was blocked out by the constantly recurring picture of Mickey's mutilated body. But he did manage to ask a policeman to phone Sir Mark and tell him what had happened to Mickey, so that the boy's parents could be told as gently as possible.

When his eyes flickered open in Tuesday morning's grim, grey-brown light, David's temples throbbed as if he'd spent the night drinking bad poteen with a Galway tinker. And the picture of the boy was still in his head.

He kept his eyes open to hold the vision at bay; took in the stark, functional furnishings of a hospital room. He moved and remembered there was nothing wrong with him, no more than a bruise or two, but – he had a vague memory – they were worried about delayed concussion, shock, trauma; he hadn't needed much persuading to stay.

He shed the hospital pyjamas. Slowly and mechanically he pulled on the beige cord jeans and checked shirt he had been wearing the night before. A nurse came in to chide him for getting up before he'd been looked at. He

17

submitted himself to a simple examination, assured her that, physically, he was in no discomfort, and declined any breakfast. He wanted to ask about Mickey, but he didn't: there was no point; he knew the answer.

He asked for a telephone and dialled Barford. Victoria answered. He could tell from her voice that her relief that David was still alive was too great to admit the full impact of Mickey's death. Sir Mark and George, she said with a hint of resentment, were already separately on their way to Portsmouth to see him.

While David waited gratefully for his father, a policeman arrived to take a more coherent statement than he had been able to extract the night before.

There was, it seemed, no blame to be attached to David. The object that had fallen from the bridge had been one of a stack of old railway sleepers which had slipped from the back of a lorry as it swung through the roundabout above the motorway.

Half a dozen more sleepers had been found on the bridge; the lorry which had been carrying them had not. It was a minor junction, not much used; no witnesses had come forward so far.

Sir Mark could barely speak when he and George arrived, so great was his gratitude that David had survived. George was full of blustering sympathy.

'I've just seen the Range Rover. I can't believe you're still alive,' he said, shaking his head.

'I wish I wasn't.'

George ignored this. 'I thought something must have gone wrong when you didn't turn up at the pub in Mere, or at Sam's. I'm afraid it was only when I got home that I realised how bad it was, otherwise I'd have come back down last night. Now, you relax and I'll look after everything. Mickey's mother and father are already here. I don't think they can cope at all. I ought to go and see what I can do for them.'

He bustled out, leaving Sir Mark gazing at David with worried eyes in a face made haggard by a sleepless night.

'I can't tell you how thankful I am that you didn't die, David,' he said huskily.

David didn't answer for a moment. 'I'm sorry,' he said at last.

'Good God! What have you got to apologise for?'

'I'm not apologising. I'm just terribly sorry Mickey had to die.'

Sir Mark didn't react. He stood. 'Look, I'm afraid I can't stand hospitals. I gather you'll be here for a while so that they can check you out before you go. Now I've seen you're OK, I'm going back home. George can bring you back.'

Though he wanted to, David didn't try to stop his father. He watched Sir Mark leave the small room with his characteristic ambling gait, grateful for the concern.

On behalf of the boy's parents, George handled details of the transfer of Mickey's body back to Devon, and the parents left for their home without seeing David.

Later in the morning, the hospital let David go. Once he was installed comfortably in the passenger seat of George's car, they drove to the recovery yard to which the mangled Range Rover had been taken.

They inspected it in silence, neither able to refer to the

blood which was still visible on the buckled pillar. Walking away, George said again, quietly, 'It looks as though you were very, very lucky to get out of there alive.'

David nodded, guilty that it had been he, and not Mickey, who had walked away.

'What a terrifying piece of bad luck,' George went on. 'The odds against an accident like that happening must be several million to one. Let's hope they find the bastard who was driving the truck.'

David nodded again, thinking about the odds. Suddenly, and for no apparent reason, he remembered his brief encounter with a man called Emmot MacClancy at Newbury the Saturday before, and the little Irishman's damp, vindictive eyes. What if it hadn't been an accident? What, for God's sake, if MacClancy had really meant what he'd said? The man hadn't looked as if he had the resources, physical or material, to carry out the threat he'd made against David, not like this – and yet ... George was right, the odds against it happening accidentally were several million, probably several hundred million, to one.

But he couldn't tell the police – not about MacClancy; that would only open up a line of enquiry which would do nothing to help Mickey Thatcher now.

David stared at the road in front of him as George turned on to the motorway which had been the scene of the previous night's horror. He could hardly bring himself to look at the newly scarred concrete walls. He glanced up at the bridge and thought about a lorry dropping part of its load, just at that spot, just at that time...

* * *

George drove into the village of Barford a little before three. David asked him to stop in the village and wait for him for a few minutes. He climbed stiffly from the car. He knew roughly where Mickey Thatcher had lived, but asked in the post office for a precise address. The old postmistress shook her head forlornly as she gave it to him. She could remember Mickey coming into the post office when he was a week old. 'You'd have seen him too, Mr David. You was often down here then, wanting them sherbet lemons.'

David nodded. 'It's a terrible thing. He was a great little lad; eager as a ferret to be a jockey.'

'And him the only child they had.'

David walked the hundred yards along the village street to see Mickey's parents. Mrs Thatcher opened the door to him. Her eyes were wet and bleak. She was only in her mid-thirties, but the loss of a son had aged her ten years at a stroke. She didn't speak at first, wanting to blame someone for what had happened; seeing David as the culprit, knowing that wasn't fair.

'Could I come in?' he asked gently.

She nodded, opening the door wider, and led him into the small front room of the stone cottage.

Her husband, a mechanic at the village garage, sat on one of two worn easy chairs with his head in his hands. When David came in, he looked up, making no effort to hide the tears dribbling down his russet cheeks.

David took a couple of paces towards him, and placed a hand on his shoulder. 'I came straight here,' he said, 'to tell you how desperately sorry I am. I guess you wish he'd never come with me to the races.'

The father shook his head. 'Nothing weren't going to stop him going. It weren't your fault, no way,' he said generously. 'And he'd have been so happy to see Groats win; he was sure he would.' The man's shoulders shook as he lowered his head.

'He was more than happy about it, I promise you,' David said. 'If there's anything, anything I can do at all...' he went on, knowing that there was nothing he or anyone could do beyond recognising the depth of their grief. As he left the cottage he considered the grim irony that Sir Mark Tredington had found his son again and, as a result, the Thatchers had lost theirs.

As George drove him the last mile to the manor, David unconsciously braced himself to handle his family. They wouldn't blame him, of course, but he couldn't stop blaming himself.

If – and it was a small 'if' – someone, MacClancy maybe, *had* caused the accident, then David could blame no one but himself for Mickey's death.

George turned the car in through the main gates to the park which surrounded the manor and drove slowly along a four-hundred-yard drive beneath an avenue of robust old oaks in the final shedding of their gold-brown leaves.

The drive curved right to reveal the house in all its classic Queen Anne symmetry of dressed red sandstone. The simple beauty of the place gave David a tingle of pleasure every time he saw it, and he still hadn't adjusted himself to the idea that one day, with all the rolling acres around it, it would be his. At that moment, though, such thoughts were a long way from his mind. His reappearance at Barford was already causing problems, and the longer he was here, the worse they would become. He should have left well alone, stayed out of trouble in Ireland.

George pulled up among several other cars scattered at the back of the house. He didn't turn the motor off. He promised to come back later. 'You'll want to see the others without my being there, I'm sure.'

David was grateful for his sensitivity. He let himself out of the car to enter the house through a back door and a warren of flagstoned gunrooms and pantries. He looked into the kitchen. Lucy glanced up from the paper she was thumbing through while talking to a stout, aproned housekeeper.

Her expression, normally good-natured but slightly cynical, was warm with sympathy. She stood up in her paint-spattered smock and came to greet her brother with her arms outstretched.

'Poor David. What a horrific thing to happen. And poor little Mickey. I'm so sorry,' she said, wrapping an arm around his shoulder.

'I've just seen his parents.' He shrugged at the inadequacy of it. 'They'll not get over it, ever. Jesus, I feel terrible about it.'

'Don't be absurd. It wasn't your fault. How on earth did a railway sleeper fall over the side of a bridge, for God's sake?'

Inside his head, David registered a picture of Mac-Clancy pushing it.

'I don't know. But maybe I was driving too fast and

23

could have avoided it. Whatever, I can't help blaming myself.'

'I don't see as how you're to blame at all, Mr David,' Mrs Rogers, the housekeeper, said. 'It was an accident, pure and simple.'

David shook his head, unconvinced. 'If he hadn't come to the races with me, those people would still have a son; there's no escaping from that.'

'I think Dad's in his study,' Lucy said. 'He'll want to see you.'

'Sure. I'll go now.'

David gently removed Lucy's arm and, with his head bowed, walked through a faded green baize door into the hall and across the polished oak floor to his father's study.

Sir Mark Tredington's eyes showed a gladness to see him that made David burn with shame. The baronet rose slightly breathlessly from his chair to put an arm around his son's shoulder.

'Thank God you're back and nothing happened to you,' he said with an embarrassing intensity of feeling. 'You look a lot better than you did this morning. Is there any damage still?'

'A couple of bruises where my head hit the wheel, that's all. Less than I deserve. But Mickey's dead, and the car's a write-off.'

'It's terrible about the lad. He could have had quite a future. It couldn't matter less about the car, though. Look, sit down, have a drink.' He walked to a small cabinet and took out whisky and glasses. As he poured, a thought occurred to him. 'By the way, I didn't want to ask you in hospital. Did the police breathalyse you?'

David took his glass and sat down. He nodded. 'They did, and it scarcely registered. I'd only had a couple of glasses of champagne with George.'

'That's a great relief. When I spoke to George last night, I got the impression you'd had a fair bit – understandable after that win.' Sir Mark gave a short laugh. 'Well done, by the way. With all this drama, I haven't had a chance to congratulate you. I watched the race on SIS; the way you kept that old villain running was tremendous. I really thought he'd thrown in the towel at one point.'

'I expect he'll take a lot more coaxing next time. Still, he won this time, that's the main thing.'

David's younger sister, Victoria, had come into the room while they were talking.

'Groats was brilliant, wasn't he,' she said excitedly, unable to disguise her priorities. Her soft brown eyes shone from her round face. 'I wish I'd been there.' The choice of Groats's sire had been hers, and she had been making a fuss of the horse since the day she had watched it emerge from its mother in the foaling box.

'He was brilliant,' David agreed soberly.

'I'm sorry,' Victoria blurted. 'How awful of me, going on about a horse after what happened to Mickey. Poor Mickey. But are you all right?' she added quickly.

David briefly assured her he was. He was saved the torment of answering her next question by Sir Mark, who promised to explain to her later just what had happened. 'I must help the Thatchers with arrangements,' Sir Mark went on, thinking of his duties. 'I'd better pop in and see them. Perhaps you ought to do the same, David.'

'I already did.'

Sir Mark looked pleased and proud of his son. 'Good.' He placed a firm hand on David's shoulder and gently rocked it. 'Good. That was absolutely the right thing to do.'

David thought about the 'right thing to do' as he walked down to the village in the weak November sunshine that pierced the clouds from the south-west.

The wind rustled crackling leaves, and gulls keened and shrieked above him in competition with the raucous calls of homing crows.

Glimpses of the stark, rolling contours of Exmoor reminded him of his home in Mayo, where his soul still lived.

When he reached the village, he headed for the old red phone-box. He had already made up his mind what he wanted to say to Johnny Henderson, but he was going to have to do it face to face. He dialled a London number. Twice he was answered by the frustrating long bleeps of the engaged tone. When, finally, he heard Johnny's voice at the other end of the line, he knew it was going to be hard to persuade Johnny to accept his decision.

'I want a word with you,' David said.

'About what happened yesterday?'

'What d'you think?'

'Are there any other problems?'

'Not yet, but for sure there could well be.'

'There was always that possibility,' Johnny said, allowing agitation to show through his normally seamless charm. 'But, OK. I'll meet you in Lynmouth tomorrow evening. I wanted to come down and see Lucy anyway. Seven o'clock, in the Anchor. We can have a drink there, then take a drive.'

Over twenty-four hours, David thought. He hoped he could keep resolved until then.

'Right. I'll see you there.'

'Well done yesterday, by the way. I won twelve hundred quid.'

'Well, Mickey Thatcher didn't,' David said angrily. 'Just make sure you're there tomorrow.'

David hung up and stood stiffly, still mentally continuing the conversation. After a moment he barged open the door of the smelly cubicle and set off for home.

Johnny Henderson sat on a stool in the saloon bar of the Anchor hotel. His long legs stretched lankily in front of him, clad in the first and, as it happened, last country tweed suit he'd had made in Savile Row ten years before. The well-worn, slightly shabby raffishness of his Jermyn Street shirt, tie and shoes indicated equally either considerable wealth or advanced penury.

Johnny was a classically good-looking type, sandy-haired and bright-blue-eyed. He was brimful of old-Etonian confidence, but he lacked the financial back-up needed to realise the potential of these attributes. At thirty, heavy drinking and minimal exercise were beginning to make their mark on his once flawless features. As the physical ravages increased, so the once easy, natural charm with which he had faced the world had developed a slightly desperate, over-stated edge.

27

He was discovering that the looks, intelligence and charm which had made life so easy for his first thirty years had not prepared him for the job of making a serious living.

He had drifted into the field of bloodstock because he knew a little about race-horses and a lot about the people who owned them. His contacts had earned him his first clients; his lack of application had subsequently lost him most of them. He had come more and more to rely on an unreliable source of income from gambling. The occasional piece of high-quality information had saved him from going under completely, but life was lived on a knife-edge, and the women he pursued, no longer in the first flush of innocence, were beginning to expect more from a man than good looks, easy charm and reasonable – though inconsistent – performance in bed.

The smile which seldom left Johnny's public face was aimed now at the appreciative girl behind the bar. He flicked back his fringe as he took another drink from a pint glass, and she laughed at the story he had just told. He was Sir Mark Tredington's godson, well known at the Anchor and, generally, well liked.

He had stayed in the small hotel a few times in his ongoing pursuit of Lucy Tredington, usually on the pretext of seeing some local trainer or potential owner. In the old days, when he'd spent a lot of time at Barford Manor, he and George had sneaked in and had their first pint of bitter together, under-age and under the indulgent eye of a since-dead landlord.

When David walked in, Johnny was still flirting with the self-possessed but not immune barmaid.

Johnny turned on his stool. 'Hello, David. Let me get you a pint, then we'll go and have a look at this horse.' He greeted him with a heartiness he wasn't feeling.

'Sure, thanks Johnny, but I'll have a Murphy's. I've still not got used to your English bitter.'

'Yours too, David, now you've returned to the fold.'

When they got outside about twenty minutes later, Johnny didn't disguise his nervousness. 'We'll take my car and drive up to the moors.'

They got into his old BMW. They didn't speak as Johnny drove out of the small town via a narrow sunken lane that led up towards the looming contours of the moor. Johnny knew what was on David's mind. He'd lain awake most of the night searching for answers. They were playing a game that needed both of them, and Johnny had no intention of letting David throw in his hand now. He slowed to negotiate a hairpin bend round a dingle and glanced at David. 'Now, what the hell's the problem?'

'I'm pulling out of the deal,' David said bluntly. 'It's gone too far. Mickey was killed yesterday; I think it was meant to be me.'

'What the hell are you talking about?'

'I think it was set up. Someone was waiting for me at that bridge.'

'Don't be crazy. Who the hell would want to do that?'

'I don't know, but it could have been Emmot Mac-Clancy.'

'MacClancy? That chap who talked to you at Newbury last week?'

'That's right.'

'Why the hell should he try to kill you?'

'I don't know.'

'I mean, what does he know about what went on in Ireland?'

'That I don't know either, but he seemed pretty damned sure of himself. Of course, I bluffed it out, told him he was talking through his hat; but he knows something.'

'Well if he did, then surely he'd have tried to get some money out of you; and you can't get money out of a dead man. Who is he, anyway?'

'He says he's a Mayo man; I don't know who he is, but I'm not going to take a chance on his blowing this thing wide open.'

The north-westerly blowing off the Bristol Channel was carrying in a bank of black clouds, heavy with rain. Fat drops began to drum on the roof of Johnny's car where he had parked it at the entrance to a deserted barn on the northern slopes of the moor.

Johnny reached for his cigarettes and lit one, trying to keep the lid on his frustration. He couldn't blame David. There had always been the chance that someone, somewhere would appear out of the woodwork to point a finger.

He inhaled a deep drag.

'You told me that no one in London knew where you went when you left for Ireland. How the hell would this chap have connected you with the twelve-year-old boy you were then?'

'God knows. But from the way he spoke, he bloody well knew what was going on.'

'It's a real bastard, this happening now, when it's all going so well.'

'You're missing the point, Johnny! For Christ's sake, a kid, a perfectly innocent kid, has died!'

'That wasn't your fault.'

'Of course it was. If someone's trying to kill me, or warn me or whatever, it's because of what I've done; there's no getting away from that.'

Johnny didn't reply for a moment. He took several more long drags on his cigarette. 'Look,' he said at last, 'there's no point in your playing the white man now. For a start, it would shatter your father if you were carted off to jail. You must know that he's chuffed to bits to have you back. I haven't seen him so chirpy for years.'

David knew this, and it mattered to him. 'OK. We'll look into this MacClancy business first and find out what the score is. Maybe it won't cost a lot to shut him up, if he really does have a line.' He made a quick decision, and hoped he wouldn't change his mind. 'Look, you saw him at Newbury. Would you recognise him again?'

'Of course,' Henderson nodded with relief.

'You'll have to hang around until you spot him at the races. Somehow you've got to find out where he lives.'

'What am I supposed to do then?'

'Don't worry. Just find out where he lives. I'll do the rest.'

Chapter Two

Later, in the small stone farmhouse where he had lived since moving back to Barford, David lay awake, alone, torn apart by what had happened.

Darkness seemed to intensify the feelings of grief and guilt which daylight had made bearable. He couldn't divert his thoughts from the images which kept flashing into his mind – images of what he had been, of what he had chosen to do, of Mickey, large as death, impaled on the seat beside him.

Tired of the torment, David groped for the switch of his bedside light and clicked it on. He sat with his back against the wooden headboard, his knees tucked up.

Was he really the cause of Mickey's death? Maybe it was, as everyone said, an accident after all.

The warm glow from the lampshade began to calm him, and his thoughts became more rational. But still he couldn't be certain. It was only a few hours before dawn that doubt finally allowed him to slip into a crumpled heap and sleep.

He was woken by Victoria jangling his brass doorbell. Bleary-eyed, he went down and let her in.

'God, you look rough. What were you up to last night?'

David ran his tongue around his teeth. It felt as if he'd been sucking cotton wool all night. His first attempt at speech was more of a croak. 'Nothing worth talking about.'

Victoria offered little sympathy and walked past him into the cottage. 'You've forgotten, haven't you, I'm coming over to Sam's with you this morning? And if we don't get a move on, you'll be too late for second lot. I was still in bed when Jason left to ride first lot.'

David groaned and pushed all the doubts and indecisions of the previous night to the back of his mind. That morning he was due to ride out on Deep Mischief, the Tredington entry for the Hennessy Gold Cup. He'd had his first race on the gelding at Newbury the previous Saturday, over the same course and distance as the Hennessy, and had ridden him into second place. He was fairly sure that, if he'd known the course, he would have won, easily. He was absolutely sure that Deep Mischief was the best horse he'd ever ridden.

'Thank God you came round,' he said to Victoria. 'I clean forgot to set my alarm. Would you ever make a pot of coffee for me while I get dressed and pull a razor across my face?'

'Sure.' Victoria smiled and went through to the tidy little farmhouse kitchen.

Later, driving his father's Mercedes the fifty miles to Sam Hunter's yard, David had to fight again to banish the images of the night before. At the same time, he did his best to keep up with Victoria's enthusiastic prattle. She noticed his reticence.

'You're a bit gloomy this morning,' she remarked. 'Sorry, am I going on a bit? It's just so great to have someone who'll talk to me about the horses, especially a brother who's turned out to be a star jockey.'

'I wouldn't say "star" was the word.'

'Well, you will be, if you win the Hennessy.'

That was more or less true, at least as far as an amateur rider was concerned, and it wasn't going to improve already strained relations with his brother-in-law. 'But I don't suppose Jason's too happy about it,' David said. 'He told me he was getting the ride, until I turned up.'

Victoria looked through her passenger window, across the misty Somerset levels. 'I don't know why he said that. I'm sure Dad didn't promise him the ride.' She turned and gave David a look of embarrassed anguish. 'I'm really sorry he's been so difficult with you.'

David shrugged. 'It's understandable. He's probably thinking of you. I guess he feels you've been sort of cheated out of what you were expecting by my coming back after you'd all given me up for good.'

'That's not true, David. I always knew you'd come back. And anyway, it isn't not getting the farm that makes Jason so tricky with you. I'm afraid he hates it when you win. I mean, if you *do* win the Hennessy, he'll be furious. I just wish he'd accept that he's part of the family now, and show a bit of loyalty.'

'Well, we've a long way to go before we win the Hennessy,' David said lightly. 'And if we do, it'll be the horse who's done it, not me.'

Victoria nodded glumly. When David didn't speak for a few miles, she said quietly, 'Sorry about my rabbiting on so much. I expect you're still upset about Mickey.'

'I am.'

She glanced at him, concerned by the tone of his voice. But it wasn't in her nature to press. 'OK. I'll shut up.'

The lads at Sam Hunter's yard liked having David out with them. He spoke their language and he'd earned their respect by showing them that he could ride the trickiest horses in the yard, as well as the best. Deep Mischief was notorious for dropping lads at the bottom of the gallops, but he'd never yet got the better of David.

That morning, the circumstances of Mickey's death dominated their conversation. The lads made it clear they considered David blameless, but all of them wanted to know exactly what had happened; how a railway sleeper could have fallen off a bridge accidentally.

A couple of them suggested it had been some stupid kids, fooling around. David wondered if they were right. He'd feel a lot less guilty if they were.

Deep Mischief strode out forcefully on the way up to Hunter's gallops on a low ridge above the River Parrett. Every so often, the horse would test David's resolve by jiggling, preparing for a buck or a plunge. David knew the signs, firmly admonished the horse, and sat hard into the saddle to show he was aware of what it had in mind.

Sam had paired him up with one of the stable's star chasers.

'Don't overdo him. If you feel him getting tired, keep hold of his head. This is his first piece of hard work since Newbury,' he shouted as the string left the yard.

Sam needn't have worried about the horse getting tired. He didn't have the speed of his workmate, but he was relentless in his stride. The four-length gap by

which the other horse had pulled clear after seven
furlongs had been reduced to half a length by the time
they reached the end. A bit further, and David knew
which one would win. If the ground remained soft for the
Hennessy, the race would become a slog, and Deep
Mischief would be in his element.

But as they clopped back into the yard, the nightmare
of the crash seeped inexorably to the forefront of his consciousness. As soon as he had jumped off Deep Mischief
and thrown the reins to a lad, he walked quickly to the
Mercedes and got in. In the quiet insulation of the car,
he picked up the phone and dialled Portsmouth police
station.

After a frustrating few minutes, he was speaking to
the constable who was handling what had evidently
been logged as a fatal accident.

'No, there's nothing new to report, sir. We put out an
appeal for witnesses who might have been on the bridge
at the time, but so far no one's come forward.'

'But for Christ's sake, surely someone must have
noticed a truck hurtling around with a stack of sleepers
on board?'

'No need to worry about that, sir,' the policeman said
frostily. 'Obviously, we're doing all we can to trace
whoever was responsible; after all, they could face a
prosecution for criminal negligence as there was a
fatality involved. If we need to talk to you again, or we
make any more progress, we'll let you know.'

Johnny Henderson stood on the platform at Ascot race-
course railway station, hands dug deep into the pockets
of his long brown coat. When he had seen Emmot

37

MacClancy at Newbury, he had recognised all the characteristics of a regular race-goer; one of that band of men who travelled from course to course, subsisting mysteriously on unidentifiable sources of income in which winning bets could have played only a small part. Johnny had to go to Ascot that day to support a client, so he drove down early to give himself a chance to spot the Irishman arriving.

His guess that MacClancy would arrive by train – no great feat of detection – proved correct. He watched him step down from a stuffy, smoke-filled carriage, and shuffle along the platform with the rest of the punters towards the path up to the course. He was carrying an already very dog-eared copy of the *Sporting Life* tucked under his arm. Johnny checked the time-table for return trains to Waterloo and followed MacClancy.

Johnny spent the rest of the afternoon talking to friends and clients, avoiding his bookmaker, and went back down to the station in time for the first train to London. MacClancy, not much to his surprise, took the second, twenty minutes later. Johnny climbed into the same carriage, two doors down.

At Waterloo, he kept a good wedge of other gloomy punters between himself and the Irishman and followed him easily to the Angel, Islington. From there, MacClancy walked a few hundred yards to a huge cathedral of a pub, where he ordered a whiskey and settled on a bench, evidently to review his day's performance.

Johnny got himself a drink. He hoped he wouldn't be there too long; he had arranged to meet a girl who worked on the front desk at Christie's that evening – an odds-on certainty, if he was any judge. He glanced at his watch in frustration as MacClancy made his way to the bar for another drink.

Moving quickly, he went and sat close to where the Irishman had left his *Sporting Life*. He picked up the tattered paper and started to read it.

'Here, that's mine.' There was a slur in MacClancy's voice.

'Oh. I'm terribly sorry. I thought it had been discarded.'

'No,' MacClancy said, mollified by the warmth of Johnny's apology. 'I keep them till I've written all the results in my little book at home.'

Johnny folded the paper neatly and handed it to MacClancy as he sat down. 'Did you go to the races today?'

'I did.'

'How did you get on?'

'Not bad.'

'Did David Tredington ride a winner?'

MacClancy's shifty little eyes focused on him like a ferret on its prey. 'Why do you ask that?'

'It's just that I've been following him. He rides well.'

'He ought to, with his background, but he didn't have a ride today.'

'Oh. I didn't have a chance to look at the card. Did you have a winner or two?'

MacClancy nodded but didn't speak.

'I had a couple of bets yesterday, but . . .' Johnny made a face to show his lack of luck. 'Anything you fancy at Kempton tomorrow?'

MacClancy perked up. 'You get me a drink, and I'll give you a horse.'

'Sure!' Johnny said, as if he couldn't believe his luck. 'What do you want?'

'A large Jameson's.'

Johnny fetched the drink and one for himself. Philosophically, he wrote off his evening with the Sloane Ranger from Christie's and settled down to drink and talk horses with MacClancy. He also managed to extract a few details of the Irishman's personal history.

MacClancy had been born in Mayo, as he'd told David, but apart from one recent visit, he'd lived in London for the past thirty years.

He was reluctant to say more, so Johnny, with a good helping of his practised charm, switched to MacClancy's current circumstances. He was the caretaker in a small convent nearby, where he had a room, two square meals a day, and a couple of evenings off each week. He had worked with the same order of nuns for many years, at one time in another of their houses in Roehampton.

Later, when the conversation had reverted to racing, Johnny said, 'I've got to go now, but if this tip of yours comes up, I'll want to know where to deliver a bottle of whiskey; I'll have a good-sized punt.'

Johnny left the pub with the address of the convent in his wallet, and the information that MacClancy would be on duty the following evening. On his way to salvage what he could from his wrecked social arrangements for the evening, he rang David to report his progress.

David asked his father if he could take the next day off to go to Kempton races and afterwards to London to see a friend.

'Why not? There'll be a couple of good races. Take the Merc if you want; I shan't be needing it.'

'Are you sure?'

'Of course I am. And why not give Lucy a ring? She's gone back up to London for a couple of days until Mickey's funeral. I'm sure she'll put you up for the night.'

Johnny was driven back into London by David after the last race at Kempton. He was in better spirits. He had sensibly ignored MacClancy's tip and picked a ten-to-one winner of his own. He waited until they were in the car before he expanded on his meeting with the Irishman the evening before.

. He told David how he'd sat and talked with the little Irishman for an hour or two. 'I got out of him that he used to work in a convent in Roehampton.'

'Good God! Now you say that, I think I remember him. Quiet little chap. Of course, he was a bit more sprightly then. I can't believe he's been with those nuns all that time. It's quite possible he put two and two together and worked out some fantasy about extracting enough money from me to get away from the convent once and for all.'

'I can tell you one thing,' Johnny said quickly, 'if your crash wasn't an accident, I think it's very unlikely he had anything to do with it. I'd say he hasn't got the nous to organise it. Besides, I had it from him during the course of our conversation that he'd never been to Fontwell. He only goes to courses he can get to easily by train.'

'He could have paid someone else to do it, though,'

David said. 'He'd have known from the papers where I was riding that day.'

'Maybe, but I doubt it very much.'

David glanced away from the road in front of him for a moment and tried to believe that it really had been an accident.

'If he didn't do it, someone had to.'

'But for God's sake,' Johnny said impatiently. 'Even the police think it was an accident.'

'They still haven't traced the lorry, though.'

'That doesn't mean it was deliberate, does it? These things do happen.'

'There's nothing I'd like more than to think that,' David said. 'But I can't. It'd be too much of a co-incidence.'

'When you go and see MacClancy, you'll see what I mean. But what the hell are you going to say to him?'

'I'll tell him that if I have so much as a sniff of a threat, I'm going straight to the police. I don't reckon he'll bother to work out how unlikely that is.'

David dropped Johnny in South Kensington and, with the help of an *A–Z*, found his way to Lucy's mews house in Chelsea.

It was exactly the sort of place he had imagined: primrose-yellow with a lovingly tended display of autumn flowers in the window-boxes. Inside it was light and bright with pictures, hanging tapestries and kilim rugs. David felt at home as soon as he walked in. Lucy treated him as if he were a brother who had never been away, without ceremony and with a lack of effort which he knew didn't signify indifference.

In fact, as they had got to know each other again, they had become closer than he and Victoria. It was only Lucy who had noticed the tension between him and Susan Butley; she had recently taken to teasing him about it.

'I think our Susan secretly fancies you, Davy, though she seems to be keeping her feelings at bay by being as hostile as possible.'

They were sitting over a bottle of Chablis that Lucy had found in her fridge. David sank back in the beige hessian-covered sofa, enjoying being her brother.

'D'you think so? I just thought she resented my coming back to Barford for some reason.'

'Yes, she does. I don't know why, either. She still fancies you though. You'd better be careful; she's very determined. That's how she ended up working for Dad. She knew he needed someone around with a thick skin and a head for figures.'

'Well, I'll do nothing to scare her away.'

Lucy looked at him, speculating. 'Did you have any girlfriends back in Ireland?'

David blushed and, knowing it, blushed harder. 'To tell you the truth, that was one of the things wrong with the place. Thousands of lonely farmers, and no women for them. All the girls get off to Dublin, or England or America, if they can. If it weren't for the television, of course they wouldn't think to go, but there it is...'

'You've set a few hearts fluttering here among the racing groupies, I can tell you. It must be that blushing modesty that does it. Anyway, who's this mysterious person you've come up to see?'

'He's just an old relation of... of Mary's. I promised I'd

look him up. But I'll not be all that long. He lives somewhere in Islington.'

Lucy nodded. David had told them about Mary Daly the day he arrived so unexpectedly at Barford Manor. 'I've got a girlfriend coming round later for dinner. You can have some, too, if you're back in time.'

'Thanks. I'll make sure I am.'

David stood irresolute outside the Convent of the Holy Infant, assailed by ancient memories.

He saw a small group of nuns arrive and go in; although they had abandoned the white wimples and black habits of twenty years before, there was a serene goodness about them that reminded him sharply of how sorry they would have been if they had known what he was up to.

Looking across the road at the painted sign of the Virgin Mary dandling the Baby Jesus on her knee, David didn't want to go in. But he had to see MacClancy.

He took a deep breath and crossed the busy road. When he reached the tall, neo-gothic front door of the convent, he pulled a worn brass handle and heard the clanging of an old bell, incongruous against the traffic noise of the street.

The door was opened by a small nun of fifty in a plain, knee-length grey dress. She smiled. 'Hello?'

'Hello, Sister,' David said. 'I wanted to see Emmot MacClancy.'

The nun scrutinised him more closely. She had certainly recognised the Irishness in his voice. 'I think I know you,' she said. 'Were you at Roehampton?'

This feat of recognition shocked David. Certainly, he

had absolutely no recollection of this particular nun. He nodded slowly.

'Well, come in then.' The nun opened the door wider to admit him. 'Emmot always said you'd gone to Ireland with Mary, but try as we might, we never found out. How is she?'

'I'm afraid she's not well.'

'I'm so sorry to hear that. Is it serious?'

David nodded. 'It is. I'm afraid she has multiple sclerosis.'

'Lord bless her, the poor woman. We'll pray for her. When you've seen Emmot, you must come and see the other sisters. They'll want to hear all about it.'

She led him along a musty corridor, past a number of large closed doors, to a smaller door at the back of the ground floor. From the other side of it came the sound of a television. The nun knocked. After a moment, it was opened by Emmot MacClancy. He was dressed only in a vest and a pair of ancient flannel trousers, and stood for a moment, blinking with disbelief at David.

'Look who's come to see you,' the little nun announced cheerily.

David attempted a smile. 'Hello, Emmot.'

'My God! What do you want?'

'Can I come in?'

MacClancy hesitated, unsure whether or not he should be frightened by David's visit. Eventually, he stepped back with a nod, and David walked into his hot, stuffy bed-sitter. David turned to the nun. 'I'll come and find you before I go, Sister.'

The nun smiled and went on her way. MacClancy closed the door nervously.

'Why have you come here? Did you know who I was when I saw you at Newbury?'

David didn't answer.

'I'm sorry,' MacClancy went on. 'I didn't mean no harm. I was a bit down on me luck that day, and you looked like a gift from heaven.'

'Was it worth an innocent young lad dying?' David asked quietly.

MacClancy's eyes opened wide with horror. 'What are you talking about?'

As he spoke, David tried desperately to detect signs of subterfuge in the man's manner. 'The lad who was killed when I was driving home from Fontwell on Monday.'

'I read about that. It was a terrible thing. They said it was an accident.'

'I know they said it was an accident. But you know it wasn't, don't you?'

MacClancy sat down with a thump on his iron-framed bed to show his indignation at the idea that he might be implicated. 'What in God's name are you saying?'

David looked at him. This would be his only real chance to assess from MacClancy's reactions if he was involved or not. There was a guilty shiftiness about the man's manner, but David had no way of telling if this was due to his half-hearted attempt to blackmail him at Newbury, or a full-blooded attempt to murder him on the M27. He was going to have to press harder.

He stared at MacClancy with hard, uncompromising eyes. 'You know damn well what I'm talking about. The thing was set up while I was riding. That sleeper didn't drop out of the sky by accident. Either you did it or you paid someone else to do it.'

'I don't know what you're talking about, I swear by Almighty God. I've never been to Fontwell. It's too far for me. I've no car and I don't drive. I've told you, I'm sorry about what I said to you at Newbury. I was only trying, like. I'll cause you no more trouble, I promise.'

David wanted to take MacClancy at his word; it would have been far more comfortable to believe that the crash was the accident everyone else seemed to think it was. He sighed. 'I hope to hell I don't have to come and see you again.'

He wanted to leave the convent without seeing anyone else, but the nun who had let him in appeared from the shadows before he reached the front door.

'Are you going so soon?' she asked.

'I'm sorry, Sister, I have to.'

'What did you want with old Emmot?'

'It was nothing,' David said, then a thought occurred to him. 'But tell me something, how does he get around? He says he's no car or driving licence?'

'He hasn't. He always takes the train. One of his brothers is a track-layer for British Rail. Whenever Emmot wants to go anywhere, I'm afraid to say he borrows his pass so he can go for nothing.'

'And where does he go?'

'Just to the races. It's his only real interest now,' she added defensively, 'so we turn a little blind eye to it.'

Driving back across London, David tried to persuade himself that unless the Hampshire police came up with anything that proved otherwise, MacClancy wasn't involved. But he knew that his mission to extract a clear-cut confession or denial from him had failed.

He arrived back at Lucy's house in time for dinner, and tried temporarily to put the crisis out of his mind.

The sight of the girl leaning back on Lucy's sofa helped. She had, David thought extravagantly, the legs and eyes of a Greek goddess. She was in her twenties and looked better than a model in a fashion plate in one of the glossies.

Lucy watched David as she introduced them. 'Emma, this is my brother, David. Emma works for *Harper's*.'

A few months before, David would have had no idea what *Harper's* was. They certainly didn't stock it in the paper shop in Louisburgh. But since he'd arrived at Great Barford, he'd been a quick learner.

He still wasn't prepared for girls like Emma, though. Beneath her exquisitely presented exterior he sensed there lurked a kind of anarchic hedonism which alarmed and excited him. At first, David assumed they wouldn't have much in common, but she seemed fascinated by the idea of an heir to a large English country estate taking more than fifteen years out on an Irish small-holding.

David found himself describing the farm and the Mayo hills where he had spent the greater part of his life with a lyricism that made him wonder why he had been prepared to leave it behind.

Emma was delighted by him and encouraged him. He guessed, though, that hers was a professional, journalistic interest. He had no way of knowing what a refreshing contrast he was to the smug, self-centred men with whom she spent most of her time in fashionable London.

Over the small round table, while they ate a simple but skilfully prepared meal of *moules*, monkfish and more Chablis, it became clear that Emma had more than a passing academic interest in David. Sitting next to her, he felt her bare foot on his leg and her hand on his thigh at the slightest excuse.

It was only with great self-control and an instinct that it would yield the best long-term results that he restricted his response to mild flirtation and a light glancing kiss on the cheek when she left.

As the door closed behind Emma, Lucy grinned. 'You've had it now,' she said. 'She's an absolute sucker for a brush-off.'

'She'd no brush-off from me,' David protested.

'She did, by the standards she's used to. It'll take a lot to turn her off now.'

David shrugged. 'Well, I'm never in London, am I? And I didn't have the impression she was much of a country girl.'

'We'll see,' Lucy laughed. 'Anyway, it was great to see you in action; you're obviously not half such an innocent as you pretend.'

'I don't pretend anything,' David said emphatically. 'What you see is what you get.'

'I've been meaning to talk to you about that. What I see is OK, but it could do with a bit of polishing. The Val Doonican cable-knit and cords are a bit homespun, don't you think? Would you like me to take you shopping tomorrow? And to a proper hairdresser?'

David laughed. 'I didn't think you cared.'

'Of course I do. It's not that I don't love having a brother again, but I wouldn't mind one who looked a tad less as if he'd just finished a gig with the Dubliners. And while we're at it, I could mark your card, as they say, on a few other English habits you seem to have forgotten.'

'You wouldn't want me to confuse my own identity, would you?' David asked.

'No more than it is already.'

'Earth to earth...'

The vicar's sober words of burial were plucked up and scattered by the blustering wet wind that drove across the graveyard outside St Kenelm's Church in Barford. And the wind, whining through the ancient yews, drowned the sound of Mickey's parents' sobbing at the graveside.

David stood on the edge of the small crowd huddled around the trench in the damp earth, and he mourned the young man's death with the rest of the village.

Sir Mark stood closer to the grave, sombre and silent with his daughters, leaning down when invited to drop a trowelful of reddish soil on to the coffin lid.

Afterwards, in the village hall, David drank tea among the murmuring villagers, feeling the eyes that were on him, aware that loyalty to the son of the big house was being severely tested. Across the hall, he saw Susan Butley looking at him and talking to Mickey's tearful mother.

Lucy found him. 'Don't look so guilty. No one's blaming you.'

'Aren't they? Most of them are looking at me as if I were a saboteur at the hunt ball.'

'It's natural enough to want to blame somebody, but they'll get over it.'

Driving back with the rest of the family, David was aware just how much it mattered to him that the people in the village should get over it, now that he was once more considered a part of the place and committed to it.

By the time they reached the gates of the park, though, Sir Mark and Victoria were discussing horses again. David was to ride a novice chaser at Newton Abbot the following day. The horse was keen, green and wilful; it wasn't going to be an easy race. Lucy and Jason were in the car too and, for their different reasons, didn't join in. David's own contribution was less than half-hearted. He had found that Mickey's funeral had forced him to review in sharp focus everything that had happened since he had arrived in Devon two months before.

Chapter Three

England: early September

It had been on a bright, late summer Sunday that David had set off from his home in Mayo to fly from Dublin to Bristol. He hadn't told the family he was coming. After fifteen years without a single communication, it was hard to know how best to make the initial contact. However it was done, it was going to come as a shock. There was bound to be some doubt that it was really him.

For the last few weeks, David had tried to guess what their reaction would be. Would there be resentment? Indifference, maybe? Sometime in the next twenty-four hours, he would find out.

Now that he had embarked on the journey, animated as he was at the prospect of seeing the family and Barford, his courage began to ebb. Like a nervous diver making his way to the top board, he was torn between a fear of what might lie ahead and the knowledge that there was still time to turn back.

But he knew he couldn't back out; there was too much to lose.

He tried to read during the short flight, but found

himself looking blankly at the pages of his paper as he fingered the small blemish on his neck. A stewardess offered him a drink. He asked for a Coke. He wasn't much of a drinker and, from now on, he'd want his wits about him.

The Aer Lingus plane landed at Bristol Airport just after midday. David hired a small car and set off south on the M5. An hour and a half later he was driving through the late afternoon sunshine between the brown rolling bulk of Exmoor and the craggy cliffs of north Somerset.

When he reached the steep hill that dropped down into Lynmouth, he pulled into the side of the road and stopped. This was the point of no return.

For five minutes he gazed down at the small port, recognising landmarks, wondering what had changed. He asked himself why he was doing this and then whether he had any right to be doing it. And he thought of Mary Daly and the never-ending struggle to survive amidst the craggy beauty of the Mayo hills.

He took a deep breath and made a sign of the cross. He started the car and moved off down the hill once more.

He had already booked a room for the night at the Anchor. The young woman who came from the back of the hotel to deal with him gave no sign of realising the momentousness of what he was doing. He grinned at her and relaxed. The real test wouldn't be until the next day.

He took his bags up to the small room he'd been allocated, and lay on the bed for a while. He reviewed the past few weeks of his life, the decisions and plans he'd made and the extraordinary activity which made arriving here now seem like a long-delayed case of *déjà vu*.

Feeling fit and suddenly confident that he could handle whatever happened over the days to come, he swung his legs off the bed, changed into a pair of jeans, and went downstairs to let himself out into the street. The town was quietly busy with strolling tourists and locals. David drew deep breaths of fresh, salty air and set off on a quick tour to find out what had changed in the past fifteen years.

Down near the front, he went into a paper shop to buy himself a packet of small cigars to help deflect the slight nausea he was feeling. As he walked in, a tall, dark, striking girl, a few years younger than himself, was coming out.

She glanced at him as she passed, then stopped for an abrupt moment to take a second, closer look. David nodded with a friendly smile which acknowledged her without admitting acquaintance. If he should have known her, it was perfectly excusable not to recognise her after at least fifteen years. He carried on towards the counter and asked for his cigars. When he turned to leave, the girl had gone.

The encounter gave him a sharp stab of excitement. He was sure she thought she knew him, even though she couldn't have been more than nine or ten at the time of his disappearance.

In an hour's walk around the town, he twice more saw people half recognise him; even though this had been predictable, his confidence grew. His temporary anonymity gave him a strange sense of power. Evidently, even after all this time, his face fitted. That was going to make it a great deal easier to deal with the family the next day.

He went back to the hotel and ate a steak and salad in the dining-room before walking through to the bar. There were under a dozen people there, none of whom showed more than a passing curiosity about him.

At a table in the far corner, two girls sat huddled in private conversation, one with her back to him. It was only when she stood and came over to fetch two more drinks that he recognised the girl he'd seen earlier leaving the tobacconist's. He looked at her with interest and a slight quickening of his pulse. Her build was a cross between a dancer's and an athlete's; she had long legs and neat, well-moulded breasts. Her gleaming dark hair was well-cut and cared for, and there was an impressive forthrightness to her manner.

She didn't notice him at first; he was sitting at a small table in a corner. As she waited for her drinks, she glanced across. She smiled at him this time, with a curious excitement in her eyes. The barmaid put the drinks on the bar, but the girl ignored them and walked over to him.

'Hello. Are you who I think you are?'

David smiled back. She really was a tremendous-looking girl, he thought; certainly as beautiful as any he had ever met. His eyes sparkled. 'That would depend, wouldn't it,' he said, 'on who you think I am.'

The look of certainty on the girl's face faltered. 'I ... I'm not sure now. You sound Irish,' she added doubtfully. 'Are you?'

'In a manner of speaking.'

'I'm sorry. I thought you were someone else, then;

someone completely different, from round here, but I haven't seen him for years.'

'Well, I'm sorry too. I'd like to have known you. Would you ever let me get you and your friend that drink, to make up for the disappointment?'

'Thanks very much,' the girl said in a soft Devon accent. Whoever he was, she thought, this man had lovely eyes and a nice wicked smile. 'Do you want to join us?' she ventured.

'Only if I'm not muscling in on some vital private discussion.'

'You won't be,' the girl laughed. 'I've been Marje Proops long enough for one evening.'

David carried his glass of stout to the corner table from which the other girl had been watching with interest, smiled at her and settled down for a chat.

The second girl had few of the obvious physical attractions of her friend, but she had a friendly, appreciative face. David's life in Ireland had scarcely brought him into contact with English girls, and his knowledge of them now was based on all the usual clichés. He was surprised and pleased by the response he seemed to be getting from these two.

They asked him what he was doing in Devon.

David, not wanting to lose this limbo period of anonymity, adopted a deliberate vagueness. 'Bit of horse business.'

'Are you in racing then?' the first girl asked with obvious interest.

David stretched a point, and nodded. He told them some of the more outrageous stories about his point-to-pointing in the west of Ireland, knowing that this aspect of his previous existence would probably soon be common knowledge around here, and the girls would learn who he was soon enough.

During their conversation, he gathered that the good-looking girl was called Susan, and her friend was Wendy. But he managed to avoid offering any clues to his own identity.

With a firm resolve not to let on the real reason he was in Devon – at least until after he had seen his family – David bought two more rounds of drinks while they talked and laughed, until Wendy announced it was time for her to go. 'But you stay, Sue,' she said. 'I'll be all right.' She had seen the clear signals of a strong rapport growing between her glamorous friend and the dramatically good-looking Irishman; she didn't want to be accused next day of deliberate gooseberrying.

Susan didn't protest. When Wendy had gone, she insisted on buying two more drinks.

An hour later, looking into her strong, black-coffee eyes, David found himself reluctantly pulling back from the brink. Unless he wanted to get himself into tricky explanations before he'd even arrived officially, he'd have to wait a few days, until everyone knew that David Tredington was back. Then he would have plenty of time to follow up this very promising relationship.

'Well,' he said reluctantly, 'I've to be up early tomorrow to be about my business. Maybe I'll see you around?'

'How long are you staying, then?'

'Who knows,' he answered enigmatically. 'If all the women round here look like you, I could be here for ever.'

The girl wasn't sure how to take this, but she smiled encouragingly. 'Well, if you're in the horse business, you

58

ought to come up to where I work, at Barford Manor. They've got a big stud up there and they keep a lot of horses in training.'

David abruptly looked down and fiddled with his empty glass to hide his reaction. When he looked up, he managed a reckless grin. 'Well, there's a thought,' he said as he got to his feet. 'Now, can I take you home?'

'No, it's OK. I only live down the road, with my mum,' she added meaningfully and with a hint of regret.

Next morning, Monday, soon after ten, David parked his hired Ford Escort on a large circle of gravel in front of the handsome weathered stone bulk of Barford Manor. For a moment, before he climbed out of the car, he gazed at the place. Even though he could recall every nook and corner, he couldn't calm the convulsions in his guts.

He walked self-consciously, not with his usual easy stride, towards the great oak front door. Before he reached it, he stopped and stared at it. If he was going to change his mind, he had to do it now. If he didn't want to disrupt the lives of the people inside, and change the whole course of his own life, he would have to turn back before he rang the bell.

In the stillness, he heard a thrush fluting loudly in the bushes by the side of the house. He took a deep breath and stepped up to tug the worn, wrought-iron bell-pull.

A few moments later, the door was opened by Susan.

'Hello again,' David grinned. 'I didn't know you were the butler here.'

She laughed. 'You're not slow to get off the mark,' she said.

'I knew about this place. It was on my list. Meeting you just pushed it to the top.'

'Have you ever met any of the Tredingtons?' she asked in a voice which hinted at some uncomfortable doubt.

'As a matter of fact, I have,' David answered.

Susan opened the door wider to let him into the cool mustiness of the main hall. 'Did you want to see Sir Mark, then?'

'If that's possible,' David nodded.

'He's in,' she said, more guarded now. 'But you really need an appointment if it's stud business.'

'Would you mind asking him for me, though? And, er . . . just tell him it's some Irish chap, OK?'

She looked at him, half wanting to return his smile to let him know she hadn't forgotten how well they'd got on the evening before, but already suspecting that he hadn't been entirely honest with her.

'I'll go and see if he's free,' she said.

She left him standing where he was and walked to a door at the back of the hall which she opened and closed behind her.

As David prepared to meet his father, he looked around, recognising the statues, the hangings, and the huge painting of his great-grandfather's Derby winner which adorned one wall.

The girl reappeared. 'Sir Mark says he'll see you,' she said with undisguised curiosity and suspicion.

David shrugged an apology for whatever he had done to sour her view of him, and walked towards the study door. He tried to quell his nervousness, and uncon-sciously wiped his sweaty palms on his trousers.

He knocked.

'Yes. Come in.' The instruction was issued in the crisp tone of a man used to giving orders.

David pushed the door open and stepped into the high-ceilinged, panelled room. One large window gave on to a fine westward view of the park. In front of it was a large desk and chair. Besides these there were a couple of big armchairs, a large, low table covered in sporting magazines, and a television.

The man sitting at the desk had his head down, reading some papers in a folder. 'Won't be a moment,' he said without looking up.

David didn't speak.

Receiving no reply, Sir Mark Tredington raised his eyes from what he was reading sooner than he would otherwise have done.

Looking at David was a man in his mid-sixties, whose face, once handsome, had faded, but still displayed features unmistakably the same as the younger man opposite him. His eyes, dimmer than they had once been, were honest but cautious beneath a thick crop of silver hair.

David remained silent. He took a couple of paces towards the desk.

Sir Mark was gazing at him, astonished and bewildered. He glanced back down at his papers in confusion, as if to clear his head, before he looked up again.

'Good Lord!' he whispered. 'David?'

David smiled, but he didn't speak.

Sir Mark stood up and walked around his desk towards David. 'David? David?' He came closer, glanced at David's neck and, motionless for a moment, faced him a few feet away. 'David! Good God! I can't believe it!'

He stood, almost rigid with shock and an apparent reluctance to believe, in case he was wrong.

'Hello, Father,' David said at last. He smiled with affection, and apology.

The man in front of him, up until that moment utterly self-possessed in his display of emotion, abruptly stepped forward and put both his arms around David, hugging him to himself while his chest heaved with the release of over fifteen years' pent-up feeling.

It was a full minute before he stepped back, unashamedly sniffing away his tears and wiping his eyes with the heel of his hand.

He smiled and shrugged. 'Forgive me; it's been a long time. I can hardly take it in.' He stepped forward and hugged David again.

This time David returned his embrace.

'I'm sorry. I should never have gone,' he said quietly, surprised at his own emotion. 'But somehow, the longer I was away, the harder it was to come back and face what I'd done.'

The older man moved away, looking at David proudly, taking in his son's handsome face, sturdy physique and black curly hair. He shook his head slowly, as if he still couldn't believe what was happening. 'Some time – not now,' he said, 'you must tell me why you went. All that matters for the moment is that you're back.' Sir Mark was gazing with unbounded affection at his only son. 'And, by God, you look very well, fit as a fiddle.' He laughed with a touch of hysteria. 'And you sound like an out-and-out Paddy. You've been living in Ireland?'

David nodded. 'I have.'

'What have you been doing there?'

'Messing around with horses mostly,' David grinned. 'Nothing very grand; didn't have the money for it, but I won a few modest point-to-points.'

'Did you, by God? You mean my son turns out to be an Irish jockey!' He chuckled. 'Could have been a lot worse.'

He stopped suddenly, and the laughter died on his lips as if he was suddenly overcome with the enormity of what had happened. He shook his head. 'God, this is going to take some getting used to. And we must be sensible about it.' David had the impression he was talking to himself, had suddenly realised that he should hold himself back, at least until he'd checked everything out.

But David had no doubt that all Sir Mark's instincts were to believe that his son had come home.

'I understand,' David said. 'I'd understand if you asked me to turn around and walk straight out, and I wouldn't blame you.'

Sir Mark looked startled, even at the thought. 'David, my dear David, there's absolutely no question of that. We all realised how bloody miserable you were at the time you left; I just hadn't appreciated how much you were missing your mother. In fact, I thought you'd got over it pretty well, but when we got your note...' He shrugged. 'I felt terrible about not talking to you as much as I should; I was away far too much of the time. I made sure the same thing didn't happen with your sisters, I can tell you.' He stopped abruptly as another thought occurred to him. He blew a breath through his teeth. 'I wonder how Lucy and Victoria are going to take this.'

So did David.

David thought that Victoria, the younger and less sophisticated of the two sisters, would welcome him back without reservation. Lucy, less trusting, would want him to be real, but wouldn't lose sight of other possibilities.

Sir Mark was making up his mind how to handle the extraordinary news. 'Look,' he said, embarrassed by the possibility of a negative reaction from the rest of the family and, more importantly, George, 'why not have a drink?' He waved at a table of bottles and glasses by the window. 'I think I'll get the girls and let them make up their own minds.' He had, it seemed, opted for the same tactic as David.

He left the room. David considered his father's offer of a drink. He went through the motions and poured himself a tiny measure of whisky which he drowned with soda.

While he waited, gazing at the landscaped grounds which dropped away from the window, David examined his conscience. The sense of guilt that had regularly plagued him since first he had decided to come to Great Barford was, for the moment, neutralised by the undoubted happiness he seemed to have provided so far.

He heard voices and footsteps approaching the study.

He had his back to them when the girls came into the room.

He turned slowly. He met two pairs of eyes and watched their mild curiosity turn to astonishment.

The plumper, darker of the two – David recognised Victoria – quickly showed signs of an ecstatic realisation of what had happened.

Hesitating at first, she took a few quick paces towards him, then stopped, unsure of how she should greet a brother she hadn't seen – guiltily assumed gone for good – for so many years. She glanced at her father. 'It is David, isn't it?'

Sir Mark said nothing, made no gesture. He wanted the girls to make up their own minds.

Victoria ran the last few paces that separated her from her brother and flung her arms around him. David's conscience was momentarily troubled by the strength of her affection; at the same time, this sense of belonging was an elixir to him.

After a while Victoria released him and stood back to look at him, shaking her head in wonderment. Behind her, Lucy stood staring in disbelief. Her brother was dead; she had been sure of it. And yet here he was, less than ten feet from her.

She glanced at his neck – looking for confirmation – searching for some sign of the discoloured blemish that had once been there. The sight of it threw her into confusion. It really was him.

David looked back at her with a rueful half-smile.

'Hello, Lucy. Here, I've got something for you.' David felt inside the pocket of his jacket and pulled out a small cardboard box which he handed to her.

Lucy took it suspiciously and opened it. Nestling in some tissue paper was a blue-green egg, a little smaller than a bantam hen's.

Lucy stared at it for a moment, then slowly a smile spread across her face. 'My guillemot's egg!' she laughed. 'You took your time.'

'Better late than never,' David grinned.

'What on earth are you talking about?' Sir Mark asked.

Lucy turned to him. 'The day Davy disappeared, he said he was going up to the cliffs. I asked him to see if he could get me a guillemot's egg for my collection. I've never forgotten; it was the last thing I ever said to him. And now he turns up with it fifteen years later. I hope you've got a good excuse,' she said to David with mock severity.

Sir Mark laughed. 'Don't start squabbling. I'm sure David'll tell us what happened when he's ready to.'

'I will, of course I will. God knows I owe you that. I'd almost rather get it off my chest right away.'

'Let's go into the kitchen and make some coffee,' Lucy suggested. 'Mrs Rogers isn't going to believe this.'

But Mrs Rogers had already been told by Susan Butley.

David met her disbelieving stare. 'Hello, Beryl,' he said to the stout middle-aged woman who had been nanny, then housekeeper at Barford for twenty-five years. 'You've lost a bit of weight. Have you still got that apron I gave you?'

Tears seeped into the corner of the housekeeper's eyes as she shot a reproachful glance at Susan Butley.

'Davy! It *is* you. Of course it is! I'd have known you even after all this time. And you're looking so well. Wherever you've been, they've been feeding you all right.'

'Not too much, mind,' David grinned. 'I can still do ten seven.'

As they talked, Lucy had filled a tall cafetière. 'Right,'

she said, 'come on, then. Sit down and tell us what happened.'

They drew up chairs around the lumbering elm table in the centre of the big bright kitchen; all except Susan Butley who stayed where she was, leaning against the Aga.

They sat silently, waiting for David to start. He took a mouthful from the cup Lucy had poured for him and shook his head.

'You've no idea what it feels like to be back here. Nothing seems to have changed, though I'm sure this kitchen used to be green.'

'It was,' Sir Mark nodded, 'but we gave it a face-lift a few years ago.'

'It all seems like I was another person then. I don't know what I was going through. I missed Mum, terribly, but it wasn't just that. I think it was when I realised that I was going to have to take this place over, the thought of it sort of terrified me; so much seemed to be expected of me. I don't know why. And you were away all the time.' He looked without accusation at his father. 'Anyway, I sort of felt I wanted to make my own life, away from memories of Mum. I took all the birthday money I'd saved over the years and went to look for Danny.'

'Danny Collins? The old groom?' Sir Mark asked.

David nodded and laughed. 'I used to love old Danny. I'd talk with him for hours, and I was sad when he went. I knew he'd gone to live somewhere near Dublin, but I didn't know exactly where. I had the address of his sister in London, so I found my way to Roehampton where she'd been living with some nuns. But she'd gone and no one knew where. Of course, the nuns wondered what on earth I was doing. I wouldn't tell them, so they pressed me to stay. They were very kind to me and I stopped there a month or so. I thought about coming back again, but I was quite enjoying not being me any more. I knew a lot of people round here didn't like me all that much; I think I must have been a terrible little prig then...

'Anyway, I made up my mind to go to Ireland to look for Danny. I knew the trains for Fishguard went from Paddington, so I walked all the way there, but there wasn't a train until the next day. I found out which would be the first to leave in the morning, and sneaked into an empty carriage and slept in it till dawn. No one caught me though and I got to the ferry all right. They didn't seem too worried when I got my ticket. I told them I was being met at the other end. But there was one woman on the boat who guessed something was up. Mary Daly, she was called. She was very kind, bought me some lunch, asked me what I was doing, and I told her. I needed to tell someone. In a way, I suppose I half hoped she'd send me back, but she didn't. She said she was going through Dublin and she'd help me look for Danny Collins – and she did.'

'But you never found him, I presume, or he would have told us,' Sir Mark said. 'Anyway, though he had a daughter in Dublin, he retired to somewhere down near Killarney, where he came from.'

'No, you're right. We didn't find him, but Mary Daly was on her way to Mayo; her uncle had left her a farm there. When we couldn't find any trace of Danny, she asked me if I wanted to go back to England. I wasn't sure, but I told her I didn't, and she said would I like to come and stay with her for a while. She told me it was very beautiful and there'd be lots of horses.'

David shrugged. 'I guess it avoided facing up to what I'd done. When I got there, I thought it was heaven – a bit like here, though the mountains are higher, and the coast more rugged, and all the lakes . . . I fell in love with the place, fell in with the rhythm of it, I guess. I helped Mary with the farm and she'd no trouble persuading me to stay. She sent me to the school in Louisburgh and told everyone I was her son. They'd no reason not to believe her; she'd not been there since she was a young girl herself, and none of them knew what she'd been doing in England.'

David's eyes became thoughtful as he looked back to those years. Lucy poured him another cup of coffee before he went on. 'I was quite content, quite happy; I was one of them. But, I suppose, underneath, I knew I wasn't. I began to feel a terrible guilt, as if I'd duped these people – not Mary, of course, but I began more and more to feel as if I was there under false pretences. But then again, I got on well enough with everybody and I was enjoying the horses.

'After I left school, I worked on the farm, but I found time to bring on a few poor-bred animals we had about the place, started to ride them in the local races, even caught the eye of one or two Englishmen that strayed to them, but I made damn sure to avoid them, especially when Mary got ill. She urged me to come back here, but I couldn't just leave her after all she'd done for me.'

They were all looking at him intently, needing to know what had finally persuaded him to come back now.

David knew he must break it gently.

'Poor old Mary's been told she has to go into hospital, or find a way of being cared for at home.' David shrugged. 'With the way the farming is over there, it's not much more than subsistence now. We got by while the subsidies were on, but there was no way we could afford what she needed. My only hope was to use the skills I'd learned with the horses. So, I've come to England to see if I can make my way here – riding, maybe, or training, whatever. I knew that I'd have to come and see you all first, though.'

'You mean, you haven't come back to stay?' Victoria said.

'No,' David said firmly, 'I've no right. I turned my back on you all of my own free will. There's no way I expect to be taken back. I wanted no more than to see you again, and to let you know I was alive and in England before you found out some other way. I knew my face would give me away soon enough otherwise.'

The father and the two sisters stared at him. His Tredington features were unmistakable now. Victoria looked like a child who had been offered a wonderful new toy only to have it snatched away from under her nose.

Sir Mark looked worried, and Lucy puzzled.

'What on earth was the point of coming back, if you're not going to stay?' she demanded. 'This is your home.'

David shook his head. 'It was once, of course, but now my home's in Mayo.'

'I understand that, of course,' Sir Mark said, 'after what you've told us; but there's no reason why you shouldn't look on this as home too.'

'It's not possible. I'm a stranger here. Of course, it

70

would be great to come and visit now and again, once I'm on my feet. But I plan to go to Lambourn or Newmarket. I've a couple of strings to pull there.'

'But what are you known as in Ireland?' Sir Mark asked.

'Aidan. Aidan Daly. It was Mary who suggested it – though you've got to understand, she never put any pressure on me.'

Sir Mark looked hard at him. 'Aidan Daly? An Irish jockey, for heaven's sake! Well, from now on, you can go back to being David Tredington.'

'Oh no. I forfeited all claims to being David Tredington when I left. Aidan Daly I've been for the last fifteen years, and Aidan Daly I stay.'

David spent the rest of the warm, early autumn day at Barford Manor. Sir Mark walked round the grounds with him, pointing out landmarks and changes that had taken place since David had left. As they walked, he tentatively tried to persuade him to stay, but David was adamant.

Sir Mark didn't refer again to David's plans to keep his adoptive name and identity. Nor, when David saw them later, did the girls. But they begged him to stay for dinner. The talk was all reminiscing about events in David's childhood – some remembered, most forgotten. He made no excuses for his forgetfulness; the family understood that the act of running away had been a watershed in his life, and what had gone before had become in his consciousness a misty period of pre-existence.

Quite early, before his father and sisters were ready

to let him go, David insisted that he was going back to his room at the Anchor. He drove off in his small hired car with the family's exhortations to collect his things and move back into the house the next day.

David had little sleep that night. He was regretting already that he wouldn't see Great Barford again for some time. But he knew he had made the right decision, and he was going to stick with it.

At six, giving up any hope of more sleep, he got out of bed, dressed, and let himself out into the empty streets to walk down to the harbour and organise his thoughts. Shortly after half-past seven, he arrived back at the hotel, planning to have some breakfast. He found Susan Butley waiting for him outside.

Chapter Four

'Hello, Susan. What a lovely sight on a beautiful morning,' David said, stopping outside the front door of the hotel.

'Hello ... David.' She stood, long legs apart, hands on hips, barring his entrance. 'I want to talk to you.' She nodded her head to suggest that they walk up the street, away from the comings and goings in the hotel entrance.

David gave a puzzled shrug and started to stroll with her along the narrow pavement.

'You're a crafty devil, aren't you?' Susan said with disdain. 'Playing hard to get with them.' All trace of their intimacy of Sunday evening had vanished.

David looked at her in amazement. 'What's come over you? What are you talking about? You heard what I said yesterday. I'm going to make my own way. I realise what I did to them by going when I did. I expect nothing from them, but I had to come back to put the record straight. It would have been cruel to let them find out by themselves.'

'Put the record crooked more like, you mean. I just wanted to warn you: they may believe you, but I don't; and you won't get away with it if I can help it. That family's been very good to me, and I'm not going to see them taken for a ride by some Irish con-man.'

David shook his head with a disarming smile. 'Look, I knew some people would find it hard to take my coming back, but I don't see how it makes any difference to you. OK, I'm sorry I didn't tell you everything when I saw you on Sunday evening, but I couldn't, could I – not till I'd seen my father. But you already knew who I was; you as good as said so in the bar.'

Susan looked back at him doubtfully. 'I admit, I did think you were David for a few minutes, but now I know I was wrong,' she said.

'I'm sorry you feel like that, especially after we were getting on so well the other night.' The corner of his mouth twitched into a mischievous smile. 'I thought we were to be friends. But then, I'm not staying around here, so I guess it's not the end of the world.'

'You can't fool me. There's one thing I know for certain about you: you'll be back.'

Annoyed by her stubbornness, David abandoned his attempt to charm her. 'If I do come back, it'll only be when there is not a shadow of a doubt about who I am. Do you think I didn't realise people would be sceptical? Do you think my father would accept me back without being utterly certain? Frankly, that's one of the reasons I'm not staying; I don't want to be the focus of everyone's gossip and speculation while there's still any question of who I am. So, when I next see you, you won't have anything to worry about, and maybe we can carry on where we left off.' He gave the girl a dazzling smile.

She shook her head. 'I don't think so,' she said, but

with enough doubt in her voice to leave David confident that the relationship which had started so well could yet be salvaged.

He watched her walk away, wishing he hadn't had to lie to her when they'd first met. He guessed it was the very fact that he was David Tredington – and not the Irish jockey he'd introduced himself as – that had so radically altered her attitude towards him.

When David didn't reappear at Barford Manor that morning, Sir Mark Tredington telephoned the Anchor. The Irishman had checked out at half-past eight, they told him.

The post arrived a little later. There was a letter for Sir Mark from a firm of Australian lawyers. Anxiously, with a slight trembling of his hands, he tore open the envelope. He quickly read down the two pages and relief flooded through him.

He had instructed the firm to check the identity of a young man, named as David Tredington, who was reported to have been a member of the crew of *White Fin*, a small yacht which had gone missing off Norfolk Island over a month before.

They could tell him no more than the fact that a man of approximately the right age had booked into a hotel in Sydney a few days before *White Fin* had set sail, and that his name appeared on the harbour register as a member of the crew.

But they could get no further back than that. They had found no record of his entry into Australia, nor of a previous address or domicile. It was possible that this man was their client's son, but they had exhausted every avenue trying to prove it and could offer no serious hope. They would keep their files open; in the meantime, they enclosed their account to date.

Sir Mark rang the senior partner at his London solicitors' and told them to expect him the following morning.

At about the time Sir Mark was telephoning his lawyers, David was booking into a small hotel in East Garston, three miles east of Lambourn, in the name of Aidan Daly.

Making no mention of his connection with Sir Mark Tredington, he set off in search of the one trainer who had advertised in the *Sporting Life*, offering employment with the chance of rides to the right applicant.

Ian Bradshaw was a young trainer in his third season. David knew a little about him from what he had read in the Irish racing papers. The horses he saw while he was waiting to see the trainer didn't inspire him. Neither did the scruffy, unscrubbed yard. Still, he couldn't afford to be choosy.

Neither could Ian Bradshaw. He came out of his house in a hurry, wearing dirty brown jodhpurs with broken zips where they met his filthy boots. He was a wiry individual with a sour look about him.

'You the lad who's come for the job?' He spoke quickly, eyeing David up and down as he carried on walking.

'Yes, sir.'

'Well, you look as though you can ride. Start tomorrow.'

David wanted to ask about the chance of rides, but before he could speak, a horse had been brought out and the trainer had disappeared from the yard.

David shook his head in disbelief. A lad walking across the yard saw, and grinned in sympathy.

'Ah, well,' David said to him. 'I suppose I have to start somewhere.'

By lunchtime, David had returned his hired car to a depot in Newbury and moved his bags into the run-down cottage where he had been billeted with half a dozen other lads.

Three days later, he sent a postcard to his father, letting him know that he was working in Lambourn and giving the address of the hotel where he had stayed the first night.

The following evening there was a telephone call for him at the cottage.

'Hello, David. I got your card.' Sir Mark didn't disguise the hurt he was feeling.

'I thought I should at least let you know what I was doing this time,' David said apologetically.

'I'm at the hotel where you stayed. The chap here told me you'd gone to work for Bradshaw. Look, let's talk. Let's have dinner, at least, and if you insist on following a career in racing, let me see if I can't get you in somewhere with rather better credentials.'

'There's no need for that. I know what I'm doing, Dad. I told you, I've no claims on your goodwill.'

'For God's sake, David, have a heart. I'm your father. I've forgiven you the hurt you caused us all. Why prolong it?'

'Because your forgiveness doesn't purge my guilt, I

suppose,' David said, reflecting the style of the old priest in Louisburgh.

'Well, it damn well should. Come on, old chap. At least let me buy you dinner and discuss the matter sensibly.'

'OK,' David said, giving in willingly. 'I could do with a decent meal. I think we get worse fed than the horses here, and that's saying something.'

They arranged to meet at seven-thirty in the hotel at East Garston. David changed into a clean pair of cords and shirt and scrounged a lift in another lad's battered old Capri.

Sir Mark was waiting for him in the bar, sitting at a table, flicking through the pages of the evening paper. He greeted David with no less warmth than when he had said goodbye four days before.

'You don't look as though you've been doing too badly on a lad's diet,' he said. 'What'll you have to drink?'

David asked for a glass of stout and the two men went to sit in a corner where they wouldn't be overheard.

'I'd far rather you came back to Barford,' Sir Mark sighed, after David had briefly described the slipshod manner in which Bradshaw ran his yard.

'How can I? I told you, I made my choice when I was twelve years old, and it's not fair to go back on it now.'

'But that's absurd,' Sir Mark said testily. 'You were young; you were obviously emotionally disturbed. I have to take some of the blame, going away so much after your mother died, leaving you to the grooms and Beryl Rogers. I should have been there for you and I wasn't. I was too busy pandering to my own grief.'

'The other thing is,' David went on as if he hadn't heard, 'I want to be sure I'll be happy back here in England. Whether you like it or not, I'm Irish at heart now – a simple Catholic, west coast boy.'

'Simple you are not, that's very evident, and I've no objection to your being Catholic, if that's what you want. The point is, you belong at Barford.'

'Are you sure about that?' David searched into the old man's eyes.

Sir Mark looked embarrassed, circling the top of his glass with his finger. He sucked a deep breath through his nostrils. 'I went to see my solicitors in London on Tuesday. Their preliminary investigations bear out everything you've told me.' He shuffled awkwardly in his chair. 'Not that I had any doubts that you were David, but for legal purposes, and to quell any rumours that might get about...'

'I understand,' David said. 'To tell you the truth, I was amazed you all accepted me so easily – well, all except Susan, and maybe Lucy. I mean, I thought there was bound to be some resentment, even doubts. But I've told you, I've not come to make any claims. That's why I've got to make my own way, earn my own living. As far as I'm concerned, you owe me nothing.'

'Fair enough. I realise that. That's why I've come to offer you a job. I haven't seen you ride yet, but I don't doubt you know what you're doing, and I need a stud manager.' He raised a hand to pre-empt David's protests. 'No special treatment. You'll get the going rate for the job and the cottage that goes with it – no more. For heaven's sake, that's got to be preferable to living in some scruffy lads' hostel.'

David couldn't keep a grin off his face. All other considerations of his current position apart, the prospect of running a stud like the Great Barford was in itself an overwhelming temptation.

'That's a hell of an offer,' he admitted.

Sir Mark beamed. 'And don't worry about the girls. They'll come round soon enough.'

When Sir Mark had told his daughters that he was going to find David and try to persuade him to come back and live at Barford, he had all their support. Lucy decided to stay on down in Devon so that she would be there when her brother returned. The sisters couldn't stop talking about this momentous event in their family: there was no question that it felt like the filling of a void in their lives which they had been unwilling to admit had been there for the fifteen years since David had run away.

When he came back five days after his first appearance at Barford, they helped him settle into the stone cottage, two hundred yards from the house, which had been the stud manager's house since before the war.

Afterwards, the sisters walked back to the manor together.

'What do you think of our prodigal son returned to the fold, then?' Victoria asked.

'At least Dad has had the sense not to kill any fatted calves.'

'I don't think David wanted that at all, anyway: he's very unassuming.'

'Yes,' Lucy said thoughtfully. 'He's changed a hell of a lot – not just physically, of course – but then I suppose we all change a lot between pre-pubescence and adult-hood. I know I was a ghastly arrogant little prig when I was twelve.'

'You still are,' Victoria laughed. 'No, you're not,' she added quickly, to be sure her sister knew she was joking. 'But I know what you mean. He really is a very nice man, now. I'm afraid Jason doesn't think so, though.'

'No, I don't suppose he does.'

'I wish you wouldn't use that tone when you're talking about him.'

'I'm sorry, Vicky, but you know he and I don't really get on.'

'Poor Jason, however much I tell him he's part of the family now, he can't seem to just accept and enjoy it. After all, Dad's been pretty fair with him.'

'Oh, I dare say he'll get over it,' Lucy said, unconvincingly. 'But what has he said about David?'

'When I told him it might mean we won't get Lower Barford, he was furious, said Dad was cheating me and God knows what. It was awful.'

'Poor Vicky. Frankly I couldn't care less about not getting any land; it would just be a lot of hassle.'

'And you're really pleased about having David back?'

They had reached the front steps of the big house. Lucy didn't answer for a moment. 'Yes, I think so.'

'What? Aren't you sure?'

Lucy opened the door and they walked into the hall. 'I suppose I've still got a lingering doubt that it's really him.'

'Don't be ridiculous, Luce. What about the guillemot's egg? Of course it's him. Dad started getting it all checked out right away. He's not in any doubt at all.'

'But he wanted his son back very badly.'

'Let's go and talk to him, see if he can convince you.'

Victoria led the way past the library to Sir Mark's study. Their father was sitting at his desk.

'Dad, we wanted a word, now that David's back for good.'

'Come in then. Shut the door. What's the trouble?'

'Lucy's still not sure he's David.'

Sir Mark looked at his elder daughter. 'I can understand that. Believe me, even though all my instincts were to accept him, I didn't want to make a disastrous mistake. Everything he's told me adds up. I've had his story checked in Ireland, and when I took him to London, he made no objections to giving a blood sample.'

'Oh no,' Victoria said, 'you didn't make him go through that, did you?'

Sir Mark raised an eyebrow. 'I had to, to be absolutely sure.'

Victoria turned to her sister. 'There you are, Luce, it really is him.'

Lucy nodded with a smile. 'I suppose so, but it's just such an extraordinary thing to happen. I couldn't help thinking of that chap who came back – when was it? some time in the 1860s – claiming he was Sir Roger Tichbourne, and even his mother believed him. He turned out to be a butcher from Wapping called Arthur Orton.'

Sir Mark smiled. 'Well, don't worry, I don't think David's going to turn out to be a butcher from Wapping.'

A week after he had first turned up at Great Barford, David Tredington was sitting in his small, chintzy sitting-room, on his own for once. It was a quiet, windless evening. He listened to the birds chirruping in the small grove of oaks outside, and thought about the wealth of high-grade bloodstock that he had been invited to oversee. So far, he had only glanced briefly through the stud book, but every pedigree had a top-class horse in it.

He unwrapped one of the small cigars that he liked occasionally, and lit it. As the blue smoke wafted towards the low ceiling, he thought that, even if he never inherited the huge house and estate – which anyway seemed a surreal, distant prospect – he'd be quite happy running the stud and living here for the rest of his life.

Then, with a twinge of guilt, he thought of Mary. It was her condition that had first made him decide to come to Barford. Her illness had prompted his leaving Mayo, and yet he hadn't thought of her all day. He got up from his squeaky armchair and sat down at a small bureau. He found a pad of writing paper and began a long letter to her. He was reaching the end when there was a light knock on the door followed by the sound of it being opened.

'Who is it?'

'It's Victoria. Can I come in?'

'Of course you can.' David got to his feet and walked through to the flagstoned hall to greet his sister.

Victoria, if she thought she had made a mistake by marrying Jason Dolton, was very loyal in not letting it show. But they lived in a cottage only a hundred yards from David's and she was obviously delighted to have her new brother so close at hand.

David saw that she had grown into the kind of woman he had learned to respect. Despite her dumpy looks, she had her attractions. She had a sharp sense of humour and was fond of saying exactly what she thought. David was impressed by her sincerity and gentleness, particularly with the horses. He recognised in her his own fondness for the animals, and this was fast forging a bond between them.

'I was just wondering what you thought about everything down at the stud, now you've had a really good look round.'

'Potentially, I think you must have one of the best studs in England.'

'*We* must have,' Victoria corrected. 'Yes, it could be. It's great to have an extra member of the family to help, especially as you seem to understand so much about breeding.'

Nothing triggered David's enthusiasm more than a discussion about the requirements for producing good race-horses, but there was something he was curious to know.

'Why did the last stud groom leave?'

'Because he never had a feel for horses. He knew pedigree well enough, but he didn't understand about temperament – and that's the most important aspect, don't you think?'

They happily discussed the stud until they got round to the subject of David's racing.

'Dad's been talking about you riding some of the horses in training,' Victoria said.

'Has he? Well, he hasn't talked to me about it yet. After all, he's not even seen me on a horse, and if

I'm to run this stud, I won't have time to be gallivanting around race-courses. To tell you the truth, though, I wouldn't mind a chance to ride some of the horses he has at Sam Hunter's. A couple of them look useful.'

'And he was talking to George, who's bought a horse from Ireland. It's a beautiful gelding, but apparently they can't get him to jump. Letter Lad, he's called. Maybe you should have a look – see if you can tell George what he should be doing.'

'I wonder what he'd think about that, taking advice from me after all these years.'

'I'm sure he wouldn't mind. He's no genius where horses are concerned. He's only decided to train a few because he thinks it's the right thing to do.'

'We'll see. I think, on the whole, it would be better to wait till he asks for my advice before I offer it, don't you? After all, I've not spoken to him for fifteen years. He may not take too well to my bursting on the scene and telling him what to do.'

David spent the next few days getting to know everything he could about the mares, the foals, yearlings and assorted young-stock on the stud. He relished the chance to use all the knowledge he had accumulated over the last dozen years of breeding horses in Ireland. Up in the Mayo hills, he had spent many hours pipe-dreaming as he pored over the stallion books, gazing at photos of animals which he would have given all he had to send his mares to. His knowledge of breeding was as good as that of people in the mainstream of the industry on both sides of the Irish Sea. Now – it seemed almost incredible – he found that he had the opportunity to deal at first hand with a quality of bloodstock which exceeded his most extravagant fantasies.

He quickly learned which mares were in foal to what stallions, when they were due, which colts were off to the sales, and which fillies Sir Mark intended to keep and run. He had fitted quite naturally into the place, and the other four members of the stud staff found no difficulty in accepting him – not just as Sir Mark's son, but also as an able boss in his own right.

David got into the habit of having all his meals in the house. Susan Butley was usually at lunch; even though she was no more friendly than she had been outside the Anchor, she had evidently decided to play down her own scepticism so as not to antagonise the family. But David, frustratingly, was hampered in his campaign to win her over by the physical thrill her presence always seemed to cause him.

Life quickly settled into a pattern. David had been working on the stud for a week. It was early evening, all the horses had been fed and bedded for the night. All but one of the staff had left for the day. Only Mickey Thatcher had stayed on to chat to his new boss.

Mickey was seventeen, in no doubt where his future lay. As soon as his parents would let him leave home, he was going off to become a jockey. And there was nothing he liked more now than to listen to David telling stories of racing in Ireland. He hung on to every word, savoured every snippet of David's experience.

David had already grown really to like Mickey. He

recognised the boy's utter commitment to horses and his own particular charges in the yard. Besides, he admitted to himself, it was gratifying to have such an eager listener.

They were still talking half an hour later when Sir Mark appeared.

'Evening, Mickey. Still here?'

'Yes, sir. Mr David's just telling me a bit about racing in Ireland.'

'You've probably heard more than I have, then. As a matter of fact, David, I thought it was about time we saw you up on a horse. Do you think that Nashwan filly's ready for you?'

'I'd say so,' David nodded.

'Well then, let's see you up on her tomorrow morning.'

Bred by a Derby winner out of a mare who had won a Group Two race, David had never sat on such a precocious youngster. She had only been ridden away three weeks earlier, but she carried him around as if she were an old hand. He worked her round the small indoor school and took her for a gentle canter on the sheep-cropped pastures that separated the stud buildings from the cliff-top.

His father watched him every yard of the way until he had brought the horse back to a walk on the track down to the stableyard.

The baronet greeted David with a broad smile. 'What do you think of her?'

'If confidence counts for anything, she'll be unbeatable.'

'It could be the man on board, of course. I'd say

you've got as fine a pair of hands as your Great-Uncle William.'

'The fella who won the Foxhunters in the twenties?'

'That's right. He was one of the best amateurs of his day. How would you like a few rides in England?'

'So long as it's on something bigger than this, I'd love it.'

Sir Mark nodded, pleased. 'Right. We must get straight on to Portman Square and get you an amateur licence. In the meantime, why not go over to Sam Hunter's and ride out a couple of days a week? I'll tell him you're going to have a few rides in some suitable races.'

David slipped his feet out of the irons and swung himself off the horse's back to lead her into the yard. 'If you don't mind messing up your horses' chances, then I don't,' he grinned.

George Tredington arrived for the weekend a day earlier than usual. Sir Mark had telephoned him to tell him the good news about David's return. He turned up at the manager's cottage on Thursday evening while David was in the bath, scrubbing off the day's accumulation of equine smells. He called up the stairs.

'Hello, David? George here – your cousin George.'

'I'll be right down.' David had been anxious about this first encounter with his cousin, knowing George had expected to inherit. He braced himself as he climbed out of the bath, dried himself down and pulled on some clean clothes.

He came down the stairs with a friendly smile on his

face, and the confidence that already belonging had given him.

'Hello, George. How are you?'

George's bright little eyes, buried in his chubby red cheeks, met David's directly. There was a moment's scrutiny and hesitation before, with a look of relief, a smile broke out on his thick lips.

'My God, David! It really is you! How bloody marvellous!' He held out a sweaty hand in greeting. 'I didn't believe it when your father told me you were back.'

David returned his firm shake. 'It's good to be back,' he said with a nod.

'I hear you're already stuck into the stud. Frankly, it could do with a bit of strong management.'

'It seems like a pretty tight set-up to me.'

'Yes, well, I suppose it's a bit different to Ireland. Your father tells me you're going to ride some of his horses under rules.'

'Maybe. I hope so.'

'I'm training some pointers myself. I've bought a few from Ireland. Or rather Johnny Henderson bought them for me. You remember Johnny?'

'Of course. How is he? What's he doing with horses?'

'He's a bloodstock agent; not a bad one, though he never seems to make any money at it. And he's not always reliable. One of the horses he got for me came from the part of Ireland where you've been living, as a matter of fact; lovely-looking animal, plenty of speed, but won't jump a straw bale.'

'That's the way it goes,' David said sympathetically.

'Come over and take a look some time.'

'Where do you live?'

'Didn't your father tell you? I took over Braycombe when my father died. I'm in London most of the week, scratching a living in corporate finance, but my heart's down here. Of course, the farm doesn't make much – wouldn't make anything at all if it weren't for the dear old CAP. But I've managed to buy myself an interest in a wholesale butcher's and an abattoir; vertical farming you could call it. I'm running the shoot on the estate now, too. I dare say you'll want to take a gun.'

'Maybe, though I've not shot a driven bird for a very long time.'

'You always had a good eye as a boy,' George said.

'It's probably deteriorated since then,' David said modestly. 'Anyway, I'd be glad to come and look at your horses and, of course, if there's anything I can do...'

'That would be marvellous,' George said heartily. 'Right!' he slapped his thigh. 'I must get on. There's a hell of a lot to do and I'm having dinner back up here this evening.'

'See you then, then,' David said blandly.

George beamed a smile and let himself out of the front door. With a palpable easing of tension, David watched him through the window as he walked to a big BMW parked outside the front gate.

For a man who faced having a substantial inheritance lifted from under his nose, George was behaving with admirable civility. David guessed that this was what was called being a gentleman; that he was prepared to accept without rancour this change in his own prospects.

When he was next alone with Victoria, David asked her about George's attitude.

'I suppose he's rather old fashioned, at least in some ways,' she said. 'I'd say he's got such respect for the rules of correct succession that he's quite happy to welcome you back as the natural heir. Besides, he's got quite a bit of money in his own right, and he seems to be making a pile in London.'

On Sunday, David went over to Braycombe, at George's urging, to look at Letter Lad.

Although he didn't tell George, David immediately recognised the horse. A big, powerful chestnut, almost roan, with a black stocking on its off-hind, it was in far better condition now and it was already half fit. Jan Harding, George's groom, had been preparing it to qualify with the Exmoor hounds. She rode it round the paddock to show its paces.

'He looks like a nice horse,' David said. 'And he moves well.'

'Yes, he does, or Johnny wouldn't have bought him. Trouble is, as I said, he won't even think about jumping a fence. I think I'll have to get rid of him.'

'I wouldn't be too hasty. Something could be made of him. He looks an honest sort of a horse. Could I just get on him for a moment?'

'Sure,' George gestured generously, beckoning Jan to bring the horse to the gate where they were standing.

David swung himself over the horse's back and geed it forward. He worked it round the field, trotting, cantering and finishing with a short burst of speed.

He jumped off and handed the reins to Jan.

'He feels the part. I'd persevere with him if I were you. You'd have to go a long way to see a better one.'

George showed David the four other horses which had recently arrived in his yard.

'Johnny Henderson bought all these in Ireland for me,' George said. 'And bloody cheap.'

They all looked capable of winning modest point-to-point races. Johnny Henderson had done a good job for George.

'Point-to-pointing's getting tremendously popular round here,' George went on. 'The cost of keeping a horse in training for National Hunt is so high now. I thought it might be fun to try and make a bit of a mark – and just as much fun as racing under rules for half the cost.'

Half the prize money, too, David thought; and it also depended on your idea of fun.

As George showed him round, David's first impression that his cousin was genuinely glad that the rightful heir had turned up at Great Barford was confirmed. He even deferred to David, as eventual owner, when talking about his plans for the shoot. As David drove away from Braycombe, he should have been grateful that George had accepted him without reservation, but, guiltily, he found himself already thinking of a plan to ease the big roan from George's yard. One thing he was sure of, on the evidence of his own eyes in Ireland, was that the horse had a colossal jump in him.

Since David had arrived at Barford, nearly everyone he had met had accepted him. Old estate workers, the villagers, local land-owners and farmers, the shop-keepers in Lynmouth who had known David the boy, all recognised him as David the man. Susan Butley, Jason Dolton, and possibly Lucy, remained the only people to show any scepticism. He knew what Jason's reasons were; he could understand Lucy's; he wished Susan would tell him hers.

As he settled in, David deliberately kept his own needs modest, settling for the use of one of the older Land Rovers on the farm as his personal conveyance. At the same time, he worked hard and was conscious that he was making a measurable difference to the running of the stud. He was able to send most of what he earned to Mary. He had plans to start making larger sums by buying, bringing on and selling horses on a scale he could not have attempted in Ireland. His father had already agreed that he would help with the modest funding this would need.

A fortnight on, his amateur licence was confirmed and he was booked to ride his first race in England under Jockey Club rules.

Sir Mark was determined to see his son succeed. He had told Sam Hunter, a small but effective trainer in neighbouring Somerset, to find some suitable races for David to ride in. The first was arranged at the end of September, at Wincanton, on a small mare from Hunter's yard.

Sam Hunter put down the telephone in his office wearing as close to a smile as he ever got. Thin, weather-beaten, he was a Devonian through and through. He was tough, honest and independent. He had only moved to Somerset reluctantly, and in the pragmatic hope that it would provide a bigger catchment area for owners.

Perhaps it had, but now, he recognised, he had reached a plateau in his training career beyond which he would never rise. At fifty-two, he had settled into a comfortable routine that produced an average of thirty-five winners a year. The burning ambition to be champion trainer with which he had set out had now cooled to a warm contentment in knowing that, given the right horse, his training skills were a match for anyone's.

He'd gone into racing as soon as he'd left school. His dreams of becoming a top-class jockey, however, had come to a painful end at Newton Abbot. Looking back, the fall had probably saved him a few wasted seasons coming to terms with the fact that his abilities in the saddle would always be limited.

Over the years, he'd watched dozens of youngsters start out with the same ambition. They had come and gone as regularly as the seasons, and always there had been something missing. Some rode well but wouldn't work for their chances. For most, it was the opposite, and all the hard work in the world couldn't produce natural talent.

In eighteen years as a trainer, he'd had only two lads in his yard who could have made it. Both rode well and grafted hard, but they'd missed reaching the very top because they lacked the confidence and the canniness to make an impression with owners; and owners paid the bills. 'No conversation – no rides,' is what Sam had emphasised to every budding jockey who had passed through his care.

Although he had never watched David race-ride, Sam could see that all the essential qualities were there and, of course, he had that Irish charm to go with it. He had found that David was guaranteed to improve whatever horses he put him on at home. They jumped better and worked harder for him. He relaxed the nervous ones and encouraged the moderate. All the man needed was luck and the right opportunities.

Only fate would decide if Lady Luck would turn out for his side, but it was within Sam's power to provide him with the chances.

He had promised Sir Mark that David's first ride in England would be a winner, and he was determined to do everything he could to deliver on that promise.

He had a small, narrow bay mare in his yard called Bideford. She was a shade over sixteen hands, with a big splash of white across her face. When David had first seen her, he hadn't been too impressed, but the moment he had schooled her over fences, he had changed his mind. She rode as if she were a hand higher with a long, easy stride. At the same time, she was as nimble as a pony and loved to jump. She could weigh up her fences and sort out her stride quicker than any other horse he'd ridden.

Bideford had been off the race-course for more than a year, since she got cast in her box and managed to pull a tendon over her near-side hock. Sam had slowly brought her back to fitness. She'd done fourteen weeks of roadwork before setting hoof on a gallop. After another six weeks' cantering, she'd begun working. Two race-course gallops had put her spot-on for her return.

Sam had entered her in a claiming race at a price ten thousand pounds below her value. She'd need to fall twice to get beaten.

* * *

It was a mild day at Wincanton. Big clouds billowed in from the south-west, but the sun shone through and the rain held off. The going at the windy race-course was on the soft side of good, and a big crowd of West-Countrymen turned out to watch large fields in all seven of the day's races.

Despite the hundreds of rides he'd had in Ireland, and even with all the self-assurance the last few weeks had given him, David couldn't calm his nervousness at his first English race. As he walked into the paddock with the other jockeys, he found himself needlessly fiddling with the strap on his helmet and tapping his whip on his boot. David knew, like Sam Hunter and his father, that his mount was running a few grades below her mark. He also knew that he would need a very good excuse not to beat Jason Dolton on a moderate animal from a small local yard.

Sir Mark, Victoria and George had come to support David in his first appearance. David found them with Sam Hunter, standing in a group close to the exit on the far side.

'Where's Lucy?' he smiled as he doffed his cap in the customary manner.

Victoria was standing, legs apart, wearing a brown fur hat and an unflattering overcoat. 'She's busy, but she wishes you the best of luck. Are you nervous?' she went on, twisting the strap of her binoculars tightly round her fingers. 'I am.'

'I'll be fine as soon as I'm in the saddle,' David answered honestly.

The bell rang for the jockeys to get mounted. David

and Sam walked across to Bideford, who was fidgeting, eager to get on.

'She'll stay longer than a tattoo, so make plenty of use of her,' Sam said as the mare's lad legged David on board. 'And good luck.'

The start of the two-mile five-furlong course was just around the bend from the stands, beyond the water jump. David eyed the jump apprehensively. This would be the first time he had jumped water in a race. In Ireland, they'd been banned as a result of the number of horses who had injured their backs jumping them.

Bideford was clearly excited by the prospect of racing again. Cantering across the middle of the course to the start, it was all David could do to stop her running away. When they had reached the start and were waiting to have their girths checked, she refused to walk quietly with the others. She jig-jogged and shook her head, rattling the rings of the bit. Sweat began to drip from her neck. David wished he'd worn gloves, but it was too late for that now.

Eventually, the starter called them in. Almost before he had released the tape, Bideford had set off for the first fence as if the devil were after her. David knew better than to fight her. He just kept a firm hold of the reins and sat as still as a mouse.

But her speed increased. If she failed to take off for some reason, David guessed his next ride would be in an ambulance. Almost subconsciously, he began counting the strides to the fence as they galloped towards it like an express train. With two full strides still to cover, Bideford did little more than bend her tiny knees and propelled herself towards the top of the fence. It was an action that frightened her almost as much as David. She was travelling so fast, she lost her footing as she landed, her nose banged into the turf and, for an instant, David thought he might be pulled over her head.

In the stands, Victoria gasped and fiercely grabbed her father's arm. She relaxed her hold a little as Bideford managed to find another leg from somewhere and galloped on, ears pricked, towards the next.

The shock of almost falling brought Bideford back to her senses. The fizz disappeared and she settled into her normal stride. David could barely hear her feet touching the grass as she bounded up to the next. This time she measured it perfectly. David gave her a pat on the neck but she was enjoying herself too much to notice. She galloped on, eating up the ground, springing over the fences as they came, leaving the other runners trailing in her wake.

The water jump came and went without incident. David let her get in close and she made nothing of it.

Hard as the others tried, they couldn't get within ten lengths of her, until, as they turned for home and all but two had given up, David felt the mare begin to tire. Her long stride shortened and her honest head began to bob wearily. She was like a car running out of petrol. David sat still and let her freewheel for a dozen strides, giving her time to suck some oxygen into her lungs. It was all downhill to the finish, which would help, but she couldn't freewheel for ever. The moment he felt her recover, David began to squeeze and push, holding the reins firmly to help her balance. With a gasp of relief, he felt her respond. Her stride didn't lengthen but it became stronger. She pinged the second last fence, but

David could sense another horse beginning to close on his outside. There was less than a furlong to run and one fence to jump when a grey head appeared at David's left leg. Bideford had seen it before he had. He felt her strain every sinew. She just didn't want to be passed, but her short legs were weary and her body was burning with exhaustion. David helped her all he could, galvanising her, urging her not to give up.

As they raced down to the last fence, the crowd were on their feet, roaring encouragement. What had started off looking like a formality had now turned into a fierce battle. It was all or nothing.

David drove the mare hard at the final obstacle, as if it weren't there. With one final effort, she put every last part of her energy into a leap that landed her a length clear of her rival. And there she stayed, until the winning post rushed by in a blur.

Lucy Tredington's decision to steal into David's cottage had taken all her courage. Snooping through somebody else's belongings, even her brother's, was completely alien to her nature. In some ways, the fact that it was David's cottage only made the act more reprehensible. But it was something she had to do; she had to be certain he was really the brother he claimed to be.

Using the spare keys from the manor, Lucy nervously let herself in through the back door. Her heart was racing as she stepped lightly across the stone floor, through the narrow hallway and up the staircase to a landing which led to two small bedrooms. Both doors were ajar. Hesitantly, she pushed the first, which creaked as it swung open.

Lucy leaped back at the sound. She waited a moment, scolding herself for being so jumpy, and then summoned the courage to walk into what was obviously David's room.

The bed was made, but his jodhpurs were lying in a heap beside an upright chair. Lucy wavered again before she began her search, then, resolved now, she started to feel inside every pocket and lining. She turned over mattresses and delved into every place where something could conceivably be hidden.

After an hour of scouring the cottage from top to bottom, all she had found of interest, in a small bureau in the sitting-room, was a neatly written list of the rides David had taken in Ireland – far more than she had realised. She also found a note-book containing a list of horses with prices beside them, presumably those at which he'd bought and sold. He appeared never to have lost any money, but then again, he hadn't made much either. Lucy was just putting the book back into the drawer of the desk where she'd found it when the phone rang.

The sudden break in the silence startled her, she'd been so engrossed in her task. She sat rigid while, after four rings, the answerphone cut in and began to rewind itself to play back a single message. The disembodied voice of a woman with an Irish accent wished David luck in his first English race. Lucy glanced at her watch. It was five to three. David would already be on his way down to the start at Wincanton. How could he be calling his home to pick up his messages?

Lucy was still puzzling over the mystery as she walked quickly back to the manor.

* * *

David's heart was pumping like a boxer's punch-bag as Bideford crossed the finishing line with two lengths to spare.

It was as if the win finally confirmed his identity. He was cheered into the winners' enclosure by a crowd who appreciated the significance of an amateur newcomer beating a dozen professionals, albeit on an obviously underrated horse.

Among the people waiting in the bar to celebrate his first win was Johnny Henderson.

Sir Mark introduced them.

'David, I'm sure you remember my godson, Johnny Henderson?'

David nodded. 'Of course I do. How are you?'

Johnny shook his head in disbelief. 'My God, David, of course I'd heard you were back, but somehow I couldn't really believe it. But there was nothing make-believe about that finish.'

David was impressed with Johnny's performance. David and he had been friends as children, and there was no reason why they shouldn't be again. The difficulty was going to be not letting it show just how well they knew each other now.

Beforehand, they had agreed not to talk too much to each other on this first meeting. But there seemed no harm in letting it be seen that they were going to get on.

After half an hour or so, when the party had settled down and another race had been watched, David was on the stand between Johnny and Sir Mark.

'George tells me you bought most of the horses he's going to send pointing this season,' he said to Johnny.

'All five of them, and all bloody cheap. Well, except one. They all ought to win a race somewhere. With any luck that'll confirm his taste for the game.'

'He asked me over to look at them a couple of weeks ago. He's not happy about the expensive one – Letter Lad – won't jump, he says.' David gave a hint of a smile.

'Just needs a bit of schooling, I should think,' Johnny said.

'That's what I reckoned. I tell you what, if he wants to sell him for what he gave, he'd be worth getting. If I could borrow the money to buy him, I think I could do something with him.'

Henderson grinned, also unable to resist the irony.

'Sure. I'll see what I can do. Maybe George will let the horse go for what he cost plus his expenses so far.'

Over the next few weeks, David rode in several races, chalking up a respectable number of wins and attracting some attention from the racing press. He took it all in his stride, working hard at the stud and enjoying every moment of his new life. When his father asked him if he'd like to ride Deep Mischief at the end of October in its warm-up race in preparation for the Hennessy, he was pleased and flattered, even though privately he didn't think he merited the ride. When Sir Mark hinted that he might even have the ride in the big race itself, he could barely contain his excitement. If the horse performed in the Hennessy, its next target would be the Cheltenham Gold Cup.

But he thought often of Ireland, and knew that soon he would have to set about seeing what he could do to ease Mary's circumstances. Knowing how the next relapse would hit her, he had tried to persuade her to undergo a five-day course of methylprednisolone injections to hold back the deterioration of her spinal cord, but Mary was adamant that she wouldn't go into hospital. At least, for the time being, her condition had got no worse, as she told him in their weekly phone-calls.

At the beginning of October, his father asked him to go to Newmarket, where they had two colts entered in Tattersall's yearling sale. To his surprise, he found that Susan was coming with him as groom.

'She loves going to the sales,' Sir Mark said. 'I hope you don't mind.'

David didn't mind at all, but he was surprised Susan wanted to make the journey, given her continued hostility towards him.

David volunteered to drive the lorry, so that he and Susan would be alone together for the six hours it took to get from Devon to Suffolk. At least it would give him a chance to find out what it was that still made Susan distrust him.

The two yearlings were due to be sold in Tuesday's morning session. That meant getting them to the sales complex for Sunday, in order to give prospective buyers time to view them.

Susan and David, with the help of one of the stud grooms, loaded the box first thing after breakfast on Sunday and set off east for Newmarket. Susan behaved in her usual businesslike manner and with apparent indifference towards David. It was only after they had passed Bristol that he noticed a change in her attitude. She had become polite, even friendly, but she spoke to him as if they had only just met. David wondered what had altered her disposition.

They had been travelling and talking for another hour or so before he realised. She had been so subtle about it that he hadn't noticed until then that she was quizzing him, sometimes in minute detail, about his knowledge of Barford and Tredington family history.

And it became clear from another slight shift in her manner that he was doing a lot better than she'd expected.

David smiled to himself. He wasn't seriously annoyed by her persistent scepticism, especially as it was now generally known that Sir Mark had had professional confirmation of his identity, but he still wondered what caused it. To amuse himself, he decided to pre-empt some of her questions.

'How's your father, by the way?' he asked after a short lull in the conversation as he turned on to the M25.

Susan gave him a quick look and didn't answer at once.

'I hardly ever see him,' she said eventually.

'I was sorry to find he'd gone. I used to really like old Ivor. He taught me how to ride.'

'And he told my mum you weren't much good,' Susan countered quickly.

David laughed at the ambivalence of her answer which seemed to create a temporary truce between them. But however hard he tried to recapture the buzz there had been between them the first time they'd met, Susan's aloofness persisted.

David found that he and Susan had hardly any time alone together once they'd arrived. There seemed to be a lot of people at the sales keen to look at the two lots Great Barford were offering. This kept Susan busy, while David was besieged by stallion owners eager to strike up a friendship with him in the hope of selling a nomination or two. Each of them was ready to reduce the fee for the chance of getting a good class mare on the books. David listened to them all politely, but he wouldn't let the prospect of cut-price deals blur his own views on breeding.

Although Newmarket, the sales, and the whole razzmatazz of the bloodstock sales were new to him, David didn't feel out of place. Back in Ireland, he'd been reading reports of the sales for years. But it was with a mixture of relief and anxiety that he watched their first colt enter the ring. He knew that each yearling had only one chance to sell well. If any mishap prevented it from keeping its allotted sale time, its value would be drastically reduced; buyers were always wary of any excuses for withdrawal, however valid.

As Susan led the young horse round the ring, David made a mental note never to allow her to do it again; she was much too attractive. He could tell from their faces that a lot of the bidders crowding the entrance and along the ringside were discussing her, not the yearling.

The sum which the auctioneer chanted increased slowly. Unconsciously, David tensed up. He knew that the colt had to make fifty thousand pounds simply to cover the cost of the stallion fee, its own keep and the depreciation of its dam. But the bids were coming sparsely now. It looked as though the colt was going to be knocked down for half its cost when an agent with close links to one of the large Japanese owners stepped in. The auctioneer quickly stepped up the bids to five thousand guineas a call as he sensed that the new bidder was there to buy.

It took less than two minutes for the price to soar to a hundred and twenty thousand guineas, at which point the underbidder – that most important but most neglected ingredient of any sale – called enough. The hammer fell, and Susan led the yearling away to embark on a career which might or might not prove that the new owner had bought wisely.

Although he'd had little to do with the preparation of the yearlings, David was elated by the sale. As manager of the stud, even as the owner's son, it was his responsibility to make sure that it ran at a profit. Their next lot could now sell only moderately and the kitty would still look healthy; though this animal was more of a race-horse in David's opinion. An hour later, his view was confirmed as their second offering topped the sale at three hundred and sixty thousand guineas. The bidder was the rich widow of a shipping magnate who had recently won a Classic with a grey colt with similar markings to the one she'd just bought. David made his way round the side of the ring to her seat beside the auctioneer. He shook her hand. 'Best of luck with him, and let's hope lightning strikes twice for you.'

She acknowledged his good wishes with an appreciative smile; David beamed back and went on his way to organise the smooth transfer of the young horses.

First he checked that both yearlings had passed the mandatory test for defects in their breathing, then he found the people who would now be responsible for their welfare and gave them a brief summary of the colts' characters. This done, he made his way to the stables and gave the horses a carrot each. He'd known them less than two months, but it felt like saying goodbye to a child.

Susan had tears in her eyes as they loaded their tack on to the lorry. The formalities were completed, and David climbed up into the cab to drive them back to Devon.

Susan didn't take long to recover. 'Congratulations,' she said sarcastically. 'Your first sale's been quite a success.'

'Come on, Susan. You know that I know I've been back far too short a time to have made any contribution to those yearlings.'

'I didn't mean that,' she said. 'I meant in convincing everyone in racing that you're David Tredington.'

David didn't rise. He glanced at her with a grin. 'Do you know, Susan, I've come to the conclusion that you're a bit of a snob. Just because I've the manners and the accent of a Mayo farmer, you think it's impossible for me to be a Tredington.'

Susan didn't reply.

'That's it, isn't it?' David said triumphantly. 'I've finally hit the nail on the head, haven't I? Well, I'll tell you one thing, I'm not going to suddenly change just to fit in with your idea of how an English land-owner should behave. If I was more like George, would that suit you better?'

Susan grinned, despite herself. 'No, it bloody wouldn't,' she said. But she wouldn't expand and, despite his encouragement, she wouldn't talk about anything but horses and the stud for the rest of the journey back to Devon.

After the conversation he and David had had at Wincanton, Johnny Henderson had been quick to get to work on George, persuading him to part with Letter Lad, though not, unfortunately, for 'a penny less than a monkey profit'.

David knew the gelding's arrival at Great Barford might create tension between him and George, but he was prepared for that. At the same time, there was considerable satisfaction to be earned in discovering why a horse which in Ireland he'd seen jump an iron gate as if it wasn't there, now found difficulty in getting from one side of a straw bale to the other.

The morning after Letter Lad arrived at Barford, David got to work on him. He started by popping him over a couple of cavalettis no more than a foot high. As he had suspected, there was no point in going on. The horse was obviously in pain each time it landed. It had only attempted the small jumps out of natural bravery. Its front feet barely left the ground before David felt it snatch them down again.

He took Letter Lad back to his stable and fetched a pair of metal calipers with flat ends. The horse had been jumping out to the right, favouring his off-fore to land on. David picked up his near-fore and held it between his legs with his back to the horse's shoulder. He began squeezing the wall and sole of the foot. He worked his way round, pressing gently, fairly sure of what he would find.

About an inch back from the point of the frog, he scraped away some dead sole with his finger and picked up the calipers again.

He had barely begun to ease them together when Letter Lad leapt backwards, snatching his foot from between David's legs and snorting with pain. He stood trembling, with his nostrils flared, looking fearfully at David and ready to run for his life.

Slowly, quietly, David held out a hand. 'Come on, old son. I didn't mean to hurt you.'

Letter Lad gave a sharp snort but, warily, allowed David to stroke his muzzle. After a couple of minutes of soft talking, the trust between them began to return. With a few gentle words of encouragement, David left the horse and went off in search of a blacksmith's paring knife and a small bucket of warm, disinfected water.

He also found Victoria and brought her back to the stable. She held Letter Lad's head while David picked up his near-fore again.

The semi-circular end of the wooden-handled knife was designed for cutting narrow grooves in horses' feet, as well as for trimming in preparation for a new shoe.

Being as careful as he could, David began to cut away the sole of Letter Lad's foot. The corn he had identified might have been festering slowly for some time, building up pressure like a bruise beneath a fingernail. The height of the shoe had given the corn some protection and it had taken time to come to a head. As David cut closer to the bottom of Letter Lad's sole, the big roan became anxious to get his foot away. David squeezed his knees tighter together to prevent the horse from snatching his hoof back. He could see a small vein of light-coloured flesh begin to appear. He gave one last short cut, and a fountain of blood burst out over the straw.

Victoria gasped softly. The relief of seeing an end to the pain was as welcome to her as it was to the horse. 'No wonder he didn't want to jump.'

David shoved the paring knife in his pocket and reached for the bucket. He began to swab the opening he'd made. 'I'm surprised he even *tried* to jump with this. I guess he must have trodden on a sharp stone or a nail or something soon after he arrived at George's. I'll put a poultice on it for a day, then get the blacksmith to put a leather pad across his foot to protect it for a while. He's got a really thin sole; if we're not careful he'll get a corn every week.'

When Letter Lad had had the pad on for five days, he began to regain his confidence. A couple of days later, he was jumping the way David knew he could, and loving every moment of it.

The following Sunday, George discovered where his horse had gone.

He found David in the tack-room. 'Is that Letter Lad two boxes down?'

David laughed. 'Sure. I thought you'd recognise him.'

George's red face showed signs of growing curiosity. 'How's he jumping?'

'Getting better. I was just thinking of selling him on,' David said, 'when I found a corn in his foot. He's jumping like a salmon in spring now his confidence is back.'

'Why didn't you tell me you were buying him?'

David grinned. 'Come on, George. If you'd known I was after it, you'd have asked double the price.'

With an effort, George forced himself to take it with good grace. 'Ah, well,' he said, 'I suppose all's fair in love and racing. I was rather pleased with myself for getting rid of him at a profit.'

David raised his eyebrows. 'You must have bought him damn well,' he conciliated.

'I gave Johnny a pretty precise brief,' George answered, pleased with himself. 'Still, I do think he might have told me who was buying it,' he added peevishly.

Once a week, David telephoned Mary Daly. She gave no signs of impatience at his absence, receiving the news of his progress and successes with audible pride. She assured him that she was able to cope for the moment with the bad spells when they came. There were two neighbours always ready to come and help when she needed them.

Johnny Henderson had once said of a fiancée who had gone away for six months, 'Absence makes a fond heart wander, and that's what mine did.' David hadn't found that his heart had wandered so much as his memory of Mayo and Mary. It troubled his conscience. He could forgive himself for losing his love of Ireland, but not Mary; she had been everything to him for so long.

It was six weeks after his first ride in England that David rode Deep Mischief in his pre-Hennessy run at Newbury.

111

'Whatever happens, I don't want this horse to have a hard race.' Sam Hunter's instructions to David as he stood with him in the paddock had an unusually stern edge to them. In the week leading up to the race, there had been a niggling doubt in his mind that the horse hadn't done enough work for his first run of the season.

Sam had considered missing the race altogether and going straight to the Hennessy, but Deep Mischief badly needed experience. He had only run five times over fences, and never in top-class company. It would be unfair to throw him into the deep end when he had barely learned to swim. What Sam did not want was the horse to come back exhausted, unable to recover in time for his main objective. Deep Mischief was an honest individual and always gave everything; Sam knew that if David didn't take care, he would run himself into the ground.

David knew it wasn't going to be easy to carry out Sam's instructions. Deep Mischief was always enthusiastic about everything he did. Whatever was asked of him, he did willingly, with ears pricked and a wish to please.

There were nine runners for the two-and-a-half-mile chase. The distance was on the short side for Deep Mischief. Under normal circumstances, David would have set him off in front, but there was a pair of other jockeys anxious to make the running. David didn't want to get into a battle in the early stages of the race. As they settled down and got under way, he deliberately primed the breach and let his horse tag along at the back.

The leaders set a modest gallop until they passed the stands and jumped the second fence down the far side. At this point the tempo suddenly increased, and Deep

Mischief was caught a little short of speed. Sam's instructions were still fresh in David's ears: he sat as still as a mouse while the horse tried to adjust to the change of pace in his own time.

Shortly after they reached the next, David found himself more than a dozen lengths adrift and going nowhere. Deep Mischief had misinterpreted David's lack of movement and, quite out of character, had begun to sulk at not being part of the action. Intuitively, David sensed the animal's mood, shortened his reins, and started to push.

It took another five fences to persuade Deep Mischief to start trying again. Slowly but surely, though, he pegged back some of the ground he'd given away, as his long, steady stride began to find its rhythm. He flew the downhill fence and hugged the rail tightly, his ears flat back as he raced on into the straight.

Three fences from home, David felt Deep Mischief increase his effort as he drew encouragement by passing another runner.

A couple more horses began to fade, enabling Deep Mischief to overtake. Despite this, it was obvious to David as the horse put in an enormous leap at the second last that victory was out of the question. He was making ground all the time, but the leaders were gone beyond recall.

When he had let Deep Mischief run on for another half-furlong to make sure he'd done enough work, David took a tight hold of his head, before they got so close that they would be involved in the race for the minor placings.

Deep Mischief passed the post in sixth place, twenty

lengths behind the winner. David grinned to himself.
With this race under his belt, and the extra distance, he
had no doubt that, provided all went well, Deep Mischief
would have a great chance in the Hennessy. Sam
Hunter and his father would be more than happy with
his performance.

Later, when David had changed and was walking
towards the members', he had been drawn up short by a
voice behind him.

'Aidan!'

He had turned involuntarily, but not particularly
perturbed. He had made no secret of his previous Irish
existence.

He was caught in the gaze of the damp, melancholy
blue eyes of a small man in a long, grimy raincoat. David
guessed the man was in his late fifties, nicotine-grey
hair, balding slightly, with a patch of missed stubble
beneath his left nostril. David had recognised the type,
but not the man.

'Hello?'

'Hello, my friend. Could we have a little talk?'

The man spoke with a Mayo accent. David nodded.
'I'm on my way to meet someone in the bar.'

'It'll not take long.'

David shrugged as the small man came alongside
him, matching his stride. 'We should get out of the
crowd where we won't be heard.'

'Look, what do you want?' David tried from natural
politeness not to let his impatience show.

The man caught hold of his arm and gripped it with
unexpected strength. 'My name's Emmot MacClancy.

I'm from Mayo, too, and I used to know Mary Daly when she was in London.' He charged the words with heavy significance.

Mary had always assured David that there was no one from those times who would be aware of her flight to Ireland and change of name. He believed her, but this man's words had his nerves tingling. He looked at him bemused.

'I don't know what you're talking about.'

'Oh yes you do.' He held up a battered hand. 'Don't deny it. But don't worry; I'll not tell a soul where they've to look to find out the truth, provided you show your appreciation of my discretion.'

David stared at him with amazement. 'I think you've got your wires crossed. It's someone else you're thinking of.' David was determined to go, to leave this confrontation before it developed but, before he could, he was assailed by a stare of such bleak, self-pitying resentment that he was almost hypnotised by it.

'My wires aren't crossed at all, and if you turn away now, I promise, you'll regret it. I know as well as you do, you're no more David Tredington than I am. And if you go on denying it, I won't answer for what will happen.'

Summoning up all his will-power, David spun abruptly on his heels and walked back towards the entrance to the members' enclosure. His heart was thumping as he cursed himself for his inadequate performance. The success of the last few weeks had almost made him forget his vulnerability; even Susan Butley had shown no signs of renewing her attack.

Now, this one assault from a watery-eyed, scruffy music-hall Irishman had rudely jerked him back to where he had been five weeks before he had arrived in Devon, to a time when he had never even heard of Barford Manor.

Chapter Five

Ireland: August

The winds of fortune often blow when they're least expected, arriving to surprise, and scatter plans into the air. To Johnny Henderson their coming was sudden, but not unexpected. He had been sitting at a rusty black table outside Brady's Bar in Westport, County Mayo. The sleeves of a red and white striped shirt, once crisp, were rumpled up to his elbows. The creases he had pressed on to his fawn cotton trousers had long since disappeared, and his brown brogues were coated with dust. From beneath the rim of a high-crowned Panama, he surveyed the passing townspeople, tourists and visiting farmers with easy detachment and well-disguised frustration.

Johnny had been in Ireland for two weeks, flogging his weary old BMW along hot empty roads in the full discomfort of a rare Hibernian heat-wave. He had driven over a thousand miles, and had got nowhere.

He had orders – at least vague verbal instructions – to look for a dozen or so jumpers with potential as yet unrecognised by their breeders. He had never met an Irish breeder who had not recognised the potential of their horses, however slight or, indeed, non-existent it might have been. He didn't hold out much hope of ever finding one, but he was prepared to be as adventurous as he was eager to do some deals.

This was one of the reasons he had come to the mid-west of Ireland, well off the beaten path normally travelled by English buyers of bloodstock. The breeders here, generally less exposed to those opportunities, he hoped, might be a little less complacent in their attitude towards a genuine buyer.

He had decided to sink his last few hundred pounds into a trawl round Ireland for cheap horses for the meaner or more impecunious of his clients. He would be lucky to make a thousand quid a horse, if he ever found anything suitable.

Looking at the farmers in Westport, in town to buy or sell or just to meet their friends and drink, he wondered if any of them harboured some sturdy youngstock in their wind-blown barns; some talented Pegasus looking for a real challenge across the Irish Sea. Surely some of them did.

As he mused and fantasised, ordering another Jameson's to help, his eye was caught by a man – a farmer, by the look of his clothes and the scarred muddy pick-up which had brought him to town. But it wasn't the man's occupation or the possibility that he might have an undervalued colt in his paddock that fired Johnny's excitement. It was the man's un-Irish, uncanny resemblance to the Tredington family of Barford in the English county of Devon that almost stopped his breathing for a moment or two.

Not too tall, with the same straight, dun-coloured

hair and grey eyes, this individual, now strolling across the street towards him, also had the same square chin, straight nose and well-proportioned face which had characterised Tredingtons for the last four or five generations. Other, not immediately specifiable features would have allowed him to step straight into a Tredington family photograph with no questions asked.

Johnny's heart thumped; his right hand, still grasping his glass, twitched and sloshed whiskey on to the table as he realised what he was looking at.

The farmer was only a few yards from him now.

'Good morning!' Johnny called. 'How are you?'

The man faltered a step, looking to see where this greeting had come from. He didn't identify Johnny at first, assuming, from the tone in which he'd been hailed, that it had come from someone he would recognise.

'Good morning,' Johnny said again, determined not to let this man by without accosting him.

The man glanced at Johnny and saw the friendly, knowing smile on the Englishman's face.

'Good mornin' to you,' he said, with habitual Irish affability and an accent that could not have been confused with a Tredington's.

Johnny looked surprised. 'Good Lord! You're not David Tredington, are you? I'm sorry, but you're an absolute dead ringer for him. I do believe you could have fooled his own mother. You must let me buy you a drink.'

A drink was just what Aidan Daly wanted in this unaccustomed heat. He wasn't in a hurry – nothing happened in a hurry on the thin-soiled, rocky farm which he worked under the shadow of Croagh Patrick. 'Sure,' he said, pulling out a chair opposite Johnny, 'I'll admit, I am a little dehydrated.'

Surprisingly, the exuberant, self-assured Englishman and the unassuming Irishman turned out to have a lot in common, led by their shared interest in bloodstock.

Johnny told Aidan why he was in Ireland.

Aidan, without much hope of interesting this obviously well-connected bloodstock dealer, did admit that there was quite a decent colt, going on four, still growing, though not what you might call classily bred, gobbling up a lot of his best hay at home, where there was scarcely a blade of grass to be seen in the fields.

'Sounds nice,' Johnny said, 'but probably too expensive for me. Fact of the matter is, I operate in the rather lower echelons of the business. Pointers for punters without a pot to piss in is really my line. Do you think you could help me there at all?'

Aidan heard this and recognised that he might well be able to help this sympathetic Englishman, and at the same time make a bit of money without taking too much advantage of him.

The Dalys' farm was not a profitable enterprise, even with the subsidies that still dribbled down from Brussels. Aidan's mother had told him only a few weeks ago that the hospital had confirmed that she was approaching the advanced stages of multiple sclerosis. Soon, Mary had lamented, she would be presented with the options of going more or less permanently into hospital, or somehow finding the money for a full-time, live-in carer at home, so that Aidan would still be free to run the farm.

As things stood at the moment, there was no prospect of finding that money. Perhaps, Aidan thought with excitement, if he could build up a relationship with this Johnny Henderson, he could supply a steady stream of horses to what he had always heard was an endless queue of aspiring English owners. He also had no doubt that Johnny was being falsely modest about his own importance in the market. It was obvious that a man like that would know all the right people.

'As it happens, John, I might. I've ridden a fair number of races out here – just little point-to-points, like – and I'd know where most of the horses are coming from and which could perform if they were ridden well. Some of them wouldn't be what you'd call extortionate prices.'

From the moment he had set eyes on Aidan, Johnny's interest in horse-dealing had taken a distant second place to a scheme of far greater importance.

For the time being, though, he knew that it would suit him to wear his bloodstock agent's hat.

'Aidan, that would be fantastic. To tell the truth I was beginning to despair of finding anything suitable. But with your local knowledge, I think we could get a hell of a deal going between us.' He grasped Aidan's hand across the table. 'I know what, why don't we start with what you've got at home, and then take a look at any others you know of – as soon as you can manage it?'

'Sure. But to get them at the right money, we'll have to employ what you might call a little subterfuge,' replied Aidan, warming to the idea. 'They'll have to think they're selling to me and you're just a friend along for the crack.'

'Of course,' Johnny agreed. 'Then we'll go halves on the profit I make back in England.'

'England's a long way for me. I'll be happy just to earn a couple of hundred a horse.'

Johnny laughed. 'You think a bird in the hand's worth a whole flock in the English bush? You needn't worry. I'm an honest man, but I'm also a businessman, so I'll be more than happy to go along with your terms.'

They had more drinks, until it was too late for Aidan to do what he had come into Westport to do; he had to get back home to his sick mother, he said, who was waiting for him. They arranged that Johnny would drive out to the farm next morning, and Aidan walked a little unsteadily back to his pick-up.

Johnny had observed that his own head was more accustomed than Aidan's to alcohol in warm weather and, still relatively sober, he set about his researches before Aidan was more than a mile along the road west towards Louisburgh.

In a bar where the clientele was notoriously committed to horse-racing, he made enquiries about Aidan Daly.

Aidan, he discovered, even in this backwood, was considered something of a backwoodsman by the few men who claimed to know anything about him.

'There's a man that should be wed and breeding children,' a small, toothless man who looked like Rumpelstiltskin said. 'But eight and twenty, he's still living on his mother's farm, fifteen miles up the road past Croagh Patrick. It's seldom he'll put in an appearance here in town.'

'But,' his other informant told Johnny, 'that is a man

who could have been a prince among jockeys if only he'd let himself be a little bit more adventurous. I've seen him win races on horses that didn't deserve to start. He can do everything bar talk to them.'

'Sure, he's some kind of a jockey,' Rumpelstiltskin agreed, calling for another three pints of Guinness. ''Tis a terrible waste to see. He could have been up with the best of them over in England, earning a king's ransom. And he's a mind like an encyclopaedia when it comes to breeding. He dreams of winning the lottery and sending his poor old mares down to Coolmore to be covered for fifty thousand pounds.'

'They say 'tis his mother is the stumbling block to him. She has a small, scrubby sort of a farm – not enough to graze a goat, but she won't leave, and she can't do without Aidan. There was a husband, but he died or deserted her, no one knows for sure, before she came back from England.'

After this, Johnny judged, the information became more speculative, but if what he had been told so far was true, it would fit very well with the plan taking shape in his head. But to start with, he would stick to being a bloodstock agent, even if it meant having to commit himself to one of the nags Aidan had in mind to show him.

The sun glittered off the blue, island-spotted water of Westport Bay as Johnny Henderson drove west next morning. On his left, the dark side of Croagh Patrick loomed. It was a stirring sight, but all Johnny's concentration was on the chase that lay ahead. Having been presented with a box of gold in the shape of Aidan

Daly, he was well aware of the problems that lay ahead in forging a key to its lock.

After ten miles, he stopped to look at his map. He identified the small hill to the south, beneath which Aidan had told him he would find his mother's farm. Johnny turned up a narrow lane and soon spotted the dirty white buildings half-way up the hillside.

Even on this sunny morning, no one could have described the surroundings as lush. Whatever home-steader had been responsible, centuries before, for settling here, could not have had many options open to him. But there was a craggy beauty to the place.

Johnny turned off the lane on to the deeply rutted track that led up to the farmhouse and a few crumbling barns that belonged to it.

As he approached the house, he saw a couple of incongruously well-kept young horses grazing in a scrubby field, and the dilapidation of the place became more apparent. Even his battered BMW looked out of place among the mess of the farmyard where he came to a halt.

He turned the engine off and got out into the still, silent sunshine. It was a moment or two before his arrival produced any reaction from the house that faced him. Then, hobbling painfully with the help of a pair of old hazel sticks, a woman appeared.

She smiled. 'Good morning to you. And you'd be the man my son met in Westport?'

'That's right,' Johnny beamed. 'Good morning, Mrs Daly.'

'You can call me Mary,' the woman said. 'Come on in out of this sun. Aidan'll not be a moment.'

Johnny followed her through the front door of the house, straight into a tidy farmhouse kitchen. Mary sat down.

'Excuse me,' she said. 'I've this creeping paralysis. It comes and goes; today, it's come. Help yourself to a glass of Paddy's.'

'Thanks. I will.' Johnny reached down the bottle she had indicated and filled a glass that was already on the table.

'So,' the woman went on, 'Aidan tells me you're from England, looking for horses.'

'That's right.' As he spoke, Johnny studied Aidan's mother. Grey-haired, with bright blue eyes, she was probably not yet fifty, but illness had aged her. It was obvious that she had once been a very good-looking woman. She also had the look of someone who had known a lot of pain in her life. 'Good, well-nurtured stock is what I'm looking for, not grand pedigrees.'

'You'll find nothing grand in our bloodlines, but Aidan knows what he's doing. I sometimes wish,' she said quietly, 'that he'd the chance to make use of his talents, but he's a good son and he'll not leave me here alone.'

Johnny identified the stumbling block in his path and mentally adjusted his approach. 'I saw two nice-looking colts in the field outside. Are those yours?'

'Yes, but I'll let Aidan tell you all about them ... here he is.'

Aidan tapped the dust from his boots as he came in through the front door. 'How are you?' he said to Johnny. 'You've not let my mother tell you the truth about the horses, have you?'

Johnny got to his feet and shook Aidan's hand. 'They look pretty good to me anyway.'

'We'll deal with them later. I've in mind to show you a few animals ready to race. When you've finished your drink, we'll head off down to Doo Lough where there's a few to look at.'

Aidan insisted that they drive in his pick-up, on the grounds that Johnny's car was too flashy.

'That's encouraging,' Johnny remarked. 'If anyone thinks my old banger's too flashy, their expectations are not going to be too high.'

Aidan nodded and grinned.

They covered a hundred miles that day, including a quick foray into Connemara, and inspected more than twenty animals. At each isolated farm, Johnny did as he was told and kept in the background, looking but saying little. He heard twenty different reasons for selling horses, and twenty more for buying them.

Back at the farm, Mary insisted that Johnny should stay the night, as he and Aidan planned to visit half a dozen more farms next day. The following evening, Johnny suggested they have a drink in the bar in the nearby village of Louisburgh.

'Well?' Aidan asked anxiously as they settled down with their drinks. 'What did you think of them?'

To his surprise, Johnny had been rather impressed by the horses Aidan had been able to show him over the last two days of driving around the craggy Mayo hills. Now, though, he was non-committal. 'I don't know, Aidan. I know I said my budget wasn't all that great, but frankly I was after individuals with a bit more class. That colt of yours will make a fine strong chaser, I'd say – certainly worth a thousand or two.'

Aidan's face fell. 'Is that all you think he'd be worth in England? I've had better offers here, but I was going to win a few races with him first. The truth is, there's so little to be made on the farm, we've really to look to the horses to keep us going. My mother's a brave woman – she wouldn't let you see how ill she is – but soon I've to find the money to pay for her treatment and a nurse in the house, and I just don't know where I'm going to look for it.'

Johnny shook his head sympathetically and sucked a mouthful of air through his teeth. 'I'll buy what I can through you, I promise, Aidan, after all the trouble you've gone to. But I can't really see it amounting to much.' He also disliked himself for the satisfaction that Aidan's disappointment gave him. 'But look,' he went on, 'surely it can't be that bad? Won't the health service pay for your mother's treatment?'

'Only if she goes into hospital, and she'd rather pass away than leave the farm; it would break her heart to do that. God knows, sometimes I wonder when I'll ever get the chance to go out looking for a woman and making a life of my own. But there it is, I never knew my father and there's only ever been her and me for as long as I can remember. Now she has only between five and ten years to live. You can see why her peace of mind has to take priority.'

'Of course I can,' Johnny spoke gently and nodded. 'So you really need a lot of money if she's to stay on the farm?'

Aidan nodded.

'Well, I'm terribly sorry if I built up your expectations about the prospects for some profitable horse-trading, but it very much looks as though I'm going to have to go back to my old tried-and-tested sources.'

He ordered more drinks for them. When two full glasses were on the table between them, he gave Aidan a long, speculative look. 'D'you know, I've been thinking of another way you could make some money, possibly a great deal.'

Aidan looked up. 'What? How? Out here in Mayo?'

'You've got one very valuable asset you could use.'

'And what might that be?'

'Your face.'

Aidan stared at him for a moment, then burst out laughing. 'You think I might have some future as fillum star, do you?'

Johnny smiled. 'You might, for all I know, but that's not what I had in mind.' He leaned forward to emphasise the confidentiality of what he was going to say. 'Do you remember when we first met, three days ago in Westport – it seems like months – I thought you were someone called David Tredington?'

'The fella you said I'm a dead ringer for?'

'That's right. What I should have said was that you'd be a dead ringer for him if he were still around. Nobody's seen him for more than fifteen years.'

Aidan, trying to see where this was leading, became suspicious. 'Why have they not seen him for so long, for God's sake?'

Johnny shrugged. 'He ran away from his home – one of the most beautiful houses in Devon – after his mother died, when he was twelve. He's never been seen since.'

'How did they know some accident hadn't happened, that he hadn't been killed somewhere and just couldn't be found?'

'The police searched every inch of Devon without a sniff or a sighting. They went over the estate with a fine-tooth comb, but he'd just vanished into thin air. Then, a note arrived, posted a couple of days later, saying how miserable he'd been at Barford. I used to be there a lot in those days. Sir Mark Tredington's my godfather. I was quite a friend of David's, and his cousin George. We were all at school together. My family lived in London, so I used to go down and stay there the whole time during the holidays. I was already interested in horses then, and they've a wonderful stud there. I was at Barford when it happened. It was a few weeks after his mother had been killed out hunting. He was a bit of a mummy's boy and he was devastated. He couldn't seem to come to terms with it, and Sir Mark was away a lot in those days. David just seemed to retreat into his shell.'

'Jesus! So this little fella was so miserable that he ran away and never came back? What age would he be now?'

'Twenty-seven, twenty-eight.'

Aidan started. 'That's my age, twenty-eight.'

'Is it really?' Johnny said with excitement. Then he asked earnestly, almost prepared to believe it. 'Look, you aren't really David, are you? You so easily could be.'

Aidan shook his head. 'I lived in England till I was twelve, too, but I'm not this David Tredington, no chance. My mother was housekeeper in a small hospital run by the sisters of the Holy Infant in Roehampton, near to London. We'd a couple of rooms there. D'you know, I scarcely remember a thing about it. I wasn't happy there. I went to the local Catholic school. I didn't like it at all. The only pleasure I ever had was helping out at the livery stables in Richmond Park. When my mother inherited the farm from her uncle, there was no stopping us getting over here. I'd never been before, but it was love at first sight. I mean, the old farm may not make much of a living, but it's the most beautiful place in the world, is it not?'

'It certainly is,' Johnny agreed, happy to become sentimental about it. 'And of course your mother shouldn't have to leave and be taken off into some anonymous place to die.' Lightly, he thumped the table with his fist. 'And she needn't, Aidan, she needn't!'

'What is it you have in mind?' Aidan asked doubtfully, less inclined than some of his countrymen to believe in miracles.

'You'll probably think this is a crazy scheme, but I think you could take David Tredington's place.' He leaned back in his chair with a slight smile.

Aidan looked at him without speaking for a moment. 'Why,' he asked, 'should I want to do that?'

Johnny took a swig of his stout and began to speak slowly to underline the significance of what he was saying. 'Because he was the only son of Sir Mark Tredington whose estate when he dies will be worth something in the order of ten million quid.'

'You mean, I should turn up and claim this fella David Tredington's inheritance?'

'That's exactly what I mean.'

Aidan stared at Johnny. 'But that's absolutely crazy! And downright crooked.'

'Not a hundred per cent ethical, I'll grant you, but not

crazy. I'll have to check out a few things before I can be sure it'll work but, as far as I can see, and I know most of the facts, it's perfectly feasible.'

'But for Jesus' sake, man, I could never carry it off! Who's going to believe I'm some kind of an English nob? I'm a Mayo farmer.'

'Fine. That's what you've chosen to be since you were twelve years old, but now you've decided to come home. Your Irish speech doesn't matter a damn. I once met a full-blown belted earl who spoke broad Australian. What you will need to do is learn everything I can tell you about the place and the family.'

'John,' Aidan said, shaking his head, 'it's not on. I can't do it. It'd be theft, or deception, or whatever criminal, that's for sure, and I'm no criminal.'

'I'm not so sure. If David doesn't turn up – and as far as I know he's missing presumed dead – the whole shooting match, estate and title will pass to his cousin George. I can tell you, you'd make a far better job of it than George. He's fat, smug and pompous: Barford would be wasted on him. You'd be doing the family and Devon a favour by squeezing him out.'

'Look, I don't care what this George is like; it's his inheritance, legally, and I've no moral right to do him out of it, and that's that.' He moved in his chair as if to get up.

Johnny held up a hand to cover his irritation. 'I take your point, Aidan, but hold on. What I'm saying is true, and you'd have no more problems about what to do with your mother. There'd be enough income for you from Day One to pay for a houseful of carers.'

This time Aidan wasn't to be put off leaving. 'I'm

happy to do a bit of horse-trading with you, John, but there's no way I'm getting involved in this crazy deception. It wouldn't work, and I wouldn't do it even if I thought it would. Now, I've got to be getting back. If you'd like to take another look at the colt, and revise your offer a bit, you'll be very welcome.'

Johnny gave in with apparent good grace. 'OK,' he grinned, 'but do just think about it. You could be certain your mother would have no more worries, plus the best possible treatment and care there is to be had; and surely she'd be very grateful to you for that.'

Chapter Six

Johnny Henderson kept a smile on his face until Aidan had left the bar. Even then, it didn't disappear entirely.

As he had talked to Aidan, the impersonation he was proposing seemed increasingly plausible. Everything was in its favour, even down to the fact that Aidan himself hadn't arrived in Mayo until he was twelve. It was as if this Irish farmer had been tailor-made for the role of David Tredington.

Johnny realised now that he had sprung the idea on Aidan too abruptly, and that he had failed to take into account any moral objections Aidan might have. It was too late to remedy that but, even so, his instincts told him that these could be overcome if Mary Daly's comfort were presented as a worthy end to justify questionable means.

He had at least planted in Aidan's mind the idea that the financial problems of his mother's tragic illness could be solved. In the meantime, he'd have to be more subtle in promoting it.

'Morning!' Johnny Henderson put his head inside the front door of the Dalys' crumbling white farmhouse.

Mary Daly, sitting at her large pine table scarred and

133

stained with a hundred years' use, looked up and smiled with a serenity that gave no hint of the constant pain that afflicted her. 'Did you want to see Aidan?'

'I did,' Johnny answered; the Irish reluctance to say 'yes' was infectious.

'He'll be glad. He's out in the barn with the colt. Be sure and come back to the house for a little cup of something before you go.'

'I will,' Johnny said. 'Thank you.'

He nodded to her and turned to pick his way across a yard littered with archaic farm implements, discarded wagons, old horseshoes and empty feed bags. A tribe of countless scrawny cats lurking among the debris coexisted in truce with a flock of wary chickens.

A cockerel of incongruous magnificence stood haughtily on the pinnacle of a mountainous muck-heap outside the barn where Aidan had put up his stables.

The cock lifted his beak to the sky and yodelled to announce Johnny's approach. A moment late Aidan came out through the high double doors of the white-washed stone building.

Johnny saw at once the look of relief in the Irishman's eyes.

'Hello, John. You came, then, in spite of my lofty moral tone in the bar yesterday?'

Johnny laughed. 'Don't worry about that. I've met loftier. Anyway, forget the suggestion I made. It wouldn't work if your heart wasn't in it; if you weren't convinced, no one else would be. No,' he dismissed the idea with a backward wave of his hand, 'I came because there was one horse I thought might be worth a second look.'

'Which would that be?'

'That big chestnut roan we saw; belongs to a tinker on the other side of the mountain, by the lake.'

Aidan grinned and nodded. 'You've a better eye than I gave you credit for. That horse has only ever been ridden by a man you wouldn't trust to walk your dog, and who sits a horse over a fence like a bag of corn.'

'You said he'd never won?'

'That's right, but he has a real turn of foot, some real talent there. If I had him, I'd get him winning in a matter of months.'

'The only trouble is, that chap was talking about seven grand.'

Aidan dismissed this with a shake of the head. 'That's only his way of letting me know the animal was for sale. He'll sell it to me for half that, and still feel happy he was cheating me.'

'If you can get him for three and a half thousand, we've got a deal. I've got a client back in England who'll give me a profit on him.' Johnny thought of George Tredington's ambition to send out winning horses from his own small farm, and boast afterwards how he'd paid next to nothing for them. George had charged him with the task of finding four or five that might help him to achieve this and, incidentally, show his Uncle Mark that he had all the skill and judgement needed to run a stud like Barford. At least – as George had put it – make the old buffer say 'Well done', for once.

They were walking back across the yard towards the house now. 'You leave it to me,' Aidan said. 'If you come with me again, he'll know it's you that wants it, and your English accent would double the price.'

'Fine,' Johnny agreed. 'If you say the animal can be

bought for three and a half thousand and then made to perform, that's good enough for me.'

'You'll not regret it,' Aidan said.

They walked into the kitchen where Mary Daly still sat. 'You'll forgive me for not bustling around,' she said with gentle apology, 'but I'm not so good on my pins today. Aidan, would you ever shove the kettle back on the ring?'

He did as she asked, while a worried look flashed across his nut-brown face.

When the three of them were sitting at the table with mugs of tea in front of them, Mary Daly asked Johnny about England.

'I've not been back these sixteen years,' she said, 'not since Aidan and I left the convent. It's strange, I never thought I was leaving for good, but once we came here, I didn't want to go back at all. I was always promising Aidan we'd go; now the poor boy has never been further than Dublin, with the farm to run and all.'

'Don't worry, Mother. I'll get my chances.'

'I just hope you do. Anyway, Mr Henderson, tell me how it is back in England now.'

Johnny aimed his answers at Aidan, and dwelt on the quality of equestrian life, the prospects and pleasures to be found in the still hugely popular English sports of National Hunt and point-to-point racing. Mary Daly didn't miss the responsive gleam in her son's eyes.

Later, when Aidan went out to deal with his cows, his mother confided in Johnny.

'I don't keep him here, you know. I've never said to him that he shouldn't go, and yet, though I know he wants to – to see more, to make more of the brilliant talent he has with the horses, he'd feel he was abandoning me, for I've no real family left here now – a couple of old uncles too petrified of the devil to move.' She shrugged. 'Maybe I should insist that I go to the hospital.'

Johnny shook his head. 'That wouldn't release him,' he said. 'He'd know you'd be missing this place too much. But look, it's just possible he might be able to help me with a couple of projects. As you say, he has a superb eye and, from what I've heard, great skill with a horse. It does seem an awful shame to leave it buried up here. And, of course, he'd make enough money to pay for all the care you need.'

Mary looked doubtful, torn between conflicting wishes. 'I wish to God there were an easy answer,' she sighed.

When Johnny left later in the afternoon for the small hotel in Westport where he was staying, Aidan set off to buy the horse from a scruffy little small-holding on the other side of Croagh Patrick.

He drove up to a rickety five-bar iron gate, and parked his pick-up. Stepping out on to a muddy track, he let himself into the yard beyond, closing the gate behind him. The only thing that moved was the big dark chestnut head of the animal he'd come to see, protruding from a makeshift window in what looked like a chicken shed. Aidan walked towards it, nodding with a smile.

Without a sound, as if he had materialised from the dung-scented air, a small dark man appeared at Aidan's side. His black eyes glinted. 'Now, that's a real hoss.'

'I didn't think it was a pig,' Aidan said. 'Though it's hard to tell with all that mud on him.'

The little man looked hurt. 'The mud is only on the surface. That animal is in beautiful condition within himself.'

'We'll see,' Aidan said, unimpressed by the sales pitch. 'I'll have another look at him.'

The horse's owner let himself into the shed, and knotted an ancient halter rope around its large head. As he led it out, the horse had to duck to pass through the low opening.

As Aidan looked on, trying not to let his appreciation of the animal's obvious qualities show, a frantic squawling erupted in a corner of the yard. A lean ginger cat shot out of a barn and streaked across the yard between Aidan and the horse, hotly pursued by a pair of yapping terriers.

The powerful chestnut took one look, spun round in terror and, tugging the grimy rope from its handler, took off across the yard towards the gate. Without missing a stride, it bunched up, stretched out and flew over the top rail as if it had been a twelve-inch cavaletti.

The sound of the cat's flight dwindled into the distance behind the shed; the wiry little farmer just stood proudly with his hands on his hips. 'As I said, that's what I call a real hoss.'

That evening, Johnny rang George Tredington to let him know that he'd found a horse of suitably unrealised potential, and at an appropriate price.

Aidan arrived triumphantly later that evening with the news that Letter Lad was theirs for three thousand five hundred and fifty pounds. The extra fifty, he said, was a necessary sop to the vendor's vanity.

Johnny phoned George Tredington again, asking him to transfer half the price of the horse – seventeen hundred and fifty pounds – to a bank in Ireland first thing next morning. George grumbled a bit, but then, he'd set a budget of four thousand pounds an animal, and whatever else he thought of Johnny Henderson, he trusted his judgement of a horse.

After some persuasion, to Johnny's great relief, George agreed. Certainly, Johnny couldn't get the money from anywhere else. Aidan had agreed with the gelding's distrustful owner that the deal would be done in cash, and cash it had to be. Then there was Aidan's two hundred, and the cost of shipping the horse to Devon.

Aidan and Johnny sat at a table in the bar with a bottle of Paddy's, celebrating their first deal, until Aidan announced that he would have to get home soon.

'Hang on a minute.' Johnny didn't want to waste this chance to work on Aidan. He leaned back in his chair and looked at the lean, handsome, guileless man who looked to him more like a Tredington than ever. 'I was talking to your mother this afternoon while you were out feeding the cows. I think she'd understand completely if you were to go out and really try to make something of your breeding and training skills.'

Aidan shrugged. 'Maybe. But like I said, who'd look after her? And anyway, where would I get the money to set up a decent yard?'

'If you really wanted it, I've told you how you could get the money. There's no question about it, believe me.

Why not sound her out on it? I mean, for God's sake, you're wasting yourself flogging a few old knackers round these local tracks, and trying to rear cattle on ground that a goat would sniff at.'

Aidan sighed. 'Sure, I'd like to get my hands on some real good horses, and I'd know what to do with them.'

Johnny decided to take a punt. He drew a deep breath. 'Look, talk to her about it. Tell her that I can set you up in a yard in England, with the chance to make far more money than you could ever scratch out of the farm.'

'She's not one to put much store by money.'

'I think you'll find she's just a realist. She doesn't complain, because there's no point – it wouldn't achieve anything. But if there was the real chance of your getting somewhere, I think you'd be surprised by her reaction. And if it meant her definitely being able to stay on the farm, with someone to look after her besides you, she'd love to see you make something of yourself. I think she feels very bad about your being tied down the way you are.'

Letter Lad was to be delivered to Aidan's farm the following afternoon. In the morning, Johnny drove into Westport to collect the cash. With the notes tucked in his wallet, he headed back to the Dalys' farm. When he arrived, Aidan was out mending a fence in one of the outlying fields. His mother, more active than the day before, was looking for eggs among the hay-bales in the barn. She greeted Johnny with no less warmth than the last time. He couldn't yet tell if Aidan had talked to her about the possibility of his going away.

She ushered him inside. As soon as he had sat down,

she said, 'Aidan's been telling me about a possible opening you may have for him in Devon.'

Johnny's head jerked up. He hadn't expected Aidan to go quite so far. He wondered just how much he had told his mother. Nothing in her attitude gave him a clue as to her approval or disapproval, pleasure or sadness at the prospect.

Still, at least Aidan had talked to her. She didn't mention the subject again. It was only when Aidan came back in that Johnny had an inkling of the way things had gone. There was a new look of determination and expectation about Aidan that made him somehow taller, more confident. He winked at Johnny. 'Come on out to get the stable ready,' he said.

When they were in the barn, he asked, 'Have you got the money? Yer man'll be here with the horse soon.'

'Sure. And I've got yours.' He pulled the notes from his wallet and passed them over.

'I like to deal with a man who's as good as his word,' Aidan said as he stuffed the money in the pocket of his threadbare cords.

'Your mother said you spoke to her about going to England,' Johnny said.

Aidan nodded.

'Well?' Johnny asked quickly.

'I told her the whole scam.'

Johnny couldn't believe Aidan had been so naïve. 'What? Everything? About the Tredingtons and Barford?'

'Sure. She's all for it.'

'Good God. I hadn't meant you to discuss the whole thing with her, but . . . she didn't disapprove?'

'It is a little surprising,' Aidan agreed, 'but when I told her about the opportunities with horses I would have, and that the whole lot otherwise would go to this pompous cousin...'

'The same pompous cousin who's just provided you with your two hundred quid finder's fee.'

Aidan laughed. 'Well, there's what you might call a sort of poetic injustice to that.'

'So,' Johnny asked, 'are you going to do it?'

'D'you mean become Mr David Tredington?' Aidan pretended to prevaricate but his eyes gave him away. They were sparkling in a way Johnny hadn't seen since he'd met him. 'What the hell?' He shrugged with a laugh, then became more serious. 'It's the only way I can see to be sure that my mother can stay here. And she's desperate to, though she'd never say as much to me. To answer your question, I am going to do it. I just hope I don't have to wait years before I can get something back to her.'

'I've told you, it shouldn't be hard to swing it so that you're getting enough to make a difference very early on. You'll be the son and heir, after all.'

Three days later, Johnny Henderson and a handful of Irish point-to-pointers arrived in Devon at more or less the same time. As Johnny was urging his car up Porlock Hill, a horse transporter drove through the gates of George Tredington's farm.

Braycombe Farm consisted of a cluster of white-washed buildings – long-house, barns, cattle-sheds and stables – which lay in a small valley in the middle of four hundred low-grade, upland acres. Ten miles from the great estate at Barford, it had once been an outlying part of it. George's grandfather had given it to George's father, Peregrine, in a moment of paternal guilt.

As a gift, it was of questionable generosity. It had a value, but its income never matched the effort needed to run it. Nevertheless, when George had inherited it, he had insisted on keeping it. George now had all the bluff, hearty mannerisms of a countryman, and liked to joke that he was merely serving time in the City – where he was said to be making a substantial amount of money – to allow him to come and live full-time at Braycombe when finally he had found a wife to live in it with him.

On the hot August day on which the horses arrived, George was at Braycombe. He had taken a few days off from the bank in London to oversee arrangements for the Barford shoot, a task with which his uncle had recently entrusted him, and which he took seriously.

He was in his small study, on the cool side of the house, when Mike Harding tapped on the half-open door.

Mike was a red-haired, stocky Devonian in his forties, who ran the farm for George almost single-handed.

'Those horses have come from Ireland, Mr Tredington.'

'Great!' George got to his feet eagerly. There was a gleam on his podgy, russet face – inherited from his mother's family – as he lifted his bulky frame from the leather desk chair which almost entrapped it. 'I can't wait to see this Letter Lad. Johnny Henderson found it on some farm in the back of beyond in County Mayo. It's run in a few point-to-points over there, but never won because it's always had a rotten jockey. Johnny thinks we could do really well with it. I'm going to train it myself, though I might need a bit of help from Jan.'

Jan was Mike's wife.

'You'll have to ask her,' Mike said, reluctant to commit anyone to anything until terms had been agreed.

George walked with a busy, short-legged stride through low doorways, out into the clean cobbled yard where a driver was lowering the lorry's ramp.

'Last of the load,' the driver said with satisfaction.

'Did you have any others for Henderson?'

'Nope. Just these.' He clattered up the ramp to swing a partition back to reveal Letter Lad. A moment later he was leading the dark chestnut roan down to its new home.

'Blimey,' he said. 'I've never seen a race-horse this colour.'

Mike Harding eyed it critically. 'He could do with a bit of grass, but he's got the frame of a proper horse.'

George nodded. He would need to hear a few more people's views before he formed his own. 'Moves well,' he ventured as Mike led the horse away to a row of cage boxes in one of the long barns. 'Anyway, get him in and settled down, then we'll put him down in the river meadow. There's still a bit of grass there.'

The telephone rang in the house. George hurried back inside.

'Hello, George. Johnny Henderson. Have those horses got to you yet?'

'Yes. They've just arrived.'

'What do you think of Letter Lad?'

'Looks a bit scrawny, but otherwise all right.'

'If I'd bought him from someone who knew how to get a good bit of condition on him, he'd have been a couple of grand more. Don't worry about it. Chuck him in a field and give him plenty to eat for a few weeks. Try and get a lot of flesh on him before you start exercising him.'

'That's just what I planned to do. Where are you now?'

'In a call-box, coming down into Lynmouth. I'll be with you in half an hour for the rest of the money.'

George laughed. 'I thought you might be. I might even give you a drink as well.'

Johnny blinked through the grimy glass panes of the phone-box at the sun gleaming off a pale blue sea and thought about George. Specifically, he wondered how he would take the reappearance of David Tredington. It was hard to guess.

After fifteen years, and many thousands of pounds spent on searching and advertising for the missing heir to Barford, it was now generally accepted that George was heir to his uncle's baronetcy. The family had not actually applied to the court for presumption of David's death, but the possibility had been raised several times. Whether or not the great estate would come with the title was a source of constant local speculation. Johnny had never heard Sir Mark or George say anything about it, but he was less intimate with the family now than he had been fifteen years before. Nevertheless, he was still in fairly regular contact with Sir Mark and, with no pretensions to innocent motives, Lucy.

'Lucy! Phone!'

Irritation flickered across Lucy Tredington's deceptively soft features as she glanced up from the canvas propped on an easel in front of her. She was sitting in the shade of a mulberry tree, trying for the hundredth time to capture the subtleties of Barford's walled garden. She had attacked the project in almost every month of the year. It seemed constantly to change, and there was a wonderful incongruity about the old stone walls, the espaliered peach trees, the elegant decaying Victorian greenhouses, and the rows of domestic vegetables in their midst which she wanted to reproduce but which always seemed to elude her.

Shaking a curtain of fine brown hair from her face, she got up and walked towards the house.

Inside, she flopped down on a hummocky old sofa in the sitting-room where the family spent most of their time, and picked up the phone.

Her sister, Victoria, who had called her in, watched her face for reaction, but Lucy gave nothing away. She spoke with neither animation nor boredom as she fingered the buttons of her paint-spattered, embroidered Indian blouse.

When she put the phone down, Victoria asked, 'That was Johnny, wasn't it?'

Lucy nodded.

'What did he want?'

'Invited himself to stay for a few days.'

Victoria's eyes lit up. 'Great. It's ages since we've seen him.'

'Yes. I wonder what he wants.'

As it happened, Johnny had seen Sir Mark Tredington,

146

though not his daughters, only a few weeks before. They had been staying in the same house-party for Goodwood. Johnny had extracted from Sir Mark some idea of the kind of horses he was looking for over the coming year. He had asked if he might have the opportunity of looking for some for him.

Sir Mark, shrewd, and familiar enough with Johnny Henderson's strengths and weaknesses, had agreed to consider anything that Johnny came up with. He still had an affection for Johnny anyway: as one of his own missing son's few close friends at the time of his disappearance, he enjoyed the occasional references to David which their conversation produced.

When Johnny arrived in the middle of that warm afternoon, he found Sir Mark in his study with Victoria, watching the racing from Newmarket. Sir Mark waited until the race in progress was finished before he spoke.

'Hello, Johnny. I didn't know you were back.'

'I phoned earlier; spoke to Luce. She said I could stay for a few nights. I hope that's all right.'

'Fine by me.' Sir Mark turned down the volume on the television. 'Well, how did you get on in Ireland?'

Johnny glanced at Victoria. 'I think I might have found something for you.'

Sir Mark gave him a quick glance. 'Good, you must tell me all about it later. Now, it's a bit early for a drink, I suppose. I'll ask Susan to get us some tea.'

He stood up, and Johnny followed him through the welcome cool of the dark hall into the back of the house. Beside the kitchen was a more utilitarian sort of an office which housed Sir Mark's secretary.

Johnny met Susan Butley's eyes with difficulty. Although Susan was a local girl, she had the kind of looks and presence that would have excited the producer of a Hollywood soap. Johnny knew that she guarded the family she worked for with fierce devotion. Once, without thinking, he'd made a play for her. She had summarily rejected him out of loyalty to Lucy, who she thought was still interested in him.

'Here's Johnny,' Sir Mark said, 'come to stay for a few days. You might tell Mrs Rogers if Lucy hasn't already. You wouldn't be kind enough to bring us a pot of tea, would you?'

'Of course, Sir Mark.' The girl swung her long legs from beneath her desk and rose to her feet. She was wearing a pair of saffron leggings that showed every curve of her well-shaped haunches. Johnny couldn't help grinning with approval as she strode from the room.

When she had brought tea into the study and Victoria had poured them all a cup, Sir Mark seemed prepared to spend a while chatting.

'So, what horses did you find for me in Ireland?'

'Not a lot. I bought a nice pointer for George, though.'

'Did you indeed? And what's he planning to do with it?'

'He says he's going to train it himself.'

'Oh dear.' Sir Mark raised his eyebrows. 'I hope he didn't pay too much for it.'

Johnny laughed. 'He did not,' he said with an Irish brogue. 'But,' he probed, 'why do you say, "Oh dear"?'

'You know as well as I do that George doesn't know the first thing about horses.'

'Maybe not,' Victoria said, 'but there's no harm in him learning. After all, if he's ending up with the stud here...' She left the implication trailing.

Sir Mark nodded in answer to Johnny's quick glance. 'It does rather look as though George will end up with the stud. I don't know; it seems unfair on the girls, though I'll make sure they'll always have enough, but the estate should really go with the title.'

'You haven't heard anything new about David, have you?' Victoria asked with a tremor in her voice.

The older man nodded again. 'Yes. I haven't given up hope, of course, and it's all being checked out now, but I was contacted by the Australian High Commission last week. They've had a report of someone called David Tredington going missing in a small yacht somewhere off Norfolk Island. There was a crew of three, all lost, sailing from Sydney to Fiji.'

Johnny couldn't speak for a moment. The unfairness of the timing was too hard to swallow.

Sir Mark saw the disappointment in his eyes. 'I know; it's hard to take – even after all this time. But as I say, it's by no means certain yet. I've got a firm of lawyers dealing with it. I shouldn't really have told you, not before they're a hundred per cent certain of the identity. I just pray it's not him.'

'God, I hope not,' Victoria said fervently. 'I still feel sure he'll come back one day.'

'Well, you never know,' Johnny humoured her, 'there could easily be some mistake, so keep praying.'

'You're quite right, Johnny; never say die. Come on,' Sir Mark said, achieving an abrupt change of mood, 'let's go out and look at the horses.'

'I'd love to. Would you mind if I just fetch my video camera from the car? I'd rather like to get a few shots of what you've got in the yard, just for my records.'

'Why not?' said Sir Mark. 'Good idea.'

Later, Johnny found Lucy up in the small attic room which she used as a studio when she was at Barford.

'Hello, Luce.'

She was squinting at the canvas she had brought in from the garden. She looked up when he came in, smiling despite herself. 'Hello, Johnny. You're looking nice and tanned; whose villa have you been squatting in?'

'No one's. I've been working. For once the sun was shining in Ireland.'

'It's been amazing, hasn't it? I was supposed to be down in Aix, but it's so beautiful here.' She waved through the mansard window behind her at the green hills rolling down towards a distant view of the sea.

'What are you working on?' Johnny asked, walking around behind her to look at the canvas.

'Don't say anything,' Lucy said. 'I'm not interested in your opinion.'

'But it's wonderful. I love the way you've handled those vegetables.' He put a hand on her shoulder and kneaded it gently.

'Don't start getting all smarmy with me, Johnny. And if you think you can come down here just for a quick leg-over, forget it.'

'Oh no! Don't tell me there's a new man in your life?'

'No there bloody isn't, and I'm not interested in a re-run of our last scene.'

Johnny straightened up. 'Oh, all right,' he said with an exaggerated pique which wasn't entirely false. Now he was close to her and could smell her warmth and the sun in her hair, he felt the old familiar churning in his guts and a twitching in his loins.

Lucy laughed. 'I wouldn't mind if you weren't such a spoilt shit. You're too used to getting your own way.'

'Only with women,' Johnny protested.

'Anyway, what have you come here for?'

'To see you, of course.'

'Balls! I presume it's because you want to try and sell Dad a few horses.'

'There is that, too. But to be honest, I had to come and see George, and I felt like a few days loafing, and,' he waved out of the window as Lucy had done, 'where could be better?'

Johnny decided that any serious attempts to get Lucy back into bed with him could easily backfire and curtail his visit. His vanity, though not his sexual urges, was amply served by Victoria's admiring attention. He responded to her with kindly charm; there was always the chance that this would arouse Lucy, and it would make it harder for them to kick him out before he was ready.

With an effort, he made himself useful about the place, helping with the horses in the stud, pottering around the pheasant pens with George, and poring over the stallion books with Sir Mark.

And all the time he slipped in questions, references to the changes that had been made to the place over the years, trying to establish what had been the status quo at the time David had disappeared. He took photographs and videos on the slightest excuse, and buried himself in old family albums in the library. He achieved all this with a naturalness and subtlety that evoked no questions from his hosts.

Only Susan Butley, ever vigilant for the family, showed any suspicion about his motives. He kept his contact with her to an inoffensive minimum. When he once found himself alone with her for a while, he reminded her that when he had stayed in the house as a boy, her father, Ivor, had been a groom on the stud. Innocently, he asked after him.

'Never see him,' she said curtly. 'Hardly have done since he left Mum.'

But with a little encouragement, she was prepared to reminisce about her childhood in one of the grooms' cottages, and Johnny was able to establish exactly what had been the personnel on the estate when David had last been seen there.

As he compiled his dossier on the Tredington household, a history of the family and their friends, Johnny managed to push to the back of his mind the possibility that the real David Tredington might yet be proved to have drowned in the South Pacific. That would have been a terrible waste of Aidan Daly's remarkable likeness to the Tredingtons.

Two weeks after George had taken charge of his point-to-pointers in Devon, Aidan Daly climbed into his old pick-up to drive to Westport. As he drove along the empty road between the mountains and the sea, he was experiencing the same kind of nervous tingle he had before his first few races. He felt more vibrant and purposeful than he had ever done, now that he was presented with a real alternative to the impasse that his mother's illness had created.

Johnny perked up when he saw Aidan's handsome face enhanced by a new, confident smile and bright, eager eyes.

'You look as though you've just won the lottery.'

'To tell you the truth, now I'm committed to this ruse, I'm looking forward to it.'

'Great. I've got more than enough to kit you out with David Tredington's boyhood memories.'

They were in the dark, empty bar of the small hotel on the outskirts of town where Johnny had established his HQ for the purposes of turning Aidan Daly into David Tredington.

They spent the first afternoon in his cramped bedroom, looking at the videos Johnny had taken and the maps, plans, and photographs of the house, the grounds, the other farms on the estate.

Johnny had also produced a family tree, and lists of names of all the neighbours, the doctor, stud staff, maids and housekeepers young David would have known. He also drew on his memories of their time at school together. From the stud records, he had drawn up a list of the horses which had been there at the time. As an additional stimulus, he played the video of the thirty or so horses currently in occupation.

Now that he was committed, Aidan was quick and keen to learn.

Johnny himself became more animated after a few days, as the Irishman reeled off the names of the cousins and connections of the entire Tredington family, and demonstrated his familiarity with every aspect of the estate. Johnny could see no point in mentioning the small yacht missing with its crew off Norfolk Island. He also decided that it was time to broach one of the trickier obstacles.

'You're doing fantastically. The more you know, the more convincing you become.'

'I've been thinking,' Aidan said. 'I'll have to have a fool-proof story of what I've been doing for the last fifteen years. The simplest thing would be to stick more or less to the truth. The problem is how to deal with my mother. She's agreed to say that she and I met on the boat when I came from England, and that she sort of adopted me as I had absolutely no wish to go back to Barford then. That way, everything will tally.'

'Great!' Johnny nodded. 'I can't see much difficulty there. The only thing that could stump us is if they do a blood test on you. But I'm convinced that, if you handle it right, Sir Mark won't think it's necessary. After all, if you're a convincing enough David, it would be very insulting. But even if he does ask for a sample, I'm pretty sure if you've offered it willingly, he won't use it; we'll cross that one when we come to it. Obviously there are going to be things that I simply haven't been able to find out about – small incidents within the family, but my guess is that after so many years, you won't be expected to remember everything.' He paused and nodded encouragingly. 'There's one problem which we are going to have to deal with, though. David had a small birthmark, just here.' Johnny pointed to a point half-way down the left side of his neck.

Aidan's face fell. 'How the hell am I going to deal with that?'

'It's OK. It won't hurt, at least, not much. I've arranged for a tattooist here in town to make it look as though you've had the thing removed, some time ago. Then, if the family ask about it, you say that you'd been told it might become malignant in some way.'

Johnny held his breath as he waited for Aidan's reaction.

Unexpectedly, Aidan grinned. 'Ah well, I don't suppose I've got any choice. In for a penny, in for a pound.'

'That's what I like to hear. The chap'll do it tomorrow.'

By the following weekend, Aidan agreed with Johnny that he was ready to go. The uncanny experience of seeing photographs of David and himself at the same age, looking almost interchangeable, had removed most of his last doubts. Besides that, he'd immersed himself so completely in the life and surroundings of the young David Tredington that he sometimes found himself thinking he really had become the missing boy.

With a guillemot's egg in his pocket, which Johnny knew Lucy had asked her brother for over fifteen years ago, Aidan said goodbye to his mother, promised her that he would do everything he could to make sure she spent her remaining years in comfort, and set off for Dublin, fully prepared to step into another world and another man's shoes.

Chapter Seven

Devon: November

The morning after Mickey Thatcher was buried in the graveyard of Saint Kenelm's Church, Ivor Butley stirred two heaped spoons of sugar and a slug of whisky into his tea. He sat at a chipped formica-topped table in the grimy kitchen of a council flat on the outskirts of a small Devon town twenty miles from Great Barford. There was a smile on his face. It was dole day, and he was going racing.

He heard a rustle and thump at his front door and shuffled in his slippers into the hall to pick up the *Sun* and the *Sporting Life* which a paper-boy had just pushed through the letterbox. He turned to page three of the *Sun*, gave a quick, lewd chuckle and pushed it away. He opened the racing paper and leafed through to that day's card for Newton Abbot.

He ran his finger down the columns of jockeys' names until his eyes reached the words 'David Tredington', where they lingered as his mind travelled back through fifteen years.

It seemed to him that every second of the day Sir Mark's son had gone missing remained clear in his head. Every tiny detail was etched on his memory as if it had only just happened. There was good reason for this, for the boy's disappearance had been the fundamental cause of all his troubles since. It was the reason he had started to drink; almost before he realised what was going on, he'd lost his job and then his family. The bottle that had been his downfall had become his comfort.

He closed the paper with a groan and a shake of his head. He was very curious to meet David Tredington; Newton Abbot would be as good a place as any, and watching him ride would prove that his mind hadn't been playing tricks on him.

Aidan Daly let himself into the back seat of Jason Dolton's Subaru. Victoria, sitting in the front with her husband, had offered him a lift to Newton Abbot.

Jason had four rides, including the one in which Just William, owned by Sir Mark and to be ridden by his son, was running.

As Jason drove too fast along the sinuous back road to South Molton, Aidan avoided any awkward conversation and thought about David Tredington.

In the nine weeks that had passed since he'd first appeared at Barford, Aidan had thought almost continuously about the man whose identity he had assumed. He had tried, like any good actor, to get inside the mind of the character he was playing. He had succeeded to such an extent that sometimes he almost convinced himself that he *was* David Tredington.

He felt somehow that he had a lot in common with the boy who had disappeared, though he had soon realised from other people's reactions to him that the David they remembered as a twelve-year-old boy had not been universally liked and that, over fifteen years later, the new David was in most ways a great improvement. Aidan had the impression that they thought the self-imposed exile in Ireland had done nothing but good. He was helped by the fact that, with very few exceptions, no one showed any sign of doubting his identity. Word had gone round very soon after his arrival that Sir Mark was completely satisfied that this man was David. He had even told Aidan to his face, looked him straight in the eye as he'd said it. It had been Aidan's greatest challenge so far. He'd almost come clean, so strong were the feelings of guilt at his deception. If the old man hadn't sounded quite so convincing and looked so happy, Aidan was sure he would have confessed.

The biggest potential problem that he and Johnny had feared had not materialised. There wasn't so much as a lock of David's hair or a nail clipping that could be used to establish a DNA match. When Aidan had been asked to give a sample of blood for comparison with Sir Mark's, he had shown no sign of the great trepidation he felt. Presumably, though, Sir Mark had taken his apparent composure as confirmation that he was genuine, and had pursued the test no further, because no mention had ever been made of it again.

After that hurdle had been side-stepped, Aidan had felt completely confident in his role, and determined to do everything he could to justify the trust of his new 'father'. At the same time, he didn't lose sight of the whole purpose of the exercise. He planned to go back to Ireland as soon as he plausibly could to start making arrangements for his mother's care. He saved all the salary he received from the estate, and had started to earn supplementary and legitimate income from some skilful horse-dealing.

The biggest difficulty he had was containing Johnny's impatience. Aidan had agreed that Johnny would get five per cent of whatever assets found their way to Aidan as a result of his impersonation.

So far, Aidan had taken and received nothing tangible that he hadn't earned. He didn't deny that he'd received other great advantages by being David Tredington, but he also felt he was giving something back. He had been enjoying himself enormously, and had managed most of the time to quell his conscience – until Emmot MacClancy had shuffled into his life, and Mickey Thatcher had been killed.

Although the police had been unable to establish any real evidence that the falling sleeper had been anything other than a horrible accident, Aidan was still convinced that it wasn't – and that he was responsible for Mickey's death. He didn't have the impression that the police were doing much more to investigate the circumstances. Somehow, he was going to have to find out the truth himself – he owed that to Mickey – but for the time being he was going to have to do it without official help.

For two or three days after Fontwell, though, all his instincts told him to drop the deception and own up, before anything else happened. So far, to Johnny's immense relief, he had delayed the decision, but life as David Tredington had suddenly become a lot less comfortable for him.

* * *

Aidan, Victoria and Jason arrived at Newton Abbot shortly after Sam Hunter's lorry. Jason went off to change for his ride in the first race. Victoria and Aidan walked to the lorry park and watched apprehensively as one of Sam's lads started to lead Just William down the ramp.

The chestnut gelding was in an agitated state. It was looking around wildly with its ears back and a lot of white in its eyes. It made a fuss about negotiating the ramp, then leapt down the last few feet, almost dragging the lad over.

Victoria was standing beside Aidan. 'Crikey!' she said. 'He's in a filthy mood today. Are you sure you still want to ride him?'

'Why? Do you think Jason'd like the ride?'

'He's already got one.'

'I know, but it's even nappier than this one. Anyway, of course I'm going to ride him. If I can stop him pulling himself up as he passes the stables, he could win. Mind you, that's a big "if".'

Their race was the fourth on the day's card. Fifteen maiden chasers ranging from five to nine years of age, most of whom were likely to remain without a win until they retired to the point-to-point field. Aidan was the only amateur, Jason the only full professional in the race. All the others were conditional jockeys at various stages of their claiming allowance.

Walking round at the start, it wasn't difficult to spot the riders to steer clear of. They had their goggles pulled down long before the starter had finished checking their girths. Their mounts were sweating and edgy from the tension transmitted by their riders' hands and legs.

'Anyone want to make the running?' Aidan called out as the starter walked across to mount his rostrum. Nobody answered. Aidan moved Just William across to the inside; two young jockeys pushed in front of him, stirring up their horses for a quick start. Neither looked at all safe. Aidan quickly weighed up the possibility of going round the outside to avoid them, but that would have given Just William too much of a chance to duck out. If he were going to get this horse round the course at all, it would only be by keeping it well and truly boxed in until they were heading for home. He didn't have a choice. He would have to follow the two spacemen and hope to God that the horses they were riding knew how to jump.

It was Aidan's first ride at Newton Abbot. He had walked the course and guessed the race would be run at a fast pace on such a sharp circuit. Jumping would be important. He could see that if he lost his position, it would be hard to make up the ground again. And that was how it turned out.

The fifteen runners set off towards the first fence as if they were sprinters. It still surprised Aidan just how fast even bad horses could gallop. He followed the first two, who were racing far enough apart for Just William to see something of the fence between them. If Aidan could keep him on their quarters, Just William wouldn't be able to run out, unless he took one of them with him.

As they thundered forward, Aidan felt his horse cock his jaw and look for the right-hand wing. Before he had travelled three more strides, Aidan had lifted his whip and leathered him hard down his right shoulder, welting his skin. Just William rushed up between the two leaders. Two strides from the birch, he dug his toes in. He was travelling too quickly to stop altogether but, as he took off, in what appeared from the stands to be slow motion, another horse cannoned into him from behind and knocked him over. Aidan shot from the saddle like a rag doll, right in the path of the horses to his left. He had curled instinctively into a ball, knees tucked tightly to his chest, even before he had touched the ground.

Watching from the stands, Victoria froze as she saw her brother tumbling and bouncing across the grass, with horses galloping past on either side of him. Miraculously, it seemed, he escaped any real injury, until one of the last horses trampled right over the top of him and its flailing hooves prised open his defensive curl.

Victoria cursed the jockey who had made no attempt to avoid him. When she recognised the colours, she gasped. It was Jason.

By the time Aidan had been driven the short distance back to the ambulance room, Victoria was waiting for him. The back doors of the ambulance swung open and Aidan was standing inside, smiling. He was plastered with mud and a bruise was blooming on his left cheek. Apart from that, he looked fine.

'Are you OK?' she asked anxiously, not really believing what she was seeing.

'Sure. Slightly battered by your husband, that's all.'

Victoria didn't miss the sarcasm in his voice. She

thought about trying to make an excuse, but her loyalty to Jason didn't stretch that far. She said nothing.

'Give me a few minutes and I'll see you back in the weighing-room,' Aidan said lightly, guilty now at having embarrassed her.

Victoria nodded, tight-lipped, as a couple of St John's ambulance-men insisted on helping Aidan inside.

Five minutes later, after the doctor had checked him over, he picked up his helmet and whip and walked outside. He was heading for the changing-room when a short, red-faced man in an old waxed jacket and grimy cloth cap shambled up to him.

'David!' the man hailed him in broad Devonian. 'Young David Tredington! I'm glad you got up after that fall.'

Aidan looked at the small, rustic individual and wondered who the hell he was.

'Hello. How are you?'

'Still pickin' a few winners, but out of work. Have been for a few years now with all these yards closing down.'

Aidan nodded sympathetically, while his mind raced through the mountain of information with which Johnny had supplied him back in Ireland. This chap was evidently involved in horses in some way. Perhaps he was one of the grooms who had been at Barford at the time of David's disappearance. Aidan racked his brains for a name. Meanwhile, the other man was looking at him with an indulgent, shifty grin.

'You don't know who I am, do you? Not s'prisin', after fifteen year, and o' course, I heard tell you was back.'

Triumphantly, Aidan lighted on a name and took a gamble.

'Of course I know who you are, Ivor. The number of times you legged me up on to those moody ponies.'

Ivor Butley stared at Aidan in startled amazement for a moment before he recovered himself. 'So you remember me, do you?'

Aidan looked at him carefully. He heard a hint of sarcasm in the man's voice. Maybe, he thought, he hadn't got it right, and this wasn't Ivor. But he didn't panic; it would have been perfectly excusable to have confused the man after all this time. He didn't let his relief show when the man went on. 'But I bet you never heard what happened to me after you'd gone from Barford?'

'I'm afraid not.'

'Sir Mark got rid of me. Said I was drinking too much. Bloody rubbish it was. I never let the horses down. O' course, Sue's there now, but she won't even talk to me, nor do her mum.'

So, Aidan thought; this was Ivor Butley – Susan's father, who had been sacked, abandoned his wife and daughter, and wandered from job to job in livery yards and riding stables around the West Country until there was no one left who would tolerate him, even at the negligible wages he demanded. Aidan inspected him with greater interest. It was just possible to see, through the broken veins and damp drinker's eyes, something of Susan, though they had nothing obvious in common as far as personality was concerned, except, perhaps, for a streak of stubbornness.

'Well, will you have a drink,' Aidan offered, 'as soon as I've dumped this stuff?'

'No. I won't embarrass you. But I'm glad you recognised me – must have taken a bit of doin', after all that time, like.'

On the way home with Victoria and Jason, Aidan mentioned his meeting with Ivor.

She nodded. 'He's often around the local courses, poor old chap. It's rather pathetic. Sue says he's ended up living in some grim little flat in Tiverton, drawing the dole and studying form all day. Still, he manages to keep himself in whisky somehow.'

'What happened to him, after I left?'

'I don't really know. I mean, he'd been with us for years, hadn't he, certainly as long as I could remember. It must have been very odd your seeing him. He was your great chum in the yard, wasn't he? Didn't he teach you to ride?'

Johnny had told Aidan this. He nodded. 'He did. But what happened to him?'

'Well, after you left, he went to pieces. I don't know why. But he started really hitting the booze, and I think Dad just got fed up with having to get him out of bed to do the horses. Shirley, Sue's mother, tried to cover up for him, but I think they started rowing the whole time, and Shirley and Sue moved out, down to Lynmouth. Shirley got a job in one of the hotels, and I'm afraid Ivor got the boot.'

Aidan nodded. 'He seemed a bit of a sad case. Frankly, I'd not have recognised him if he hadn't come up to me. I offered him a drink, but he turned me down, said he didn't want to embarrass me.'

'Would it have embarrassed you?'

'Not a bit, though he is a pretty scruffy-looking little individual now. It's hard to see how he sired someone like Susan.'

'Yes, isn't it? She's turned out to be rather a star. Her mother worked like hell to make sure she went to the sixth-form college in Ilfracombe. We all thought she'd go up to London and get some high-powered secretarial job when she passed all her exams and with her rather glamorous looks, but she was determined to come and work for us. Very lucky, really.'

'I don't think she's taken to me all that much, though,' Aidan remarked lightly.

'Just the opposite, if you ask me; but anyway, you wouldn't want an efficient busybody like that, would you?'

'That I wouldn't know,' Aidan answered thoughtfully.

Jan Harding came in from doing evening stables at Braycombe Farm. Mike, her husband, who was George Tredington's farm manager, was already sitting in the kitchen of their cottage reading the local paper.

'How are they all?' he asked routinely.

'In bloody good shape. His nibs shouldn't have anything to complain about. Though I'm bloody annoyed with him.'

'Why's that?'

'I've just heard from Sam Hunter's yard that Letter Lad's there now. Apparently he had a corn. They said that David schooled him at home for a couple of weeks and he's jumping beautiful now. He's going really well and they're running him at Sandown tomorrow – and it was me as got him fit,' she added sourly.

'Who's riding him, then?'

'David, of course. I *told* George if he gave it time we'd get him right ourselves, but the silly bugger thought he'd be smart and take a quick profit on it when Johnny Henderson said he had a buyer. Mind you, I don't think he was too happy when he found out it had gone to Barford.'

'Serves him right. But you've got to hand it to David. He only rode him the once here. He must have known what was wrong with him then. Which reminds me, your blasted brother Ivor was on the phone, pissed as usual, saying something about seeing David at the races. He wanted to talk to you.'

Jan didn't answer for a moment; her husband didn't miss a worried look that flashed across her wind-worn face. 'Did he? Well, I suppose he was bound to bump into him sooner or later.'

'Why? What's the problem?'

'I don't know, but I've always thought it was David going missing that started all poor Ivor's troubles.'

'Poor Ivor, my arse!' Mike expostulated. 'He was always his own worst enemy, you know that. Everyone bent over backwards to help him after that, and they all ended up with mud on their faces.'

'What did he say?'

'He wanted you to go down and see him as soon as you could, this evening. I told him no way. Like I say, he was already half-cut. You wouldn't have been able to have much of a conversation with him anyway.'

'I'm going.'

'What! Just because your useless elder brother summons you, you'll drive thirty miles to listen to his moaning?'

'It's not often that he asks me to, is it? It must be important. Sorry, Mike. I'll try not to be back too late.'

Mike sighed. 'Do you want me to come too, then?'

'No. I'll be all right.'

Ivor hadn't really expected Jan to come, even after she'd telephoned to say she would. But when she rang the bell on his battered front door, he opened it to her gleefully.

'Hello, Jan. I'm bloody glad you've come. I had to talk to someone. Come on in. Do you want a drop of scotch?'

'No, I don't, and you sound as though you've had enough already.'

'Hardly had a drop.'

'Well, what's so important I had to drive down here?'

'It's important all right. After what I saw today. I can get my own back on those bloody Tredingtons, after they wrecked my life and stole my daughter.'

'Stole your daughter?' Jan exclaimed, incredulous. 'Susan worked like hell to get taken on there, you know that. It was her own choice.'

'All right, but she was sort of seduced, like, by their money and all that. And she's turned into a right little snob now.'

'I don't know how you know that. You haven't seen her for two years.'

'Maybe not, but I've heard.'

'Look, I don't know why you should think the Tredingtons owe you anything after the way you behaved, but how the hell do you think you're going to get even with them?'

'Not just get even with them, but make myself a tidy sum too. No more living in this bloody hovel.'

'Wherever you lived would be a hovel ... but go on; how are you going to do it?'

Ivor took a sip from a dirty glass of whisky and looked mysteriously at his sister. 'I know something Sir Mark Tredington doesn't; he can't do, or he wouldn't have had that bloke back in the house.'

'What bloke? You mean his son, David?'

'No. I don't mean his son David. I mean that bloke that's turned up calling himself David.'

'What on earth are you on about, Ivor? Everyone knows it's David. They had it checked out. I heard George telling someone over the phone, and you can still see where the birthmark was and all.'

'You don't want to be fooled by that birthmark. Whatever he's done to convince them he's the long-lost David, I can tell you, he bloody well isn't.'

Mike Harding was still up when his wife got back from Tiverton. He looked up from an old form-book he was reading.

'Well, what did the old bugger want, then?'

'He wanted to tell me that he's going to get even with the Tredingtons for sacking him and for stealing his daughter.'

Mike laughed out loud. 'That's a good one, stealing his daughter. Anyway, how's he going to do it?'

'He didn't tell me exactly. I suppose he thinks he's going to try and blackmail David.'

'Blackmail David? That's ridiculous. David hasn't been back long enough to have done anything, has he? Or does Ivor think he knows about something David got up to in Ireland? I suppose he might. After all, why did David suddenly decide to leave Ireland?'

'No. It's nothing like that. He says there's absolutely no way that David is David.'

'What the hell does he mean?'

'He says this David is an impostor; and he couldn't be anything else.'

'In that case, his mind must be completely pickled. Everyone knows Sir Mark checked it out when he turned up. I mean, there weren't just a few people who thought he must be a fake, after all. But no one's in any doubt about it now. Your brother's gone off his rocker; if he tries anything, he'll end up in bloody jail, which will probably be a relief for us all.'

'Don't say that about him. He is family, when all's said and done.'

'What's he ever done for you, besides letting you down every time you recommended him for a job?'

'Whatever, he's certain it's not David, and it wasn't just because he was drunk. He's obviously been excited about it all day since he saw him ride.'

'Did he say why he was so certain?'

'No. I tried to get that out of him, but he clammed up; just said this bloke doesn't even ride like David.'

'What's he talking about? How could he tell the difference after fifteen years?'

'I don't bloody know, Mike, but he just kept on repeating that it couldn't possibly be David, and he was going to make the Tredingtons pay for what they did to him.'

'It's all bollocks, isn't it? It's got to be. He's always been sore as a fox in a wire about what happened to him, and he thinks he can get his own back by stirring up a few nasty rumours to embarrass them.' Mike considered his own involvement. 'I'll have to talk to George about it. I mean, we work for the family, and George may be an arrogant so-and-so, but he pays well, and I don't want to be connected to anything your brother does. It could cost us our jobs.'

Mike's eyes flashed with angry concern that his wife's loyalty to her waster of a brother might threaten the cosy life he and Jan had secured for themselves on George's farm.

Jan found herself panicking slightly at Mike's reaction. She was regretting, too late, that she'd told him what Ivor had said. Disguising her own doubts, though, she laughed off her husband's suggestion. 'Of course it won't,' she said. 'No one's ever going to blame us for anything he does. Besides, like you say, it's probably all bull anyway.'

November the fifth dawned bright, clear blue. The sun, rising above the bulk of Exmoor, illuminated a faint, glittering coat of frost on the ground as Aidan walked from his cottage to the stableyard.

Out exercising a newly broken colt, Aidan's sheer pleasure at the sight and smells of the autumn morning vied with other feelings of excitement and, just below the surface of his consciousness, doubts that this life could go on for ever.

He was excited, above all, because that afternoon he was riding Letter Lad in its first race under rules. Since he'd had the gelding at Barford to school it, he had become more and more impressed with it and, though he didn't admit it to anyone, he had great hopes for the animal. A tingle of pleased anticipation ran through him as he urged the beautifully conformed colt beneath him into a bouncy, ground-covering trot.

For a while, with an unfamiliar churning in his guts, he thought about the rest of the weekend that lay ahead. Lucy was arriving for lunch with a group of friends from London. They were going to organise a great firework display on the lawns in front of the house. Among the guests would be the lovely, long-legged Emma, Lucy's journalist friend.

Since he had met her, Aidan didn't pretend to himself that her blatant interest in him had turned him on. He knew that she wasn't his type, but then Sue Butley, who was, wasn't having anything to do with him, and he had found that Emma kept sneaking uninvited into his thoughts.

Aidan's charm and strong good looks disguised his lack of experience with women. Since his late teens, there had been several covert flirtations with local girls, which from time to time had led to love-making of variable passion and quality. He was self-consciously aware of how little he knew, especially for a man of his age, about how to deal intimately with a woman. Perversely, and without his knowing it, there were a lot of women for whom this diffidence only increased his attractiveness.

He didn't know why Emma should have made it so clear that she fancied him, but he was a fit man with all the normal appetites and he didn't feel like questioning it. Now he knew he was looking forward to seeing her almost as much as riding Letter Lad, and with almost as much confidence.

Aidan was well on his way to Sandown by the time Lucy and Emma arrived at Barford with four friends, Johnny Henderson among them. When it was time for the race to be shown on television, they all settled down with Sir Mark to watch.

Aidan wasn't disappointed with his first novice hurdle race on Letter Lad, who was now so pleased at his own performance in finishing fourth that he jig-jogged all the way back to the unsaddling enclosure, eager for people to notice him.

'What a show-off,' Aidan remarked to the lad as they came back. If he hadn't over-jumped at the downhill hurdle, where he'd pecked badly on landing, he'd have been even closer.

Aidan weighed in, feeling pleased with himself and the horse. Next time out, he'd press the throttle and see what he could really do.

Walking back to the changing-room, he felt a moment's *déjà vu* as a scruffy little figure in an old Barbour and flat hat shuffled into his line of vision.

There was the same shifty, cocky smile on Ivor Butley's face as there had been the day before at Newton Abbot.

Aidan gave him a friendly nod. 'Hello there, Ivor. It's a long way you've come. I hope you didn't come to back me.'

'No, though I reckon you could have won. I wanted another word with you.'

'Fine. I'll get you the drink you wouldn't have yesterday.'

'Nope. We'll want to talk private.'

Aidan shrugged. 'OK. I won't be long.'

Fifteen minutes later he found Ivor where he had left him.

They walked out of the race-course together, towards the car-park, an incongruous couple. Once they had left the crowds behind, Aidan asked Ivor what he wanted.

'Well, let me see now,' Ivor answered with a puckered forehead. 'A decent living wage for not too much work; one of them nice little cottages in Barford. That'll do for starters.'

'You mean, from the estate?'

'That's right.'

'Look here, Ivor, you'll have to talk to my father about that. I just run the stud, and we've all the grooms we need at the moment. I heard that you fell out with Dad after I left, and I was sorry to hear it, but there's not a lot I can do.'

'There'll be plenty you can do when Sir Mark goes and you get the whole lot. And don't try to tell me there isn't something you could do now, if you wanted to.'

Aidan heard the confidence in the little man's voice, and the hard edge that was making demands, not asking favours.

'I'd like to do something for old time's sake, of course,' Aidan said tentatively, 'but I can't yet. I told my father when I came back that I wanted no special treatment, just the same pay as an outside stud manager would have got, and that's what I get, besides turning a few horses.'

'You're a crafty bugger aren't you?'

Aidan suddenly thought of Susan Butley using much the same words when he'd bumped into her outside the Anchor in Lynmouth when he'd first arrived in Devon. He looked more sharply at Ivor. 'And what makes you say that?' he asked with a laugh.

'Because you made the old boy fight to get you back. My daughter told me. I spoke to her last night on the phone, first time in nigh on two year.'

'It wasn't a matter of being crafty,' Aidan said uneasily. 'It was just that I knew how much grief I'd caused, and I didn't really feel I had an automatic right to come back and demand a place to live.'

'I should think you bloody didn't, being as you haven't got no right at all. Being as you're no more David Tredington than I'm the Duke of Edinburgh.'

Although Aidan was half-prepared for this accusation, he faltered for a couple of strides. From Ivor Butley's tone, there could be no doubt that he knew he wasn't David.

Aidan stopped walking, drew himself up and gazed at Ivor with puzzled indignation. 'And what on earth makes you think that?'

'I knows,' Ivor said firmly. 'No matter Sir Mark is supposed to have checked you out and that, and that job

176

you've done on your neck to look as though you had that birthmark taken off.'

'I see,' Aidan said, not letting his nervousness show. 'Do you mind telling me why you're so sure?'

'There's a few things, which anyone could have seen who knows what to look for. For a start, I taught David to ride, remember, and I taught him to run his reins inside his little finger. He'd have never changed that. But I've been watching you ride these last two days, and you wraps your reins right round the outside.'

Aidan laughed. 'Good Lord, Ivor, I don't think that proves much. I changed my style completely when I got to Ireland.'

Ivor shook his head confidently. 'Oh no. Once you've learned to ride one way, you won't ever change. Besides,' he added, wiping a drop from the end of his nose, 'that's only one of the reasons I knows you're not David. There's others, much bigger, you'll find out. I don't know who the hell you are, but I knows, sure as I'm standing here, there's no way you can be David Tredington.'

Aidan looked long and hard into Ivor's aggressive little eyes. Then he smiled, and shrugged. 'OK. So what are you going to do about it?'

Ivor cackled triumphantly. 'Nothing – so long as you agree to give me what I want. It ain't a lot, not to someone who'll have the money you will.' He challenged Aidan with a confident flash of his normally shifty eyes. 'But then, if you don't, I'll tell everyone you're not who you say you are. And I can prove it – no trouble. Then George Tredington will get the bloody lot and you'll end up in jail, if I don't get to you first,' he added with menacing bravado.

Aidan watched Ivor Butley shamble away across the car-park. He was feeling sick. This new threat from Ivor had far more potency about it than MacClancy's. It wasn't just a matter of the birthmark or the way he rode; Ivor's delivery had left him in no doubt that the little drunk knew as an absolute certainty that he was a fake, and could demonstrate it if he had to.

Aidan couldn't face going back into the stands. He walked round to the jockeys' car-park, climbed into the Mercedes that Sir Mark had lent him for the day, and headed back for Devon, for home.

Back at Great Barford, there was a houseful of people determined to have fun, mostly Aidan's age, confident and urbane. He was greeted with some interest by those of Lucy's friends who hadn't met him but had heard about him. Sir Mark, more privately, congratulated him on his ride and showed that he fully appreciated what he had been doing. 'Very wise to get the measure of him first time out. It looks as though you've got yourself a good horse there.'

Aidan couldn't rise to the spirit of merriment in the house-party. Most were sitting around in the drawing-room with drinks before the firework display. He saw Emma looking at him with undiminished interest as he slipped from the room. He wanted to talk to Johnny Henderson.

Johnny was playing snooker in the billiard-room at the back of the house. He was taking a shot as Aidan walked in. He glanced at Aidan and carried on lining up his cue. 'Why the hell didn't you win that race?' he asked peevishly.

'You didn't back me to win, did you?'

'Yes, I bloody did.'

Aidan shrugged. 'You should have asked me first. I'd have told you he wasn't going to win today. Next time, mind...'

'Anyone could see you were taking him for a walk. I'm surprised the stewards didn't ask you in for a chat. He'll never be that price again.' Johnny sent a long ball the full length of the spotless green baize and potted the pink. Only the black remained on the table. His opponent, an untidy, long-haired man in his late twenties, raised his eyebrows and peered with resigned disgust down his aquiline nose.

'If you pot this,' he drawled, 'I suppose I'm going to owe you a hundred.'

'Yah,' Johnny said as he walked around the table, choosing the right shot. 'Start getting your chequebook out. I'm not interested in IOUs.'

He took the shot and potted the last ball on the table. He wasn't smiling as he put his cue back in the rack.

The loser grudgingly wrote out a cheque and handed it to Johnny. 'I think I need a large drink now,' he said as he wandered out of the room. Johnny waited until his footsteps had faded down the corridor before he spoke.

'What an arsehole! Still, another four games at that price and I'll get back the money I lost on you.'

This was the first time Johnny had shown any animosity towards Aidan. He was obviously fairly drunk, and Aidan sensed that something else had upset him.

'Your betting doesn't have a thing to do with me.'

'Doesn't it? Well I'm not too happy about you muscling in on Emma, either. Anyway, she's only interested in you because she thinks you're David.'

'I wouldn't know,' Aidan said. 'I've only met her once before. But am I going to tell her I'm not David, or are you? The way things are going, she'll find out soon enough anyway.'

Johnny looked startled. 'Why? What's happened? I thought you'd dealt with MacClancy.'

'I have. I don't think he'll cause any more trouble.' Aidan heard more of the party coming towards the billiard-room. 'Come on, we'll take a walk, go and check on the fireworks or something.'

Johnny came reluctantly.

Outside, in the crisp, clear, early night-time, they walked away from the house towards the vast bonfire which had been prepared beside the old kitchen garden. In a dim light from the windows of the house and a newly risen moon, a guy was visible, perched on top of the heap of brushwood and logs. Its face was made from a turnip with a carrot for a nose. There was a sly grin on its face. Instinctively, Aidan and Johnny moved away, as if it would hear what they were going to say.

'Well?' Johnny asked. 'What's the problem now?'

'Ivor Butley. He saw me yesterday, at Newton Abbot. Came up to me and challenged me to recognise him. I was flummoxed for a moment, but I thought back over all the people you'd told me about and took a punt on it being him. He was surprised, but not for long. Then he grumbled a bit, about the way he'd been thrown out of the stud here. I offered him a drink, but he wouldn't take one.'

'So, what's the problem?'

'I haven't finished. He turned up again today at Sandown, cornered me and told me he knew I wasn't David and he could prove it. From the way he said it, I'm bloody sure he can.'

Johnny didn't reply at once. Aidan couldn't see the expression on his face, but he could tell that he was prepared to accept Aidan's judgement.

'Shit! I wonder how the hell he's so certain?'

'He said I held my reins differently from David, but he only noticed that because he has some other, much better reason for being sure. Obviously, he didn't tell me that one. Maybe he's still in touch with David. Maybe David told him where he was going; you said they were good friends in those days.'

'They were. David used to spend a hell of a lot of time down at the stables with Ivor. Ivor wasn't a bad little jockey then, and he knew his horses. It was only after David disappeared that he went to pieces and took up piss-artistry in a big way.' Johnny took a deep breath. 'What a bugger! When we've been doing so well. What the hell are you going to do about him?'

'If he's got the kind of proof he says he has, there's not a lot I can do.'

'For God's sake, Aidan!' The thought of his cut of the Tredington inheritance slipping away evidently sobered Johnny up. 'You can't give up now. What did he say he wanted to keep quiet?'

'A pension and a cottage, for starters.'

'Well, that wouldn't be the end of the world.'

'Don't be crazy, Johnny. The man's a boozer and a gambler. Once he knew he could touch me for that, he'd be after me the whole time, and there wouldn't be a thing I could do. You know, this time we're really going to have to call it a day. I mean, for God's sake, if it wasn't Ivor, it'd be somebody else. I'm never going to be able to lie in bed nights. My conscience is shot to ribbons as it is.'

Johnny struggled with his frustration. 'Just hold on, Aidan,' he said quickly. 'I know damn well you don't want to give up all this. You're loving it, being the dashing, blue-blooded amateur jockey, with all the girls looking googly-eyed at you. I just don't believe you want to go back to being an Irish peasant. And anyway, what about your mother? She's depending on you to sort out some kind of a life for her. Are you going to let her down now?' He gripped Aidan's arm. 'Listen, you've got to find a way of dealing with Ivor. I did last time – at least, I tracked MacClancy down so that you could deal with him. But please, don't do anything now, on the spur of the moment.'

Aidan grunted and kicked a mole-hill that had freshly risen in the smooth green turf. 'I don't know. Of course I like it here, and of course I don't want to let my mother down, but that Mickey being killed – it shook me . . . And I like these people, for God's sake; I hate lying to them.'

'You're not doing them any harm,' Johnny said desperately. 'Far from it. And that lad's death wasn't your fault. It wasn't MacClancy – it was an accident; these things happen.'

'I'm damn sure it wasn't an accident, and something tells me the police think so too.'

'They're just going through the motions; but as there's no possible motive, they're not going to get anywhere, are they? Stop worrying about it,' Johnny begged.

From the house, fifty yards away, floated the sounds of the rest of the party coming out into the night to light the bonfire and launch the fireworks.

'We'll talk about it tomorrow,' Aidan said quietly, then shouted across to the approaching figures, 'Lucy, who's the guy meant to be? It looks like Jeffrey Archer.'

Chapter Eight

Tom Stocker, the Barford gardener, put a blazing torch to the fire. A flame licked ten feet up into the still, cool air. Within minutes a crowd had gathered around it, glowing in the heat and dancing light.

The party had swelled to thirty or so. A dozen were staying in the house, the rest were local family friends, some of whom had known David and were taking the opportunity of seeing what he was like after his long absence.

Aidan, despite the tension caused by his encounter with Ivor Butley, took them in his stride, helped by it being common knowledge that he was fully accepted by the family. Some were struck by his apparent Irishness, at least in his speech; most seemed happy enough that this was the man who would one day be taking over Barford, an important focal point in the social life of that part of Devon.

Two of Lucy's friends brought out a gleaming copper basin full of a rum punch which they had concocted. They put it on a garden table near the fire and ladled it into beer mugs. After Aidan had had a couple of glasses of the deceptively innocuous-tasting drink, he was beginning to enjoy himself. Johnny Henderson, in an effort to appear helpful, had taken on the job of setting off the fireworks.

Rockets flared fiery-tailed up towards the stars and burst into umbrellas of twinkling multi-coloured light. Roman candles fizzed and popped, and Catherine wheels squealed. The audience, loosened by the punch, gasped and giggled as they were expected to.

Aidan found Emma beside him, and felt her hand grasp his arm as a series of rockets exploded deafeningly right above them. It seemed quite natural that he should put his arm around her.

'Are you going to keep me from the chilly, chilly dew?' she asked.

He looked at her face in the light of the fire, and grinned. 'What do you think?'

She laughed and wriggled slightly in his arm.

Beyond her, Aidan saw George Tredington watching him. George grinned and turned to the punchbowl to refill his mug. And across the fire which had soon collapsed into a pile of glowing red logs, Susan Butley was looking directly at him. Aidan gave her a smile and took his arm from Emma's shoulder.

When the fireworks were over, the punchbowl empty and the fire a pile of embers, the party drifted back to the house. There was supper and music, billiards and cards. Victoria tried to organise some games, but the London contingent weren't having it. They were more concerned about keeping the booze flowing and consolidating any promising relationships.

Over all this, Sir Mark beamed bravely, holding court in the drawing-room with those who shared his interest in racing. Aidan was brought in and introduced to the people he hadn't met before, and asked to recount his successes so far on English turf.

He lost sight of Emma until much later, when she drifted into the room with a fixed, contented smile on her lips, and curled up on the floor beside Aidan.

Later she shook his arm. 'Come on, Davy, you've talked horses for too long.'

Aidan was glad enough to get away from the racing buffs. 'I'll take this girl out and give her a bit of air. I think she needs it, and I can show her that great Irish giant in the sky.'

'What Irish giant?' someone asked.

'O'Ryan.'

He stood and held out a hand to draw Emma to her feet. As they were leaving the room, they passed Susan Butley coming in.

The sight of Emma naked came as no disappointment to Aidan; nor did the first real physical contact between them. He hadn't made love to a woman for months, since he had been in England, and making love with Emma was an entirely new experience for him.

The constant, frustrating nearness of Susan, and her *de facto* rejection of him, had built up a head of sexual energy in him which was bursting for an outlet. There was nothing about Emma's matter-of-fact, earthy attitude to induce any feelings of guilt in him, and he guessed her motives were not much different from his own.

It was some time after their first mutual and explosive climax that Aidan wondered if Emma had meant the things she had said, though he didn't much mind if her words owed most of their inspiration to the amount of punch she had drunk.

He lay beside her, serene and spent for a while, still tingling in the aftermath of orgasm.

'All right?' he asked softly.

'Mmm. Couldn't be better. I've never fucked a jockey before.'

'Ah, well, I'm only an amateur.'

'It doesn't show,' Emma murmured. She rolled half over, stretched a long leg over his, and felt for his briefly limp genitals.

Later, when they had been coupled so long that it was hard to tell whose body belonged to whom, moist with each other's sweat, they came again and she collapsed on top of him with a throaty, contented gurgle.

'That was *good*,' she whispered.

'Wasn't it just,' Aidan agreed.

Emma propped herself on her elbows so that her nipples caressed his chest. She looked into his shining blue eyes. 'You're a bit of an enigma, aren't you? For some reason or other, I didn't really expect a nice, wholesome man like you to let go the animal in him; but I had to find out.'

Aidan laughed. 'And I thought you'd be so drunk you wouldn't know if you were going or coming.'

'Tell me,' she said with a mischievous grin, 'are you really a Tredington?'

Aidan blinked. 'So far as I know,' he recovered himself enough to say lightly.

'I don't think your sister's so sure,' Emma said, not showing that she knew the effect this would have on him.

'Which sister?'

'Lucy, of course.'

'Why? Did she tell you that?'

'Not in so many words, but there's just something about the way she talks about you.'

'Good God,' Aidan said, 'I'd never have known. I wonder why?'

'Well, are you David?'

Aidan laughed. 'No, of course not. I'm just a fella breezed in from the West of Ireland and saw the chance of a comfortable living here. It was just lucky the blood tests and everything checked out...'

Emma looked at him uncertainly. 'Lucy never told me you'd had to take a blood test.'

'I don't suppose Dad told her.'

'So you really are David?'

'You look disappointed.'

'I am, in a way. I really fancied the idea of you being a complete con-man.'

'Well, don't tell Lucy what I said. I'll enjoy watching her over the next few days.'

'All right.' Emma grinned, and stroked his chin. 'By the way, I feel something stirring. Anything to do with you?'

Aidan looked at Susan's flushed cheeks and found himself blushing.

It was Sunday morning, but horses still had to be fed and mucked out. Susan always came in to help in the yard every other Sunday so that the regular grooms could have a lie-in.

Aidan wondered if she'd seen Emma leaving his

cottage half an hour earlier to get back to the house before it awoke. She looked annoyed about something, but at first Aidan kept up the affable politeness with which he had treated her since he'd arrived back at Barford after his short stay in Lambourn.

He got on with feeding the mares and foals, while Susan dealt with the yearlings. After ten minutes or so, he went into the feed house and found her leaning over a corn bin with a scoop in her hand. He walked up quietly behind her, until she turned and saw him, taken by surprise.

There was an uncharacteristic vulnerability in her eyes.

'What's up?' Aidan asked, before she could hide her feelings.

Susan hardened herself. 'What do you mean "What's up"? Nothing's up.'

'But you looked upset about something.'

Susan emptied the scoop of barley into the rubber bucket at her feet.

'I am upset,' she said without looking at him, 'because you're such a bloody fraud.'

Aidan looked blank. 'In what way?' he asked.

'In loads of ways, by the look of things. For a start, what the hell have you got in common with that tart, Emma?'

'Not a lot.'

Susan met his steady gaze. For the moment his answer seemed to satisfy her. 'OK, but however much everyone may be taken in by you here, I'm still as sure as I've ever been that you're not David.'

'That's what your father told me yesterday. Was it him who told you?'

'Sort of. When David disappeared, Dad was very upset, and when people were saying that David would come back, after they got the note from him, he kept on saying that they'd never see him again. He never told us why, just said there was no hope of him coming back.'

'Did you speak to him recently?'

'Yes, the day before yesterday, for the first time in ages. He told me he'd seen you at the races, and what the hell was going on here?' She shrugged. 'I said that you were back living here, and as far as the family and all the neighbours were concerned, you're David. He laughed and said you were no more David than the Pope.'

As she talked, Aidan was trying to decide on the right approach. There was a part of him that really wanted to tell her the truth, to remove the blockage to the relationship he knew they could have had. His feelings for her certainly hadn't diminished as a result of his night with Emma.

But he couldn't risk her reaction: she might be prepared to accept his reasons for what he'd done and go along with it, or she might not.

'I'm afraid your father's not in too good shape these days. If you've not seen him recently, you maybe don't know how far gone he is. I'm afraid he's probably a complete alcoholic now and, like most alcoholics, living in a fantasy world of his own.' Aidan sat down on a table next to the feed bin. 'Listen, he still resents what happened to him after I went.' He shrugged. Susan was looking less certain than she had a few minutes before.

Aidan went on. 'I don't know what happened. I was very fond of him. I spent a lot of time with him, you know that. He sometimes used to bring you up to the yard; you were maybe nine or ten then, do you remember?'

'Yes, I remember,' Susan faltered.

'Well then. What are you talking about? You and I were getting on so well before you knew who I was.'

'Do you think I don't know that? And even if you are David, what'd be the point of us having a relationship anyway? I'm just the secretary round here; and after what happened last night, I'm not so sure I'd be that interested.'

'What happened last night?'

'I saw that skinny tart leaving your cottage, stumbling about.'

'If it's a saint you want, I'd not be the man for the job anyway.'

The sound of footsteps across the yard reached them through the open door of the barn. A moment later, Victoria walked into the feed-store. Aidan and Susan just managed to put on a businesslike appearance as she came in.

'Hi, David. I didn't think you'd be up so early this morning, after Hugo's bloody rum punch.'

'I'm glad I'm not riding a three-mile chase today, but I'm just about up to heaving a few feed buckets, and of course Sue turned up to help.'

Victoria smiled at Susan. 'You are brilliant. I don't know how you do it.'

'Well,' Aidan said, 'I've done mine. I'm heading up to the house for a bit of breakfast.'

'Mrs Rogers will be pleased; she's been there an hour waiting for takers and no one's appeared yet – though,' Victoria added suspiciously, 'I did see Emma, that weird friend of Lucy's, wandering about. But I don't suppose she eats a lot of breakfast.'

Ten miles away, at Braycombe, George Tredington heaved himself out of his large oak bed and into a silk dressing-gown.

He creaked down the stairs and filled a percolator with strong Brazilian coffee, and poured himself a tumbler full of water and dropped three Alka-Seltzers into it.

He was just draining the fizzing dregs, when Mike Harding knocked on the kitchen door and walked in.

'Morning, Mr Tredington. Good party?'

'I'm not sure. I don't think so.'

'You should have stuck to orange juice.'

'With the benefit of hindsight, I should. What brings you in so early on a Sunday?'

'Early? It's after ten.'

'Well, what do you want?' George asked irritably.

'There was something I thought I should tell you about, to do with the family.'

'You'd better sit down, then. The coffee'll be ready in a minute.'

Mike Harding dropped into a kitchen chair and tried to decide how to start.

'It's about Jan's brother, Ivor,' he said.

'I thought you said it was about my family.'

'It is . . . about David.'

George looked at him more keenly. 'David? My cousin?'

'Yes. You know before he disappeared, when Ivor was at Barford, they used to be thick as thieves.'

'Yes, of course. Ivor taught him how to ride, though I must say, no one thought he would turn out to be as good a jockey as he is. Anyway, what's the old drunk been up to now?'

Mike took a deep breath. 'I think he might be going to cause some trouble.'

George didn't say anything.

'He's told Jan that he thinks David's not David.'

George looked flabbergasted. 'What on earth are you talking about?'

'It's not me, Mr Tredington. It's Ivor who's said it. He says he knows David isn't really David; says he's an impostor, like.'

'What? That's absurd,' George said dismissively. 'I wouldn't take any notice of the bloody fool; I mean to say, he's drunk most of the time, wouldn't know if it was Christmas or Tuesday.'

'Of course, that's what I said to Jan, but she went to see him Friday night. She said he was pretty sober, but very excited. He'd seen David at the races at Newton Abbot, and he said there was no way it was him.'

'How the hell would he remember? And for God's sake, of course David's changed a bit since he was twelve; most people do.'

'Ah, but he says he can prove beyond any doubt that it's not David.'

Slowly, George poured coffee into two cups. 'How can he possibly prove it?'

'I don't know. He didn't tell Jan, just said he could, and he was going to use the information to get his own back on the Tredingtons.'

'Get his own back? What for?'

'For sacking him, I suppose, and he says for stealing his daughter.'

George let out a burst of laughter. 'Now that really is absurd. Susan Butley was always determined to worm her way into Barford. Frankly, it's probably a jolly good thing she did; she's made the world of difference to the way Uncle Mark runs things.'

'Well, that's what Ivor says, and it looks as though he means it.'

'But he wouldn't get anywhere. My uncle had David's story thoroughly checked out. He hasn't told David, of course, though if you ask me it was perfectly reasonable. After all, he's now been officially reinstated as heir,' he added ruefully.

'I had heard that, Mr Tredington, but I'm only telling you what Ivor said, and him being Jan's sister, if he did do anything, I didn't want it reflecting on us, like – you being part of the family and everything.'

'Good God, I'd never hold it against you or Jan for anything Ivor did.'

'Well, I just wanted to be sure. Besides, I thought it was my duty to tell you.'

'Quite right. Thank you very much, Mike. And I shall certainly see what I can do about it.'

Mike looked relieved. 'Thanks, Mr Tredington. Maybe if you was to go and see Ivor...'

George put his hand to his mouth, tapping his upper lip with his index finger while he considered the idea.

'That's a very good notion. Give me his address and I'll try and get down there soon.'

After breakfast at Barford, when Emma didn't appear, Johnny Henderson and Aidan went out to the stud to look at the yearlings.

Susan had gone and there was no one else in the yard. Johnny didn't waste any time getting to the point.

'Right, Aidan, I've been thinking about Ivor bloody Butley. Why don't I go and see him, find out how much he knows? Maybe I could tell him I can help him do a deal with you. If he really does know anything, and can prove it, we'll just have to buy him off.'

'I've told you, Johnny, there's no way of buying him off. If we give anything, he'll just keep coming back for more.'

'Let's talk about that when we've discovered how much he really knows. My guess is he's got a hunch, for some reason or other, and he's blown it out of proportion, got himself excited about the possibilities. Maybe he's just trying it on; he's got nothing to lose.'

'OK, but I can tell you, he's doing more than playing a hunch. He knows all right. It's a matter of whether or not he can prove it.'

'Right, I'll get on to it. Trouble is, I've got to get back to London tomorrow – I've got a meeting with a punter who's keen to buy a couple of expensive yearlings. Then I'm shooting here on Tuesday. I won't be able to get down to see him before Wednesday. Look, Aidan,' he pleaded, 'please don't do anything until I've seen him. I bet I can sort it out.'

Aidan regarded him, resolved. 'Listen, Johnny, if he

really can let the cat out of the bag, I'm through with this. There's no way I'm having that hanging over me as long as I'm David Tredington.'

Johnny let out an exasperated breath. 'Don't worry about it; I'm sure he's trying it on. You'll see.'

The house-party at Barford Manor broke up on Sunday afternoon. Aidan watched the cars pull away with a lot of shouted 'goodbyes' and promises to keep in touch.

Johnny Henderson's was the last car to leave. There was a pleasing calm about the place when it had rolled off down the drive with Emma curled up sleepily in the back seat.

Aidan smiled to himself and walked back into the house with Sir Mark.

'Come and have a drink in the library,' the baronet suggested.

'As long as it's not that rum punch we had last night.'

Sir Mark laughed. 'There wasn't a drop of that left by midnight, thank God.'

In the library, the older man's manner became more serious and self-conscious. He poured a drink and sat with it in a favourite armchair. 'Help yourself,' he invited Aidan gruffly.

Aidan sat down opposite him, on the other side of an unlit fire. A horizontal shaft from the last of the afternoon's autumn sunshine pierced the tall window, glittering on a silver statue of Saint George, and on the bookshelves beyond.

Aidan glanced at his adopted father. 'You look tired.'

Sir Mark nodded. 'I can't take these weekends like I used to. Not that I don't like having the house full of the next generation; I still wish Victoria had met someone she liked before that jockey came on the scene. Not,' he added, 'that I've anything against jockeys as a breed.' He sighed. 'Still, I suppose I shouldn't complain. She's been a model daughter, considering she was brought up by an old blimp like me.'

'I don't think anyone would call you an old blimp.'

Sir Mark smiled, but the smile quickly faded and his face seemed to collapse into a mask of overwhelming sadness. He looked at Aidan. 'David, there's something I ought to tell you. I should have told you before, but even the girls don't know yet, though maybe they suspect.'

Aidan held his breath.

'I'm afraid I've never been a great man for quacks, and when I first started getting a pain in my guts, I ignored it. One can put up with quite a lot of pain if one feels inclined to.' He paused and looked thoughtfully at Saint George about to plunge his sword into a small, hapless dragon. 'A few months ago, just before you reappeared, it became intense enough for me to take it seriously. I'm afraid by the time it was diagnosed, it was too late to stop.'

Aidan felt himself close to tears at the bleak bluntness of Sir Mark's delivery. 'What is it?' he asked almost in a whisper.

'I'm afraid the spleen and now the intestine. They could hack a lot of it out, and subject me to monster doses of radiation, but there's small guarantee that it would work and, frankly, if I've got to go, I'd rather do it with a bit of dignity.'

'But surely,' Aidan said, panicking, hating the idea that the whole purpose of Johnny's plan was so much more imminent than they had imagined. 'Surely it's worth a try? I mean, you're only sixty; you could have another twenty or more years in front of you, and you've a lot to offer.'

'Have I? To whom? I'm just a man who was born lucky enough to be handed this place.' He waved his arm to take in the house and grounds. 'I've bred a few good horses. Hardly mould-breaking stuff. Most people would call me an anachronism.'

'You've a lot to offer the people close to you. Lucy, Victoria ... and me.'

Sir Mark nodded. There was a faint smile on his lips. 'And you. That's made me very happy. It makes the whole thing a lot easier to bear.'

'Have they given you something to deal with the pain, at least?'

'Oh yes. I'm taking a jar full of pills a day – rattling like a tin can.' He forced a smile, trying to make light of his condition. 'They take the edge off it, but they seem to make me more depressed. Or perhaps I'm just getting more depressed anyway.'

Aidan stared at the man who had trusted him, who had shown him a paternal affection he had never known. And he knew he didn't want him to die. All his instincts wanted there to be no secrets between them. If admitting to his own deception would have prolonged the man's life, even for a few years, he'd have done it. As it was, his conscience told him, it would probably have the opposite effect.

'Jesus, Dad, I'd no idea. You've not shown it at all. I wish to God there was something I could do.'

'There is. You're helping me just being here. Having a

son again.' He grinned. 'There is one other thing you could do, and that's win the Hennessy with Deep Mischief for me. And you never know, he could be a Gold Cup horse after that; I've never won a Gold Cup.'

Aidan laughed. 'We'll win the bloody race for you, just you wait. And make sure you win yours, too,' he added gently.

'Thanks,' Sir Mark nodded with no hint of self-pity. 'I'm aware that I'm not the only one with problems, though. I've been meaning to ask you how Mary is? It must be a worry for you – after all, she was virtually a mother to you for fifteen years.'

'Yes, it's a worry,' Aidan said. 'Things don't seem to be getting much better, and she has the odd bout of almost total immobility. As soon as I've made a bit of money turning a few horses, I'm planning to organise things for her so she'll have the care she needs at home.'

'I could probably help out with that.'

Aidan looked at Sir Mark, more grateful than he could express for the generousness of the offer, but he shook his head. 'No, Dad. She's not your responsibility and, I told you from the start, I want to make my own way here – and I can.'

'Yes, I believe you, but it will take a while before you can build up much of a base to start dealing in the kind of horses that will really earn you some money.'

'I should do well out of Letter Lad.'

'You're planning on selling him?'

'As soon as he's given a hint of what he can do.'

'I hope you don't do *too* well out of him; that would really upset poor old George.'

'He doesn't seem to have taken it too badly so far.'

'No,' Sir Mark agreed. 'I'm rather impressed . . . Getting back to Mary, though: don't you think you ought to pop over and see her? We can manage without you for a few days here. You're riding on Saturday, aren't you?'

'No, I'm not as a matter of fact.'

'But you told me Letter Lad was running at Chepstow. Has Sam decided to withdraw him?'

'No, but he's only to carry ten stone. I can't do that, so I'm going to ask Jason.'

Sir Mark nodded. 'Good idea. I wonder if he will? Still, I expect you'll want to be back in time to watch it. Why not fly over to Ireland after shooting on Tuesday, or on Wednesday morning, and spend a couple of days there?'

Aidan smiled. 'You're very perceptive. I'd been thinking exactly that myself.'

'I tell you what, that Taunton builder – what's his name? Bruce Trevor, the chap you won that race for – he's got a plane and a pilot. He'd always get you over there. He keeps it at Weston. I'll give him a ring. I'm sure he'll do it, if I ask him,' Sir Mark added.

After a night of patchy sleep, tussling with his conscience, Aidan woke wanting more than ever to throw himself into his work to repay Sir Mark for his generosity.

He and Johnny had agreed not to do anything about Ivor Butley until Johnny had seen him. Aidan wasn't riding out at Sam Hunter's that day, so he spent the morning working on two well-bred fillies he was breaking before they were sent to a Newmarket yard to see how they would perform on the flat.

The Tredingtons stuck to a policy of hanging on to all

promising-looking fillies, and selling the colts. Normally, the fillies would have been sent to their trainer for breaking at the end of their yearling year, but Aidan had persuaded Sir Mark that he could do it just as well, and save a few months' training fees.

He loved dealing with the young horses, and knew how crucial it was to their later performance that they were handled correctly now. He had the capacity to be utterly single-minded while he was doing the job, and several satisfying hours passed before he went to the house to face Sir Mark and his conscience over lunch.

They didn't refer to their conversation of the previous evening, and spent most of the meal discussing possible stallions for mares who were due to be covered the following spring. There was no doubt that Sir Mark derived a lot of pleasure from a task which had occupied him for over thirty years, despite the fact – of which they were both tacitly conscious – that it was probable that he would never see the progeny of the unions they were discussing.

After lunch, Aidan wanted to get out on his own, away from the house and the yard, to try to come to terms with the dilemma which faced him. The wind that had been threatening to blow up a storm all morning had relented, and there were even a few patches of blue showing through the wispy winter clouds.

He tacked up one of the older mares who had failed to get in foal that season, and walked her out of the yard towards the pasture that swept up to the cliff-top. To reach these big open fields, he had to make his way for half a mile along a track through a wood of sycamore and twisted oaks. At the end of the track, a five-bar gate gave on to the first of the fields. On any of the chasers, he'd have popped over the four-foot obstacle without a second thought; on an unfit old mare, it was too risky.

He dismounted and led her towards the big metal catch. As he reached it, he stopped. His eye had caught a movement on the far side of the field. There was a straggling, wind-swept hedgerow which led up towards the cliff before petering out.

A man dressed in a khaki jacket and leggings was walking along below the hedge; something about the cautious, uneven way he was moving suggested he didn't want to be seen.

Aidan's natural curiosity made him stop and watch as the furtive figure reached the end of the hedge and darted across the open grassland towards the cliff-top, where he disappeared.

Aidan had ridden these top pastures a few times. It was the traditional exercising ground, despite the lack of fences along the cliff-edge. Water drained fast through the thin soil, leaving a consistent surface of sheep-grazed sward.

He was about to open the gate when a second figure appeared below the hedge, moving stealthily, almost certainly following the first. Aidan strained his eyes to try to identify them, but the distance was too great. He could be sure only that this person, probably a man, was dressed in a long brown coat. He watched, fascinated, until the pursuer also crossed the open field and disappeared.

He wondered what on earth they were doing: possibly it was a game of cat-and-mouse between a poacher and a keeper. He opened the gate quietly, led the mare through, closed it and remounted, then trotted gently over to the hedge and followed it up to the top. Tethering his horse to the last sturdy blackthorn trunk, he walked the thirty yards to the top of the cliff.

There was a slight dip into a shallow, grass-lined gully where the two men must have dropped out of sight. There was no one there now. Aidan walked down to where the cliff fell away sharply. At this, the lowest point, a rough and under-used track started a switch-back course down the cliff-face.

The man in the long brown coat was just reaching the bottom of the track. Aidan flung himself down so that he wouldn't be seen against the skyline. He eased his head through the damp grass to get a clear view of the small, isolated beach below.

The brown-clad individual was now moving quickly but cautiously along the back of the beach in the direction of a naked rock headland that projected into the sea. It was clear that he was only concerned about his quarry spotting him; he didn't once look back up the cliff to where Aidan lay watching. Before he reached the end of the beach, he clambered up on to a low outcrop of rock and tucked himself into a shallow indentation scooped in the bottom of the cliff, and there he waited.

Twenty minutes later, Aidan was concerned about the old mare he had left tethered. The damp was beginning to seep through his long waxed riding coat, too, and the tide had turned and was creeping back in towards the foot of the cliff. The man in brown hadn't moved, and Aidan had given up trying to identify him from that distance.

Aidan thought it was time to go; whatever was

happening down there was probably none of his business. But his curiosity kept him hanging on. A moment later he was rewarded.

The first man emerged from what must have been a cave-mouth invisible from Aidan's viewpoint. His pursuer had also spotted him and sank deeper into the shadow of his hiding place.

The khaki man seemed confident now that he hadn't been followed. He set off back across the shrinking beach without looking back. He had almost reached the bottom of the track that led back up, when the brown-coated man, instead of following, darted down and round to the point where the other had come out of the cliff.

Aidan watched, fascinated, but quickly switched his attention to the man who was now clambering up the cliff below him. Half-way up, he was close enough for Aidan to see who he was, if only he would look up. It wasn't until he reached a tricky stretch of track, fifty feet below Aidan, where it was crossed by a stream trickling down the cliff, that the man raised his face.

It took Aidan a fraction of a second to take in who it was; quickly he pulled his head back among the cover of the damp grass tuffets. Keeping doubled up, he scrambled to his feet, sprinting back to where he had left the mare. Within seconds he was on her back and urging her into a reluctant canter, back towards the gate into the woods.

This time, Aidan had to risk the mare's rusty limbs. He put her squarely at the gate, helped her with her stride, and kicked her up and over it. She flew into the gloomy opening without any hesitation. Aidan grinned and slapped her neck. He pulled her up as quickly as he could and wheeled round to see if Ivor Butley had reached the top of the cliff.

To Aidan's intense relief, it was a few seconds before a silhouette appeared on the skyline. He heaved a sigh of relief and watched Ivor head for the cover of the hedgerow and start back down towards the woods.

Aidan walked the horse back through the trees, guilty that he had pushed the old mare harder than he should have done, but she seemed none the worse for it and was still sound when he arrived back at the yard.

He handed her to Billy, one of the stud-grooms, and asked him to give her a good dressing over. 'Any messages?' he added.

'No, Mr David, except Jason was here looking for you earlier.'

Aidan stopped walking. 'How long ago?'

'Dunno. Half an hour?'

'What did he want?'

'Didn't say.'

'If he comes back, tell him I'm up at the house.'

Aidan checked some of the horses before jumping into his Land Rover and driving the few hundred yards to Jason and Victoria's cottage. Victoria opened the door to him.

'Hi, Davy,' she beamed, 'you look rather damp. Do you want a cup of tea or something?'

'No thanks. I just wanted a word with Jason.'

'He's not in. I'm not sure where he is. He was out when I got back.'

'When was that?' Aidan asked, more sharply than he'd intended.

'Is it important?' Victoria asked, worried.

'No. It's just that he was looking for me. I thought it might have been about him riding Letter Lad.'

'He was wondering why you wanted him to.'

'He can do the weight; I can't,' Aidan said simply. 'Anyway, tell him I'm up at the house.'

Mrs Rogers made Aidan some tea. She told him that Sir Mark wasn't feeling well and had gone up to his room. Susan had driven down to Lynmouth to pick up some stationery. Aidan tried to chat to the kind old housekeeper, but his mind was full of Ivor Butley, coming clandestinely to Barford, clambering down a slithery cliff-face to spend half an hour in a cave in what he had been told was one of the most inaccessible beaches on the North Devon coast.

Not wanting to let his impatience show, Aidan left Mrs Rogers in the kitchen when he finished his tea, and walked through the silent house towards the library. As he passed the office, he heard the fax machine in action. They were expecting details of race entries. He went in to see what had arrived.

He picked up the piece of paper that the machine had spewed out. It was a message to Sir Mark from a firm of lawyers in Sydney, Australia.

We have a report that three members of the crew of White Fin, lost off Norfolk Island, were picked up and arrived in Fiji on 2 November. We have no confirmation that David Tredington is among them, and no further information relating to the identity of this person. We will inform you as soon as possible of any further development.

As he read, Aidan grew numb with shock, until he could scarcely feel the sheet of paper between his fingers. There was turmoil in his guts as all the conflicting possibilities paraded themselves in front of him.

After what he had seen that afternoon, he had been in no doubt that Ivor Butley's visit to the cave had been prompted by his need for proof that Aidan wasn't David. And that someone else – the brown-coated man – was presumably on a similar quest. But who the hell was this David Tredington in the South Pacific? And what did Sir Mark know about him?

He listened for a moment for sounds of anyone else in the house, heard none, folded up the sheet of paper and tucked it in his pocket just as he heard a man's voice from the back of the house. A moment later, footsteps echoed along the corridor and George Tredington walked past the office door.

Aidan went out to meet him. 'Afternoon, George.'

'Oh, hello, David. Mrs R said you were in the library.'

'Just on my way there. Are you having a drink?' They carried on together across the hall towards the library.

'Thanks. I wanted to see you; I really need to know if you've decided to take the spare house gun tomorrow. I've a couple of eager paying stand-ins if not.'

Aidan nodded as he poured two whiskies. 'I thought I might, though I don't suppose I'll worry the birds much.'

'It'll be interesting to see how you shoot now. I used to be very envious of you as a boy.'

'Well,' Aidan said cautiously, 'I've had no practice at all since.'

'Never mind. Should be a good day.' The sound of

someone else walking across the hall reached them. George turned expectantly towards the door. 'I hope this is your father. I just wanted to check he's happy with my instructions to Jim Wheeler.'

Jason Dolton walked in. He was wearing muddy jodhpur boots, and a long brown waxed coat, similar to the one Aidan had hung in the back hall half an hour earlier.

He gave Aidan a surly nod. 'Vicky said you were back 'ere. What's this about me riding Letter Lad Saturday?'

'You can do ten stone without any trouble, can't you?' Aidan asked.

'Yeah, 'course I can.'

'Well, I can't get near it. He's right down the handicap, and I thought you might like the chance of an easy win.'

'That's very generous of you,' Jason grunted sarcastically. 'I'll take the ride, if I don't get offered a better one.'

'Great!' Aidan said with an enthusiasm he didn't feel. 'You won't get a better offer. Letter Lad should just about win, after his last showing.'

'We'll see,' Jason said, turning to go.

'Hang on, Jason,' George said, finding it difficult to talk to him as a member of the family. 'You still haven't told me if you're shooting tomorrow. You know you really should; it makes it very tricky to organise properly otherwise.'

Jason looked at Aidan. 'Is he shooting?'

'Yes,' George said impatiently.

'Then so am I.' Jason left the room this time without another word.

Aidan didn't speak either as he listened to the footsteps fade across the hall and through the green baize door. He was trying to relate Jason to the figure he had seen following Ivor down to the beach. George interrupted his thoughts.

'Chippy bugger. I can't think what possessed Vicky to marry him.'

'I doubt he's like that all the time,' Aidan said. 'It was probably a pretty daunting prospect for him marrying into this family. And,' Aidan added, 'maybe he's just beginning to realise that he's never going to make it to the top.'

'You think so?'

'I'm afraid I do.'

'Hmm,' George grunted. 'That reminds me,' he said, 'I was meaning to talk to you about Letter Lad. How did he go on Saturday?'

Aidan shrugged. 'Did you not see the race?'

'Yes, I did. He didn't really seem that interested.' George found it hard to keep a touch of irony from his voice.

'Ah well,' Aidan said with a grin, 'I can't expect to win them all. Maybe I was a bit too optimistic, and you did the right thing by selling him.'

'I think you'll find I did,' George said with a laugh. 'Still, best of luck with him.'

'Thanks,' Aidan said, relieved that George had mis-read the race at Sandown. 'Now, I'm still half-soaked. I'm going home to wallow in a bath for a while.'

'Fine,' George said. 'I'll hang on until your father gets down.'

Chapter Nine

Tuesday, the day of the shoot, dawned dry and still beneath a blanket of thick grey cloud.

Sir Mark had suggested that Aidan walk up and have breakfast at the house. Johnny Henderson had invited himself to stay the night before, and had turned up from London at three in the morning. He and George were already at the table when Aidan walked into the dining-room.

Mrs Rogers waddled in and out with dishes of scrambled egg and bacon, while George talked about the quality of sport they were going to have.

'I've given my gun to Johnny for the day as a tip for finding me some decent horses,' he said heartily, 'despite the fact he sold you Letter Lad. Also, I'll be able to keep my eye on Jim Wheeler's beaters. I want to make sure they do the job properly. With no wind, we should get some good high birds on the coomb drives, and there are plenty in the oak coppice woods. It would be marvellous if old Lord Barnstaple hit a few for a change.'

'Listen,' Johnny said, chewing hard on a piece of bacon, 'when those horses I bought you start winning, I shall want a few more days' shooting here.' He kept his eyes fixed on George, knowing that just the thought of training a couple of winners, seeing his name in print, was enough to have him promising the earth.

'Of course, dear boy, of course. I'll make damn sure there are plenty of birds next season, just for you.'

Aidan listened apprehensively. Apart from a few surreptitious outings with one of the keepers, a clay-pigeon trap and a borrowed twelve-bore, he had scarcely fired a gun in his life. It wasn't an activity in which he had ever participated in Ireland. And David the boy was supposed to have been something of an infant prodigy with a four-ten.

Lord Barnstaple, the owner of a neighbouring estate, and two local farmers of considerable substance, all of whom contributed to the costs of the shoot, appeared during the course of breakfast. There were to be eight guns in all. Mike Harding and Victoria, with a sixteenbore, were coming to make up the numbers.

As the table filled, Aidan was able to catch Johnny's eye and indicate that they had to talk, somewhere else.

No one took much notice of them leaving together – to sort out their guns, they said. In the gun-room they made certain they couldn't be heard.

'Look, Johnny,' Aidan said, 'things have been happening down here.'

'Like what?' Johnny asked nervously.

'I saw Ivor Butley yesterday, and someone else following him down to the beach.'

'To the beach? What beach?'

'Down below the gallops, near a point called Stanner Head on the map.'

'Why the hell was Ivor going down there?'

'I don't know, do I?' Aidan said testily. 'But I'd say it

was pretty likely to have something to do with his proving I'm not David.'

'But why down there?' Johnny shook his head.

'God knows! Maybe David left something there which Ivor's kept hidden for years. He went into a cave and came out about half an hour later. Then this other fella slipped in after he'd gone.'

'Who was that, then?'

'It was too far away for me to tell.'

Johnny looked at him keenly. 'But you've got an idea, haven't you?'

Aidan sighed and nodded. 'I can't be sure, and I can't make the connection, but I think it was Jason.'

'Oh my God. That's all we need,' Johnny moaned. 'I wonder what the hell he knows about it. Of course, he's totally pissed off about you turning up; he's made that pretty clear all over the place, because he thinks Vicky won't get her farm now.'

'Sure, I know that. But I'd like to know how he got on to Ivor.'

'I'll find out what I can from Ivor tomorrow when I go down and see him.'

'That may not be soon enough.'

'It'll have to be. It'd look very odd if I suddenly ducked out of a free day's shooting.'

'Yes, I suppose that would be a little out of character. Mark's arranged for me to fly to Shannon tomorrow, so I can see Mary but, for God's sake, you must get down there tomorrow. I don't trust that Ivor. And there's something else I've got to show you.' Aidan pulled out the fax he had pocketed the evening before and handed it to Johnny.

Johnny's mouth twitched into a grimace as he read. He handed it back to Aidan with a shrug. 'Don't worry about it.'

'What do you mean – don't worry? If the real David has turned up in Fiji, that's the end of it.'

'I don't know who the hell he is, but I'm pretty damn sure it isn't the real David and, more to the point, so is Mark.'

'You knew something about this, then?'

'As a matter of fact I did, yes. Mark told me when he first got the report that a David Tredington was one of the crew who had gone missing on *White Fin*.'

'When was that, for God's sake?'

'When I was over here in August, gathering up material for you.'

'Why the hell didn't you tell me then?'

'I didn't want to put you off your stride unnecessarily. And anyway, not long before you arrived here, Mark got a report from these lawyers saying they couldn't find a trace of any David Tredington who'd been in Australia. And since then, he's accepted you without reservation, so he obviously doesn't think this chap is his son.'

'God, you might have told me.'

'But at that stage I still wasn't sure you were going to do it anyway. I took a punt.' Johnny grinned. 'Lucky I did, or we'd never have got as far as we have.'

'I wish to God we hadn't,' Aidan said. 'I was leading a peaceful life out in Mayo until you turned up, and now Mickey's been killed, and I'm being threatened by a drunken old groom, and Jason too, if it was him I saw yesterday.'

'Look, don't worry about Ivor. I'm sure he can be sorted out, whatever he knows.'

'I hope to God you're right. Anyway, we'd better get a move on and join the others, or George will start fussing.'

As they were walking back to the dining-room, Mrs Rogers intercepted Aidan to tell him he was wanted on the phone. Johnny went on; Aidan made his way to Sir Mark's study.

'Hello?'

'Mr Tredington?'

'Yes.'

'Sergeant King here, Hampshire CID. A couple of things have cropped up on this accident in which Mickey Thatcher was killed. I'd like to come out and interview you as soon as possible.'

Aidan's heart pounded. 'What sort of things?'

'I'll tell you when I see you. When would be convenient? I'd like to come today, if possible.'

'I'm tied up most of the day,' Aidan apologised, 'but I could be free by six.'

'That'd be fine, if you could just give me directions.'

Aidan gave them as calmly as he could and put the phone down, itching with frustration. It would be hell having to wait until the evening to hear what this policeman had to say. But he was sure that, whatever it was, it would confirm his suspicion that the crash had been no accident, and that he had been the intended victim.

George had concocted a new ritual for drawing peg numbers. After breakfast, when Jason had arrived, each gun was given a small silver tumbler filled with port, which they all drained at the same time, to find their number etched into the bottom of the tumbler.

'I've reorganised all the drives and the numbering,' George declared, 'so you won't know what you're in for until you get there.'

The party set off south in a convoy of Land Rovers which left the metalled drive and lurched down a farm track to the river. There, a crowd of twenty or so beaters, keepers and pickers-up waited. They were gossiping, stamping their feet to keep out the seeping damp, yelling at their dogs, nodding to the guns they knew.

Johnny Henderson was in Aidan's Land Rover. As they pulled up beside the other vehicles, he grabbed Aidan's arm. 'Christ! Have you seen who's beating?'

Aidan looked more closely at the group of thickly wrapped men, some with dogs, most carrying stout sticks with which to beat the woodland undergrowth. Among them, hunched over his stick, Ivor Butley was blowing on his hands.

'Jesus!' Aidan hissed. 'Does he usually beat?'

'I haven't seen him out for years.'

'Can you try and find out why he's come?' Aidan asked. 'See what reason he gives?'

'Sure. I knew him well enough when he was working here.'

They climbed out and joined in the general banter between the other guns. Only Jason stood apart from the group, not feeling part of it and resenting it.

'I'll be with the beaters and the pickers-up,' George announced in the manner of a general before a battle. 'Any queries, refer them to me.'

216

Johnny strolled across to the beaters and said hello to those he knew, until he reached Ivor.

'Good heavens! It's Ivor, isn't it? Haven't seen you for years. What brings you back here?'

Ivor was on the defensive. 'Mr George came round my place Sunday. Said he was short of beaters. Says he wants to raise the standard now he's taken over the shoot.'

'Great to see you back. No dog, though?'

'Haven't kept a dog in years.'

'I expect you'd rather be carrying a gun, eh? You used to be a bit of a crack-shot in the old days. Anyway, I'll get you a drink afterwards if you make sure to flush a few my way.' Johnny gave a hearty laugh and carried on to talk to a couple more of the regular beaters he knew.

George was directing the guns to their pegs now. Aidan was already walking to a peg at the far end of the valley. George pointed Johnny in the opposite direction.

To get the day off to a good start, George had arranged to drive a conifer wood on the steep valley side both ways and, as he had predicted, a thick flock of pheasants screamed out of the top of the trees and across to the cover on the far side of the deep coomb.

Trying to remember everything that had been told him, Aidan aimed well in front of the racing birds and, to his amazement and mild disgust, downed a couple at each of the first drives.

Afterwards, George appeared by his side and made a point of coming over to congratulate him. 'Not bad for a man who hasn't shot for fifteen years. I'm afraid you won't get much of a crack on your next peg, but things will improve after that.'

Jason, who had hit everything he'd aimed at from the next peg, was less complimentary and more disgruntled than ever.

'I've had enough of this,' he said to George. 'I've got better things to do than stand around shooting these easy driven birds with a bunch of snobs.' He pointedly started putting his gun back in its sleeve.

'That's a shame,' George said, not disguising his relief. 'Still, it'll leave more for the rest of us to shoot at.'

'If you can hit them,' Jason said, striding off towards his battered pick-up without saying goodbye to any of the other guns.

Twenty minutes later, Aidan found himself completely alone on the next drive, out of sight and hearing of the rest of the shoot. He was supposed to be covering the flank of the oak coppice wood, where the birds would tend to leave by the other end. A few might fly back over the beaters, if he was lucky, George had promised.

He heard the head-keeper blow a whistle to start the beaters. This was followed by the sound of wood hitting wood. Shrieks and whoops echoed back to him from the close cover. A few minutes later, the sound of multiple gunshots reached him from the far side, where the pheasants were evidently emerging in some numbers. None came back towards him. He wasn't sure that he wanted to shoot them if they did, but he kept his gun cocked and ready.

Behind him was a swathe of thick mixed woodland

where the Exmoor deer sometimes came and sheltered. He heard a distant movement from inside the wood and wondered if there were any there now. He turned to have a look, but his gaze didn't penetrate more than a few feet into the dense woodland. As he was turning back, he heard the sound of a shot from the woods behind him. Almost at the same instant, there was a vicious burning sensation in his arm.

He had been hit, and not by a shotgun.

For a moment, he couldn't take in what had happened.

He glanced at his stinging arm where a little blood had seeped through and stained the ragged edges of a tear in his Barbour. He flexed his arm and winced, but the arm functioned. He dropped his cocked twelve-bore and leapt as the trigger caught on the branch of a small gorse bush beside him and exploded at his feet; the shot scattered harmlessly across the tussocky ground in front of him.

He pulled off his waxed coat and the tweed jacket he was wearing under it. His shirt was bloody but he was able to examine the wound. It had already stopped hurting so badly, and after gingerly prodding round it, he concluded that the damage was only on the surface. Whatever had hit him had skimmed past and carried on.

Thinking fast now, Aidan pulled his jacket back on and snatched up his gun. He rejected the empty cartridge, replaced it and ran towards the wood behind his peg. There was no obvious way in there. He ran twenty yards along the edge until he reached a narrow fire-break. The grass was long and wet between the ruts made by timber-hauling tractors. After ten yards, there was a crossing of ways and, along the track to his left, above a small clearing, he spotted a wooden platform about fifteen feet high; it was a 'high seat', used occasionally for the culling of the Exmoor deer. He ran to it, stopped below it, and listened.

He could hear nothing besides the melancholy autumn calls of small woodland birds, obliterated now and then by the alarmed honking of pheasants and the blast of guns on the far side of the big oak coppice.

Aidan scrambled up the ladder to the sturdy timber platform. As his eye came level with the floor, his heart thumped harder. There was a discarded brass cartridge case lying a few feet in front of his face. He clambered the last few steps and reached across for it. It was still warm. Whoever had fired it couldn't have gone far. He listened again, more intently, for ten or fifteen seconds. But there was no sound of human movement.

He stood up on the platform and looked through the trees towards the point where he had been standing at his peg. Though partially obscured by scantily leafed branches, there was a viable view of the spot, especially with a telescopic sight.

His mind raced. After what had happened to Mickey, he'd promised himself that, whatever it cost, there'd be no more deaths – his own or anyone else's. But then, there didn't seem any reason to kill him, not for anyone who knew and could prove that he wasn't David.

Shaking with uncertainty and anger, he climbed down to the ground and looked for signs of a departing human. But he had no tracking skills, and there was no obvious disturbance among the woodland that bordered the fire-break.

In the distance, the shots were becoming more sporadic. The drive would be over soon, and he would be expected to join the rest of the party to move on to the next. He was running back towards his peg when he heard the plaintive whistle of the head-keeper bringing the drive to an end.

He looked around to see if there was anyone else nearby who might have seen what had happened. There didn't appear to be. He rubbed some earth on to the tear in his Barbour to obscure the bloodstains, unloaded his gun and walked back round the wood to the Land Rovers.

George was fussing around, overseeing the beaters and pickers-up who were gathering up the twenty or so brace of pheasant which had just been shot. He glanced at Aidan.

'Any joy your end? I heard a couple of shots.'

Aidan shook his head with a self-effacing grin. 'Missed 'em both,' he said.

'Bad luck. Never mind, they had a good haul here.'

'Aren't you sorry you're not carrying a gun yourself?'

'I'm quite enjoying myself overseeing things, though I might take Jason's peg for the next drive.'

'He's gone, then?'

'Yes, missed the last drive, silly bugger.'

There were two more drives before they stopped for lunch in a small abandoned woodman's cottage. Mrs Rogers and a couple of women from the village had arrived before them with a large stockpot of casseroled venison, a case of claret and port. They had managed to squeeze a splendidly laid table, with silver candelabra, in what had once been the parlour of the small timber-framed house.

Johnny and Aidan walked in together. Johnny appreciatively sniffed the aroma of the venison. 'That smells fantastic, Mrs Rogers. Did you make it?'

'No. Victoria did.'

'Did she? I wondered what had happened to her. She was supposed to be beside me on the last drive. I suppose she came back to help you.'

'No. I haven't seen her. Look, here she comes now.'

Victoria walked in looking flustered.

'Hello, Vicky. What happened to you?'

'Sorry,' she said. 'Jason was having one of his moods and wanted to talk to me,' she said uncomfortably.

Aidan glanced at her sharply. He had already gathered that Jason hadn't been seen since the second drive. Looking away from Victoria, he was abruptly assailed by a series of crazy possibilities. But Johnny didn't give him the chance to ponder them now.

'Do you remember lunches in here when we were kids?' he asked.

Aidan nodded absently.

'Don't you remember, David,' Johnny prompted across the room, 'when we were about ten, trying to snaffle a bit of port?'

Aidan laughed at his non-existent memory of the event.

The party in the old cottage became rowdier as it filled up and people took their seats around the table. The claret started to flow, and carried on flowing until all the food had been eaten and the port was being passed round. It was traditional to have this lunch late, and leave only two short drives for the afternoon when the light would fade fast.

As he tried to join in, Aidan couldn't tear his mind from the fact that someone had attempted to kill him. Every so often he fingered the empty cartridge case in his pocket to remind himself it hadn't been some kind of horrible daydream.

None of the party seemed to notice his discomfort: they were past such subtleties by then. But when one of his neighbours went out to relieve the pressure on his bladder, Johnny Henderson came over and sat down beside him.

'What the hell's wrong with you? You look as though you've seen a ghost,' he said out of the side of his mouth.

'Sorry.' Aidan made an effort to brighten up. 'I'll tell you later.'

Johnny raised his eyebrows and turned to the conversation on his other side.

When lunch was over and the guns walked out of the cottage, the beaters started to climb out of the back of a Land Rover where they had been eating their sandwiches. Aidan, watching them, caught Johnny's eye. Johnny nodded slightly and walked over to talk to them.

Aidan turned to George who was beside him.

'Wasn't old Ivor Butley beating this morning?' he asked.

'Yes, he was as a matter of fact. I went down to see him on Sunday evening.' George glanced around to make sure that they weren't being overheard. 'The fact is, he's got some funny ideas about you.'

With an effort, Aidan restricted his reaction to a slightly raised eyebrow while George went on.

'His sister Jan's my groom, and he told her he'd seen you at the races and...' George paused awkwardly. 'Well, to be quite frank, he said he was sure you weren't David.'

Aidan laughed. 'Well, he's not the first to have thought that since I came back, and I dare say he won't be the last. Silly old fool; I recognised him the minute I saw him.'

'Of course,' George said. 'Anyway, I thought I'd better see what his idiotic theory was all about, you know, just in case. I told him that the family had made absolutely certain that you are David, and there was not a scintilla of doubt about it. I think I managed to convince him. Anyway, when he asked if he could come up and beat, I thought that might put an end to his story.' George looked anxiously at Aidan. 'I do hope you think I did the right thing?'

'Sure, you did, George. Thanks very much. I dare say the old fella's still bitter about what happened after I left. Maybe if he feels he's been summoned back into the fold a bit, he'll get over it.'

'Just what I thought,' George said with relief at Aidan's evident approval. 'He used to be pretty useful in the old days, so I agreed. But he must have brought a hell of a big flask with him because he was fairly pissed after the first couple of drives, and unfortunately I had to send him home.'

Aidan couldn't hit anything after lunch, but nobody took much notice. Though George, now on Jason's peg next to him, was watching him with interest, he made no comment. After what seemed to Aidan like several

224

hours, the party finally loaded their twelve-bores back into the vehicles and wound their way across the estate towards the house. Johnny Henderson went in Aidan's Land Rover.

'What's happened?' he asked as soon as Aidan had started the motor and joined the convoy.

'Someone tried to shoot me this morning.'

'Shit!'

'Yeah, and they'd have killed me if I hadn't just been turning round. As it was, I've got a small chunk of flesh out of my upper arm.'

'Is it OK?'

'I'm fine; it's not serious. But this thing is getting out of hand. Maybe whoever dropped that sleeper on the car was trying to kill me, not just warn me; maybe it was MacClancy.'

'Why the hell should MacClancy still want to kill you? You said he wouldn't cause any more harm. And anyway, how would he have been able to get anyone to have a go at you down here?'

'God knows. I don't know what the hell to think. Maybe I should have reported it to the police at once, but I've left it too late now.'

'No. You can't go to the police, not without telling them who you are.'

'Of course I can. The only reason I didn't was for Sir Mark's sake. You were right this morning when you said he's accepted me totally. And there's no doubt it's done him a lot of good. I'm beginning to feel guilty as hell about it, but I know damn well how much it would harm him if he found out now.'

Johnny looked at him cynically. 'That's a pretty

speech, Aidan, but I don't think you want to do a few years' porridge, either. And what about your mother and the money you're going to need to take care of her?'

'If there's one thing I've learned since I got to England, it's that I'd have no trouble making a decent living out of horses here.'

'There's a difference between making a living and coming into ten million quid – less my half-million,' Johnny said.

Aidan pulled up the Land Rover in the courtyard behind the house where the rest of the party's vehicles were parked.

'Well,' he said as he switched off the motor, 'I'd not hold my breath over that, if I were you.'

All the guns were invited to stay for drinks before heading home after tea. Although Jason hadn't come back, Victoria was there, trying to disguise her mortification over her husband's ill-humour. The guests were gathered in the big drawing-room to talk contentedly about the day's sport before moving on to wider topics.

Most of them had an interest in racing and took advantage of Aidan's presence to glean a few inside tips. But all the time he talked, his mind was a maelstrom of conjecture about who had shot at him.

It had to be someone connected with the shoot, or the house; at least someone who was aware that he would be shooting that morning, and which peg he would be on.

Jason hadn't reappeared since he had left after the first valley drives, and Aidan was still fairly sure that it was Jason he had seen following Ivor down to the beach.

He had no doubt at all that he'd seen Ivor on the beach, and then Ivor had turned up to beat that morning for the first time in years. But he could see no good reason why Jason, or Ivor or, for that matter, MacClancy or anyone else would want to kill him. Whilst it was true that the jockey held a grudge, and he had been at Fontwell on the day Mickey had died, Aidan just didn't think Jason had it in him to attempt murder.

Maybe it was Ivor; perhaps he had concluded from Aidan's attitude at Sandown that he wasn't going to get anywhere, and was motivated by pure bitter frustration...

These thoughts and the conversation he was holding simultaneously were interrupted by Mrs Rogers coming in to tell him he was wanted on the phone.

He excused himself and went to take the call in the office.

'Hello, Davy?' Emma's voice purred down the telephone line. 'How did the slaughtering go, then?'

'OK, provided you weren't a pheasant.'

'Were you all right?'

'How do you mean?'

'It's just that Lucy said on the way back to London that you seemed a bit nervous about shooting again.'

'Nervous, me?'

'Well, maybe she didn't say nervous, just apprehensive.'

'It was all fine. I hit a few and everybody was very happy.'

'Nothing else happened?'

Aidan hesitated. 'Like what?'

'It's just that you sound a bit odd.'

Aidan managed a laugh. 'That's fifteen years of living in Ireland for you.'

'Anyway, are you coming to London again soon?'

'God knows,' Aidan answered, then added quickly, 'Things are quite busy with the horses just at the moment. And I'm off to Ireland tomorrow morning until the end of the week.'

'Maybe I'd better come and see you racing one of these days.'

Aidan felt a stirring between his legs as an image of Emma, naked, lying on his bed sprang into his mind.

'Make sure you don't tell me you're there till after the race, then. Otherwise I might have trouble getting my breeches zipped up.'

Emma laughed. 'Just thinking about you squeezing into them turns me on.'

'You're a wicked woman. I'll be in touch,' Aidan said, 'but I'm needed back at the party now.'

Aidan winced guiltily at the edge in Emma's voice as she said goodbye. When he had put the phone down, he reminded himself that she was a girl who was quite capable of looking after herself. Besides, he was a lot more interested in Ivor Butley's altogether more substantial daughter.

He left the office but didn't go straight back to the drawing-room. Instead, he made his way through echoing corridors at the back of the house to the courtyard where the cars were parked.

He let himself out of the back door and stood silently for a moment, making sure there was no one else around. A steady drizzle had set in and the worn cobbles gleamed in the light of a single naked bulb. When he was confident that he was on his own, he selected two vehicles and walked across to them.

Both were unlocked and he was able to make a thorough search of each. He had been nursing a hope that he might find a rifle that fitted the cartridge he still had in his pocket. But he found nothing suspicious in either car, or in the other three that he searched. Jason's pick-up, which he guessed Victoria must have driven up, only contained a brace of pheasant.

He was just closing it when he heard someone open the back door of the house. He ducked down by the passenger door of the Subaru and hoped it wasn't Victoria.

He listened carefully. The footsteps, a heavy clip on the cobbles, suggested someone heavier. He peered over the car bonnet. It was George, who walked across the courtyard to a green door on the far side of the yard. This opened into an all-purpose store-room. He went in and, after some clattering around inside, came out again carrying a bulky object which he took over to his Range Rover and placed in the back. He banged the tail-gate down without locking it and walked quickly back to the house.

Once he was inside, Aidan got up from where he was crouching and made straight for George's car. Holding his breath, he lifted the tail-gate. It turned out to be nothing more than the clay-pigeon trap which he had been using himself over the last week to improve his own shooting. He guessed that George had decided after his performance that day that he also needed a bit of practice, but didn't want to publicise the fact.

Frustrated that he hadn't discovered anything to help

him, Aidan went back to the drawing-room. No one in the party seemed to have missed him particularly, now that some of them had gone into the billiard-room. He joined in the conversations going on around him as naturally as he could, while his mind raced, selecting and rejecting a dozen different courses of action.

Within half an hour, the guns began to leave, until only Sir Mark, George, Johnny and Aidan remained.

George was as affable as ever, congratulating Aidan again on his moderate performance on the shoot and chaffing him light-heartedly about Letter Lad, until he too announced that he was going home. As he drove out of the gates, an anonymous Vauxhall drove in. A few minutes later, Mrs Rogers was opening the door to a tall, shambling figure who identified himself as Detective Sergeant King. Mrs Rogers showed him into the library and went to fetch Aidan.

Aidan walked in a few moments later. 'Good evening.'

'You're Mr David Tredington?'

'That's me. Have a seat.' They sat in chairs either side of an unlit fire. 'How can I help?'

'As I told you on the phone, a couple of things have cropped up. We think we may have traced the truck which was carrying the sleepers, and forensic have established that some kind of fluorescent marker paint was sprayed on your vehicle, possibly very recently.'

'Fluorescent paint? Where? How? I certainly didn't see any.'

'Well you wouldn't have done, from the ground. Even though you're quite tall, you're probably not tall enough to see over the roof of a Range Rover.'

'There was paint on the roof?'

'Yes. A small "X". Do you recall seeing it there before?'

'God, no. And I'm sure I'd have seen it some time or other. Why do you think anyone did that?'

'To identify your vehicle as you drove along the motorway. No problem from the bridge with the sodium lights reflecting on it.'

'You think someone was waiting for me?'

'Why else would anyone go to the trouble of marking your car?'

Aidan didn't answer at once. 'Jesus! You're saying you think someone was trying to kill us?'

'I'd say someone was definitely trying to kill you.'

Official confirmation of what Aidan had felt in his guts since the incident eight days before produced another rush of guilt about Mickey. He got up and walked across the room, unable to look the policeman in the eyes. 'You're saying you now think someone tried to ... murder me?'

'That's right.'

Aidan turned to face him. 'But who the hell would want to do that?'

'I'd have thought you were in a better position to answer that than we are. That's why I'm here. Who do you think might want to kill you?'

Aidan's head was crowded with all the possibilities that had been running through it since the crash had happened. He shook it to clear it. 'No one,' he muttered. 'There's absolutely no reason anyone should want to kill me – no reason at all that I can think of. I mean, I'm a new boy over here. I've not been in England over two months.'

'So we gather. But you could still have put a few noses

out of joint since you got here. Or was it something you got up to back in Ireland?'

Aidan shook his head. 'No. There's nothing like that.'

'What were you doing in Ireland, then?'

'Farming a small place in Mayo. I'd no enemies over there. There was no reason why I should have.'

'What about someone trying to stop you ride here?'

'Why should they? If I couldn't ride one of my father's horses, there'd always be a few pros ready to do it, and probably make a better job of it than I would. Anyway, it's not as though anyone's had a big gamble on any of our horses.'

'Yet.'

'I have to tell you, I think that's a pretty unlikely scenario. Are you really sure about this mark on the car?'

'Yes, we're sure. Only found it by chance, when the security lights at the compound lit it up. You rolled the car and slid it on the roof for about twenty yards.'

'Yes, I remember.'

'And also, we've had a sighting of someone clambering on to the vehicle, in the car-park. The witness thought he was just playing a prank with a bit of graffiti. It's not a lot, but it's a start. And you're telling me definitely that you can't come up with any names for us to follow up?'

'I'm afraid not, though of course I'll do everything I can to help.'

'I'm sure you will, sir.'

'You said you may have traced the truck with the sleepers?'

'Maybe. We know where the sleepers were stolen

from.' The detective stood up and took a few paces towards the door. 'Not all that far from here, as a matter of fact. Travellers probably. The local force think they might have a line. We'll see.' He took out a note-book, scribbled his name and telephone number in it, tore out the sheet and handed it to Aidan. 'Get in touch if you've got anything to tell me, won't you? I'll probably need to see you again, so see if you can come up with any names for us, all right? Don't worry. I know the way out.'

Aidan watched the policeman stroll from the room. As the footsteps faded across the hall, he dropped back into the chair he had been sitting in and stared at the empty fireplace.

Later he went upstairs and found Johnny Henderson coming out of a bathroom. They went to Johnny's bedroom, where Aidan told him what he had heard from the Hampshire policeman.

'Look,' Aidan said, 'you'd better be bloody careful with Ivor. I mean, all these things may be connected.'

'I don't see how.'

'Nor do I. If I did, I'd know what I was dealing with. I'm being picked up at half-six tomorrow morning, so I won't see you. I'll ring you from Ireland in the evening.'

Johnny nodded. 'Sure. I'll have to go back to London after I've seen Ivor. You can reach me there.'

Chapter Ten

Bruce Trevor had not only agreed to Sir Mark's suggestion that he put his plane at Aidan's disposal, he had also offered to send a driver to collect Aidan from Barford.

When Sir Mark had described him as 'that Taunton builder,' he had been understating the property king's commercial standing. Bruce Trevor had been responsible for developing shopping malls all over the southwest of England, and had sold out the previous year for a rumoured sixty million. These days he spent most of his energy and some of his enormous resources trying to capture the major trophies of English jump racing. Aidan had twice ridden for him, and won, and Trevor was anxious for him to do so again in the more prestigious big amateur chases: he would have done almost anything to curry favour with Sir Mark.

By eight o'clock, Aidan was installed in one of the six seats of a Cessna Citation, while a taciturn pair of pilots ran their checks and prepared to take off on the short flight to Shannon.

Driving up through Galway to his old home produced an irreconcilable blend of emotions in Aidan. He felt that he was, after his two months as David Tredington, an altogether new person. At the same time, the sight of the hills and coast tugged at him, making him almost sick with nostalgia.

Mary's greeting confused him further.

She was, as he had expected, overjoyed to see him. There had been no deterioration in her health in the two months he had been away, and she had lost none of her cheerful courage.

As they sat at the old farmhouse table eating the stew she had made for their lunch, she pumped him with questions about his new life, the family and his racing ambitions; she seemed delighted with his answers.

Reluctantly, and only under pressure from Aidan, she revealed the most recent medical report on her condition. It was hard to tell exactly what the doctor who had compiled it really meant. Reading between the lines, Aidan inferred that Mary's illness was entering a new phase and was likely to take a turn for the worse soon. She might be looking at no more than a few years of uncomfortable, increasingly immobile existence. Aidan made a note of the specialist who was handling her case so that he could contact him directly and extract a more precise prognosis.

Besides this, Mary told him, the farm finances were in a dire state. The odd bits of money he had sent her had helped to stave off an immediate crisis, but the bottom of the barrel was in sight.

As he talked, Aidan did everything he could to prevent his mother seeing the strain he was under. The last thing he wanted her to know was that a lad had been killed as a result of his deception, and that just the day before, someone had tried to shoot him. As he smiled and talked about his hopes for Deep Mischief in the Hennessy and, God willing, the Cheltenham Gold Cup, he couldn't keep his thoughts off Ivor Butley, and Jason and MacClancy. Every few minutes he found himself wondering what Johnny had found out, counting the hours till he could phone him in London.

A wet north-westerly followed Johnny Henderson from the North Devon coast to Tiverton.

Cursing the puddles in the rough ground that served as a car-park for the block of council flats in which Ivor Butley lived, Johnny picked his way to the shabby building and up the open staircase to Ivor's front door.

He pressed a little-used button and heard a buzzing inside the flat. Five minutes later, he had supplemented his buzzing with hammering and yelling through the letter-box. He still hadn't succeeded in arousing Ivor, when an old woman in slippers and a frayed apron appeared at the neighbouring door.

'If you're looking for Mr Butley, he's gone out.'

'But it's not nine yet.'

'I know. But sometimes he goes out to a farm for a few days to look after some horses when they goes away.'

'But I thought he didn't have a job?'

'Are you from the social, then?' the woman asked with interest.

'Lord, no. I ... I'm a friend.'

The old woman wasn't convinced, but saw no reason not to help. 'He don't work much but, like I say, there's a farmer, sort of a friend of his, he helps him now and again. They come and pick him up, to make sure he turns up, I s'pose.'

'Do you know where the farm is?'

'Not far, just out at Washfield. Bacon, the farmer's called; suits him, too. He looks a bit porky.'

Johnny nodded. He didn't imagine any friend of Ivor's could be anything other than repellent. 'Bacon, in Washfield?'

'That's it.'

'And you're sure that's where he's gone?'

'Yes, I saw them go off together not half an hour ago.'

'I'm most grateful to you. I do need to see him rather urgently.'

'I shan't complain if you locks him up.'

Johnny didn't stay to explain that this wasn't his aim. He turned and went back down the concrete stairs, ignoring the mud which splashed his trousers as he ran through the rain to his car.

Once in, he pulled out a map, found Washfield, a few miles outside the town, and skidded off on to the road.

An enquiry at the first cottage in the village told him that Mr Bacon had a small-holding called Withy Farm a mile further on, not far off the road. He got the impression from his informant that Mr Bacon wasn't held in great esteem locally.

When he saw Withy Farm, he wasn't surprised. The fields and dilapidated buildings which it comprised showed all the signs of slack farming, apart from the quality of two well-rugged mares in a paddock beside the road.

Johnny gingerly drove his BMW along the pot-holed

track that led to the house and a range of stone-built barns with corrugated iron roofs. He drove through an open gateway and parked his car among the discarded trailers and muck-heap in the weed-infested yard.

He got out and tucked a bottle of Scotch into a pocket of his Burberry. The rain had eased to a misty drizzle. He walked carefully to the front porch which sheltered a worn and flaking grey door.

There was a rusty knocker and no bell. He hammered hard.

This time Ivor appeared promptly, shabbier than ever and chewing something. The old groom took a second or two to register who he was looking at.

He grinned, revealing a few bad teeth and a mouthful of toast. 'Hello, Mr Henderson. You come to buy a horse off Bert?'

'No. I've come to see you. I was told you were looking after the horses here for the day.'

''Sright. Bert's taken a couple to the Ascot sales. What d'you want with me?'

'OK if I come in?' Johnny asked, walking into a cluttered, dirty hall where a strong smell of frying prevailed.

Ivor let him through and pushed the door shut behind him. 'What do you want?' he asked with growing suspicion.

Johnny turned and looked at him. 'It's about David Tredington.'

'What about him?' Ivor stiffened.

'Relax, Ivor. We're on the same side. Is there anywhere remotely civilised in this house where we can sit?'

Ivor quickly picked up the way the conversation was

going. He gave another grin, less uncertain now, and pushed open a door into a front room – an old-fashioned parlour furnished two generations before.

Johnny pulled the bottle of whisky from his pocket, put it on a table and took off his raincoat.

'Any chance of a couple of clean glasses?'

Ivor nodded and went out. He reappeared a moment later with two grimy tumblers. Johnny pulled a handkerchief from his pocket and carefully wiped one before filling them both with whisky. The two men sat down in ancient chintz armchairs either side of the table.

'I gather you have some doubts about David being who he says he is,' Johnny said.

Ivor took a large gulp of whisky and exhaled deeply. 'Did he tell you that?'

Johnny ignored this. 'Why don't you think David is who he says he is?'

'It's not I don't think he's David; I know bloody well he isn't.'

'But Sir Mark had him checked out. An investigator was sent to Ireland and David's story was confirmed, and the family have formally accepted him.'

'Maybe, but it's not him, sure as you're sitting in that chair,' Ivor said firmly.

'Why are you so sure?' Johnny pressed.

'Don't you worry about that. You tell me why you says we're on the same side?'

Johnny took a sip of whisky – his first – while he watched Ivor take another big slug.

'David asked me to come and see you, to work out a deal.'

'You mean the bloke as says he's David.'

'We'll call him David, OK? If you know something that might be embarrassing to him and you can back it up with hard evidence, he's prepared to come to reasonable terms with you.'

Ivor grinned again. 'That's more like it. So, I keeps quiet, and your friend gets the estate. Serves the fuckin' Tredingtons right if they lost the lot to a con-man.'

'I also have an interest in a satisfactory outcome,' Johnny said quietly.

'You're in for a cut too, are you?' Ivor cackled. 'I always thought you was a bit of a chancer. It was you put him up to it, was it? Well, you didn't do a bad job. He looks the part, all right, and he knows what's what. Give me a real turn, he did, when he knew who I was. If it hadn't been for me knowing he can't no way be David, I reckon he'd have got away with it.'

'And now he is going to get away with it.' Johnny filled Ivor's glass with whisky again.

'It'd be worth a tidy bit, then, for me to keep quiet, wouldn't it?'

'That depends on what proof you can provide.'

'That'd be tellin', wouldn't it?'

'If you want anything out of it, you're going to have to tell me – or there's no deal.'

'I'll tell you what happened, but I won't tell you where the proof is, otherwise you might try and get rid of it, if you could ever get at it. And then where'd I be?'

Johnny sighed. 'We'll see.'

'First, what's in it for me?'

'No chance. When you've told me as much as you're prepared to, I'll tell you what it's worth.'

A smile spread over Ivor's face. He was feeling in control of the situation now.

'I know where David Tredington is, right now.'

Johnny didn't move a muscle. He stared back at the little man.

'At least,' Ivor said, 'what's left of him.'

'You mean – he's dead?'

Ivor nodded. 'Oh yes.'

Johnny gulped. 'How ... how do you know?'

Now he was talking about it, Ivor became nervous. He clutched his whisky glass for support. 'I found him, dead, on the beach, the day he disappeared.'

'Good God!' Johnny whispered at the final revelation of the truth behind the puzzle that had mystified David's family for fifteen years. 'What happened?'

Ivor's eyes misted over. He let out a long groan as he nodded. 'It was all my fault.'

Tears filled his eyes at the memory and his own guilt. 'I felt terrible. I really liked the boy; he always treated me like a real friend. But I couldn't bring him back to life, and I knew I'd get the blame.' He stopped again, looking down into his glass.

Johnny waited silently for him to go on, but Ivor would say no more.

Johnny gazed at him without speaking. The rain and the wind outside seemed louder. For the first time, he noticed a dog barking out in a barn. 'Have you ever told anyone about this?' he asked at last.

Ivor shook his head. ''Course not. I went to pieces after, knowing I was sort of to blame. I couldn't ever tell anyone why, could I? But I got the sack anyway, and Shirley and Susan had moved out. No one wanted to know after that.'

Johnny nodded sympathetically. 'Of course, you'd have done much better to tell them what happened in the first place, but you couldn't, I suppose.'

'I wish it never happened. It weren't my fault, but it ruined my life. Whatever I did wasn't going to bring him back, and I knows they'd have all blamed me.' He nodded his head slowly, relieved, it seemed, to have unburdened himself of fifteen years of guilt.

It occurred to Johnny that he'd overlooked something. 'But what about the note? Did you send it?'

Ivor looked puzzled. Johnny pressed him. 'You know, the letter David was supposed to have sent, saying how unhappy he was?'

'Oh that,' Ivor nodded. 'No. That's a mystery, that is. I put it down to someone playing a sick joke.'

'You could be right,' Johnny said. Abruptly, he changed the subject. 'What suddenly brought you back to Barford, beating for the shoot the other day?'

Ivor's eyes slid sideways as he answered. 'I told you, Tuesday. Mr George asked me, when he came down to see me. I thought I could keep my eye on this so-called David.'

'But you went after the second drive.'

'I had a couple of other things to do.'

'Like what?'

'None of your business.'

'It is, if it had anything to do with David.'

'Well, I ain't tellin' you, nor nothing else till I has something in writin' from your con-man friend.'

243

Johnny stood up. 'OK. It'll take a few days, so don't do anything to rock the boat. I'll be back at the end of the week to talk terms.'

At Barford that afternoon, as Aidan was away, Sir Mark went down to the stud to do the rounds with Victoria and the head-groom. They were half-way through the horses when Susan Butley arrived in the yard, breathless from running and with tears streaming down her face.

'Sir Mark. I'm sorry, but I'm going to have to leave early,' she tried to say calmly.

'Whatever's the matter, Susan?' He could see that she was struggling not to break down completely.

'They've just found my father. He's been kicked in the head by one of the stallions at Bert Bacon's.'

'Good Lord! Is he badly hurt?'

'Yes. They've taken him to hospital in Exeter. He's in intensive care, but they say he may not last more than a few hours. He'd been unconscious in the box for several hours at least, but there was no one there to find him.'

Sir Mark put a comforting hand on her shoulder. 'Why don't you let Victoria drive you?'

'No!' The refusal sounded sharper than Susan had intended. 'No, thank you. I'll be better on my own.'

Sir Mark glanced at Victoria over her shoulder and shrugged. 'All right, but ring me later and tell me what news.'

'Of course. Thanks.'

Susan turned and ran back to the house to get her car.

'Poor old Ivor,' Sir Mark said, watching her. 'Though God knows, he shouldn't have been allowed to deal with horses any more.'

He and Victoria followed Susan back to the house. In his study, Sir Mark picked up the phone and dialled Mary Daly's farm in Mayo.

Aidan answered, and involuntarily flushed with guilt when he recognised Sir Mark's voice.

'Hello, David. How's it going over there?'

'Not too bad, thanks. I'm glad I came.'

'Well, I'm sorry to disturb you, but I felt I ought to ring you. There's been a rather nasty accident. Susan's father has been kicked in the head, apparently very badly. They think he may not live, and she's had to rush off down to the hospital in Exeter.'

Aidan blanched. That Ivor Butley should have had an accident like that, on the day Johnny had gone to see him, was more of a coincidence than he could accept. And yet, and yet, he admitted reluctantly to himself, if Ivor did die, it would solve a problem. Unless, that was, he talked before he died.

He turned his head so his mother couldn't see his face. 'Poor old Ivor,' he muttered. 'I remember him well.'

'Do you?' Sir Mark sounded surprised. 'I'm afraid he became very unreliable and I had to let him go. I suppose, in a way, that's why I took Susan on; though frankly I don't think she had much to do with him for the last dozen years. It was a great shame. Ivor was as good a groom as you could have found, honest and conscientious, and he had a natural empathy with most horses. But the fact is, he'd become a more or less complete drunk. I can't think why Bert Bacon would have left him in charge, poor old chap. If he dies, I suppose we'd better let them bury him in the church at Barford, if that's what they want,' he added.

Aidan thought of the burial he had already witnessed there – Mickey Thatcher's. Maybe, indirectly, he was to blame for this second one, too.

'I think I'd better come back right away,' Aidan said, regretting it almost at once. 'With Susan away,' he went on hurriedly, 'and all the arrangements, there'll be no one to do my work.'

'Well, that's up to you. Can you get in touch with Bruce Trevor's pilot?'

'Sure. He gave me a number; said he'd come back and get me whenever I wanted, if he wasn't on another trip. Otherwise I'll get a flight to Bristol.'

'Let us know if you want collecting, then.'

An hour later, Aidan drove down to Louisburgh to phone Johnny Henderson in London.

Johnny answered after two rings. 'Aidan? I've been waiting here an hour for you to call.'

'Did you see Ivor?'

'Yes, I did. I had a very interesting chat with him. I can't tell you the details over the phone but, for the time being, the situation's under control.'

'Don't you know what's happened to him?'

'What?' Johnny picked up the urgency in Aidan's voice. 'What is it?'

'He's had some kind of accident. They found him unconscious in the stallion's box, and they don't think he'll survive.'

'Jesus Christ! When did this happen?'

246

'Earlier today. What time did you leave him?'

'About eleven. He'd had a skinful of whisky by then; I'm surprised he even made it out to the yard.'

Aidan couldn't tell whether or not he was lying. He didn't speak and waited to see what Johnny would say next.

'Aidan? Are you there?'

'Sure I'm here, Johnny,' he said quietly.

'Look, it wasn't me, I swear! It must have been a bloody accident; of course it was. I couldn't have asked the bloody horse to kick him, could I?'

'How do you know it was a kick?'

'Well, what else could it have been? And anyway, what did they tell Susan?'

'They told her it was a kick.'

'See!' Johnny sounded relieved. 'It couldn't have happened at a better time.'

'That's what worries me.'

'For Christ's sake, Aidan, I wouldn't do a thing like that.'

'You were mad enough when I told you.'

'Sure I was annoyed, bloody pissed off in fact, but I squared him, no trouble.'

'He may pull through; he may talk. We've got to be prepared for that.'

'Shit!'

'Well, if he does, he does,' Aidan said. And maybe, he thought, that would at least bring this episode of the nightmare to an end. 'Look, there's nothing we can do. We'll just have to wait. If I get more news, I'll let you know. I've got to get back now.'

'I'll ring the hospital and tell them I'm a relation.'

'I wouldn't. I don't think they'll believe you, and they may trace back the call. Ring me tomorrow and we'll arrange to meet.'

Aidan put the phone down. He stared through the grimy panes of the phone-box at the lights from the bar across the street glowing in the dark night, and wondered, not for the first time, what the hell he'd got himself into.

George Tredington was waiting early next morning to meet Aidan at Bristol Airport. Aidan sank gratefully into the leather upholstery of the big BMW.

'Morning, David,' George said sombrely. 'Have you heard about Ivor?'

'I heard he was in hospital.'

'I'm afraid to say he didn't pull through. He's dead. Poor old bugger. I wonder what the hell he was doing in that stallion box.'

Aidan couldn't help the relief he felt. 'Did . . . didn't he come round before he died?'

'No, he didn't. It's a bit of a mystery how he was kicked, but that horse had a bad name apparently and, frankly, Ivor probably wasn't sober.'

Aidan looked out at the grey morning, trying to gather his thoughts. 'He looked bloody rough out beating on Tuesday, and when I saw him at the races.'

'I told you, didn't I, he had this bee in his bonnet about you?'

Aidan nodded. 'Yes, you did.'

'I expect the police will want to talk to you about that.'

'The police? What have they to do with it?'

George grinned. 'Don't worry. I was joking. There's

no question of foul play, though I suppose there'll have to be a coroner's hearing, given the rather bizarre circumstances.'

'Who found him, then?'

'Bert Bacon.'

'Who's he?'

'He's a rather disreputable breeder and dealer. Oddly enough, he's bred a few good horses in his time, despite the fact his farm looks like a pig-sty. But then, he's always had a good eye for a mare. He was about the only person who'd still give Ivor a few days' work, and that wasn't often. He got back from Ascot mid-afternoon, found Ivor laid out in the box, stinking of whisky with the hell of a dent in his head.'

'Is Susan down there?' Aidan asked.

'Yes. So's his sister, Jan, my groom.'

'She's Ivor's sister, is she? I'd forgotten that. Is she upset?'

'She is rather. God knows why. Ivor caused her nothing but trouble for the last fifteen years. Still, she'll get over it.'

They talked inconsequentially for the rest of the journey. Aidan had to be alert not to show what he was thinking. To his relief, George dropped him at his cottage and said he had to be getting back to Braycombe.

It was still only half-past ten. Aidan should have gone straight up to the house to see Sir Mark, or down to the stables. Instead he went upstairs to change. When he got to his bedroom, he succumbed to the temptation to be alone for a while and lay on his bed, staring at the ceiling.

His head was reeling from the events of the past week.

Two threats to expose him.

Two accidents?

Two deaths.

Two attempts on his own life.

Even if he'd wanted to, he couldn't back out of the position he'd got himself into; not now he knew about Sir Mark's condition. Aidan was suddenly determined to get at the truth, for the sake of Sir Mark and the missing boy, as well as himself. Feeling calmer with this decision made, he went up to the big house. Sir Mark greeted him with another bombshell.

'Rather alarming news about poor old Ivor. Susan rang from the hospital. The pathologist who carried out an autopsy on him last night has declared that in no normal circumstances could the stallion have kicked him the way it did.'

'What? How do you mean?'

'I'm not too sure exactly, but apparently the angle at which the shoe hit his head was wrong. And also, the indentation is from a rear hoof, and the animal was only shod in front. I'm afraid they suspect there may have been foul play.'

'Jesus! Why'd anybody want to kill someone like Ivor?'

'God knows. Maybe he owed money or something.'

Aidan was beginning to feel as if a rope were tightening about his throat. He poured himself some coffee and took a gulp. 'You know I had a visit from the police Tuesday evening.'

'So I gather. Something to do with your crash. But that's got nothing to do with Ivor.'

'No, I was just mentioning it.'

'What did they want?'

Aidan sighed. 'They say there was some kind of mark painted on the roof of the car; they think it was to make identification easier, for someone who was waiting on the bridge to drop the sleeper on us. The fella who came asked me who I thought might have done anything like that. Of course, I told them there was no one.'

Sir Mark gave him a long worried look. 'And is there?'

Aidan shook his head. 'Of course not. Why would there be?'

Aidan spent the rest of the morning frustrated at having no word from Johnny. He wanted to see him face to face, to be sure he wasn't in some way responsible for the kick on Ivor Butley's skull. And he was desperate to hear what Ivor had said. But when he phoned, there was no reply from Johnny's London number. He wrote a card to his mother, feeling guilty about his abrupt departure, and went to the village to post it. When he got back to his cottage, Victoria was waiting there for him.

Although the grounds for his suspicions about Jason were skimpy – his possession of a brown raincoat and his disappearance after the second drive of Tuesday's shoot – in the absence of more plausible ones, Aidan still had him up among the prime suspects, especially now that Ivor was dead. But he knew that whatever the case, Victoria wasn't involved, and he found himself over-compensating and greeted her with more effusiveness than he'd intended.

She looked pleased. 'Hi, David. Where have you been?'

'Just posting a card.'

'Oh? Who are you writing to? Not Emma?'

Aidan laughed at Victoria's look of disapproval, and

the fact that Emma hadn't entered his head for two days.

'No. Only to Mary. I felt bad about cutting the visit short, though, to tell the truth, she wasn't too upset. I had to promise I'll go back again soon.'

'It must be odd for her, having treated you as a son for so long, and now you're a young English blade. Anyway, I only popped in for a chat and to ask you if you're going to Sam's tomorrow.'

'Sure,' he said airily, 'I might as well. I wouldn't mind seeing how Letter's going before Saturday.'

'Are you all right, David? You seem sort of flustered.'

'No, no. I'm fine. I was just wondering how Deep Mischief will run too. I really want him to win the Hennessy. Dad would love it.' He looked at his watch. 'I told him I'd pop back up and see him before lunch, so I'd better go. I'll see you tomorrow, if not before.'

Aidan's discomfort increased when Susan Butley arrived at the house at the same time as him. She wasn't expected. When she had rung early that morning, she had said she would be in Exeter for a few more days, until her father was buried.

She nodded at Aidan. 'I'm glad you're here; I want to speak to you.' She seemed a lot less self-assured than normal, and said no more than this as they walked through to find Sir Mark sitting in the library.

'Hello, Susan,' Sir Mark greeted her warmly. 'There was no need for you to come back so soon.'

'I've got to go back tomorrow. Jan's still there and Mum wanted me to come back with her anyway and, er' – she hesitated – 'I wanted to speak to David.'

Aidan took his cue. 'Why don't we have our discussion at lunch, Dad? The vet's down at the yard now and there's a couple of things I want to sort out with him. You come with me if you want, Sue.'

Susan looked relieved.

Outside, they walked across the spongy lawns towards the stables.

'I'm very sorry about your father,' Aidan said.

'Are you?'

'Of course. He may not have been the man he was, but he was a good man before things went wrong for him.'

'You mean before David was killed?'

Aidan stopped dead in his tracks with his heart thumping.

He forced himself to speak lightly. 'What are you saying now? I thought we'd had all this out on Sunday?'

'So did I,' said Susan calmly enough. 'But when the autopsy showed that Dad's death was no accident, my mother nearly broke down while we were driving back and told me something she'd never let out before.'

Aidan cleared his throat. 'And what was that?'

'She said that Dad had made her swear never to tell anyone, not even me, and she'd stuck to it, even though it got so bad she had to leave him.' She paused. Aidan didn't speak although his thoughts were racing. There was only the sound of their footsteps crunching on the gravel path which led across the lawns to the yard. 'I suppose,' Susan went on, 'she understood why Dad felt so bad, and perhaps she didn't blame him.'

'Blame him for what?' Aidan asked hesitantly.

'He thinks it was all his fault. David had been

pestering him for weeks to ride one of the colts that had just been backed. He was a beautiful horse, apparently, but he broke his leg a few months later and had to be put down – I don't really remember him.'

'That doesn't matter,' Aidan said, trying to conceal his impatience to hear Susan's story. 'What happened?'

Susan sighed. 'Anyway, Dad let David take the colt out. David said he was going up to the cliff gallops. He was a good rider, and strong for his age, but Dad should never have let him go on his own.' She stopped, then blurted out, 'The colt came back without David, an hour later. Dad realised he must have dumped the boy somewhere and went out to look for him, petrified that something awful had happened and he'd be blamed – Sir Mark had specifically forbidden David to ride any young horses.'

Aidan heard Susan gulp with the telling of the story. 'Poor old Dad, he must have been wild with worry. He hunted everywhere, but he couldn't find a sign of David in the fields. He went down to the beach, really panicking now. At first he couldn't see him there either, but he found him in the end, lying below some rocks by Stanner Head . . .' Susan's voice faltered. 'He must have fallen right down the cliff. You know what it's like there – he'd smashed his head on the rocks on the way down. The tide must have carried him round and washed him up by the cave. He was dead.'

'Jesus,' Aidan hissed, letting out a long breath. 'Fifteen years of mystery, and all the time your father knew what happened.'

'He thought it was his fault; he'd be blamed, sacked, lose his job, the cottage . . . And he loved working here,

Mum said, up till then. He hid the body, he told Mum. No one ever found it. They looked, of course, but when they got the letter, everyone thought he'd just run away.'

'But who sent the letter? Was it your father?'

'I don't know.'

'Does ... does your mother have any idea where he took the body?'

'None at all. He wouldn't tell her; said he didn't want her involved. I suppose he must have buried it somewhere.'

Aidan thought there had to be a connection with Ivor's visit to the beach. He considered coming clean and telling Susan right there what he'd seen the day before the shoot. But other options raced through his mind.

He could bluff it out, say that he, David, hadn't died, but had come round and walked away. There was only Ivor's word against his, and that couldn't be heard now.

But Susan *knew*. Whatever he said, however he said it, she wouldn't believe him.

They were approaching the yard now, where there were a dozen pairs of ears to hear them. He stopped. 'Let's walk on past. We can take a look at the mares in the paddocks.'

Susan nodded. She looked helplessly distressed, vulnerable in a way he had never seen before. He smiled, sincerely, affectionately.

'What are you going to do about it?' he said quietly.

Susan looked back at him with an uncertain expression that showed none of the hostility of the past few months. Inwardly, Aidan heaved a sigh of relief. He knew at last that he and Susan had reached a turning point in their relationship. Tentatively, he reached out a hand and took her forearm, squeezed it with gentle encouragement.

'I've thought about that. There's not a lot I can do, is there? Without knowing where Dad put the body, and without a body, who's going to believe me? But if Dad was *murdered*, I've got to know why. And I'm sure you want to know why, too.'

'Do you think I had something to do with it then? Since he'd told me he knew I wasn't David?'

A faint smile spread across Susan's lips, surprisingly generous lips in a woman so self-reliant. 'I considered that, of course. It seemed obvious. But I thought back and reckoned I could say where you were getting on for twenty-four hours before he died.'

'Maybe I paid someone else to do it?'

'No. You're no killer, though I don't know how the hell you ended up here, doing what you're doing. Actually, if you really want to know, now everybody assumes you are David and will inherit, there's been a lot less tension about the place. And it's made Sir Mark happy.' She gave a weak smile. 'Look, I don't think you had anything to do with my father's death, but it may have had something to do with you.'

'I hope to God it didn't.'

'You think it might?'

Aidan shrugged. 'I wish I knew.'

'Johnny Henderson went to see him,' Susan said.

'They know that, do they?'

'He was seen in the village quite early, and someone else saw him again later. I think the police want him in for questioning.'

'He never told me.'

'Why should he?' Susan asked drily.

Aidan realised he'd tripped. Maybe it didn't matter now.

'Anyway,' Susan went on, 'I'd already guessed that Johnny might be involved, especially when he told me where that horse Letter Lad had come from – a few miles from where you lived in Mayo. It seemed a bit too much of a coincidence.'

'OK,' Aidan nodded. 'But he swore blind to me that Ivor was still very much alive when he left him. He did say he was very drunk, though. We'll see what the police say, but I very much doubt Johnny did him any harm.'

'Who else do you think it might have been, then?'

'It's too early to say.'

Susan looked at him, imploring now, ready to trust him. 'Look, I don't know why you turned up here, or how you managed it, and you know I've never believed you were David, but right now I think you can help me find out what happened to Dad, because it's got to involve you somewhere along the line.' She looked at him with sudden warmth. 'And whatever you are, I know you're not a criminal, not at heart.'

Aidan looked back at her, drawing strength from her trust. 'You're right, I'm not, and I need to know as much as you do what happened to David. If we knew that, we'd probably know who killed your father.'

'You've got an idea?'

'I have a suspicion, but there's no way I'm going to tell you or anyone else about it until I'm damned sure, and then, even if it means me giving up my life as David

257

Tredington, I will. It's only right that the family should know if David really was killed. First, it would help if we could find anything that's left of David's body.'

'But Dad could have put it anywhere. He could have rowed out and dumped him at sea.'

'Maybe, but I've a hunch he didn't.'

'Why's that?'

'It's only a hunch,' Aidan said firmly.

In the afternoon, the wind picked up, and for the first time Aidan had a taste of the full force of the north-westerly blasting off the Bristol Channel. A gale howled through the trees around the yard, rattling the doors and the roof tiles.

But, after hearing what Susan had told him, nothing was going to put him off his search for David's body.

He wrapped a full-length Dryzabone round him, pulled the hood over his head, and set off for the cliff-top.

He reached the place where David Tredington must have come off all those years before. The wind whipped his eyes to tears as he gazed out at an angry, growling sky over a grey, white-flecked sea.

The gale buffeted him and whined in his ears. Way below him, he could see great waves rolling in to smash themselves savagely against the rocks at the back of the narrow beach. There was no point going down there now.

It wasn't on a day like this that David had gone missing, he knew, but even on the quietest of summer days, it was a hell of a fall down the near vertical cliff. He turned his gaze eastwards towards Stanner Head, the sheer, jagged promontory that jutted into the sea at the end of the bay. Slowly, unconcerned about the weather, he followed the cliff-top towards the naked stone crag.

When he reached it, he stood looking down, thinking about the small boy who had perished there, whose identity he had assumed as a result. He felt a new affection for the boy, an affinity with him, now that he was beginning to know what had happened to him. He owed it to David to uncover the truth, even if that meant exposing his own deception.

Making up his mind, Aidan carried on along the edge of the cliff for another mile until he was approaching the small, sporadically manned coastguard building. There was a van parked outside it, and lights glowed from the windows of the squat concrete building beneath a flat roof bristling with aerials. He walked on up and opened the door into a warm, smoky fug.

The broad back in front of him turned to reveal a man in his mid-forties, red-cheeked and blue-eyed above a mass of auburn whiskers.

'Mr David,' the man said, by way of welcome. 'Not much of a morning for a walk. I've been watching you come this last mile.'

Aidan grinned. 'I don't mind the weather, I'm used to a bit of rain, as long as I'm dry inside.'

'Cup of tea?'

'Thanks. Any trouble out there?'

'No. Not yet. Funny thing is, we usually gets more problems on a beautiful sunny day when the people who don't know what they're doing go out. Only the people who've got to be are out in this sort of shit. Still, even the pros come unstuck from time to time.'

As he talked, he organised a boiling kettle, big tin mugs and tea-bags.

'Has anyone ever come to grief from the cliff-tops here?' Aidan asked.

'Not for many a year. There was a girl, out on a hike in weather not unlike this, maybe ten years ago. She fell down the cliff by those gallops of yours.'

'What happened to her?'

'I should think she was dead before she touched the beach.'

'I mean what happened to the body? I suppose it got washed along this way, got caught up on Stanner Head, or on the rocks before it.'

'Oh no. There's no tide'd wash anything this way. It'd always take anything on towards Lynton.'

'Always?' Aidan asked casually.

'That's the way the tides run along this side of the Channel.'

The kettle boiled and the coastguard filled the two mugs. Aidan took his and drank gratefully while he absorbed the implications of what he'd just been told.

He encouraged the man to yarn on for a while, glad of the warmth. He left the hut with the dramatic details of some of the more famous wrecks along the coast, and the knowledge that either David had crawled from where he had landed at the foot of the cliff, or someone had carried him, to hide him below the rocks where Ivor had found him.

Chapter Eleven

It was nearly dark by the time Aidan walked back into the yard. He joined the grooms giving the horses their final feed, but his mind was still back on the cliffs. From what Susan had told him, and from what he had seen of the coast that day, Aidan had in his head a clear picture of the dying boy. He tried to concentrate on his jobs around the stud, and make arrangements for Letter Lad's outing on Saturday. But the vision of the boy, so like himself, lying dead on the beach, stubbornly remained.

Susan had supper with the family that night. So did Victoria and Jason. When they were all sitting round the kitchen table, Sir Mark asked Aidan where he had been that afternoon.

'I love to see the sea in a rage,' Aidan said, not entirely untruthfully and keeping an eye on Jason for his reaction. 'I walked up to the coastguard post and back.'

'Good Lord! Sounds positively masochistic.'

Aidan laughed. 'It was great, honest. And not a drop of rain seeped through my coat.'

He met Susan's eyes for a moment, and saw a glimmer of approval. He relaxed a little. If, in the end, he was to own up to what he'd done, he wanted it to be in his own time and voluntarily. For one thing, it would have to be broken very gently to Sir Mark. Deliberately, he steered the conversation away to talk about Deep Mischief's preparation for the Hennessy, and Jason's ride on Letter Lad the following Saturday.

Victoria was pressing for decisions on stallions for several of the mares who had not yet been booked in and, despite the drama of Ivor's death, the rest of dinner took its normal course. Just before ten, Aidan announced that he was going to bed as he had to be up early to ride out next morning.

The wind howled most of the night, but eased off by the time Aidan got out of bed at six next morning. Victoria, reliable as ever, was knocking on his door at six-thirty, ready to come with him to Sam Hunter's.

Aidan was riding Deep Mischief back from the gallops when Johnny turned up at Sam Hunter's yard. The gelding had shown all his usual form, striding out effortlessly alongside two of his struggling stable-mates.

Aidan spotted Johnny's well-worn car as he walked his horse into the stableyard with the rest of the string. While he had been riding, he had concentrated exclusively on the animal beneath him. Now his problems came back to him with a rush.

He slid from Deep Mischief's back. Johnny was chatting earnestly to Sam Hunter.

'Morning, Johnny,' Aidan called.

Johnny looked up, pretending to be surprised. 'I didn't know you were riding out here today.'

'Just keeping Sam up to the mark.' Aidan managed a quick grin. 'As a matter of fact, I wouldn't mind a word with you back at Barford. We've a couple of colts we may not want to send to the sales. We'd like you to look at them. I'd stay and have a chat now, but I brought Victoria over with me this morning.'

Johnny nodded, acknowledging that they couldn't speak now. 'Fine,' he said. 'I was coming over anyway.'

'I'll see you back at Barford then.'

As Aidan drove home, he listened to Victoria enthusing about Deep Mischief's progress.

'Did you have to put him under any pressure to pull past those other two on the gallops?' she asked.

'No. I gave him no more than a squeeze. He's a very classy animal, but he'll not need to miss any work between now and the Hennessy. He puts on weight just looking at food. But don't worry, Sam doesn't need to be told what to do. He's probably forgotten more about training horses than most people ever know.'

Victoria beamed excitedly as she let her hopes for Deep Mischief have some rein. 'It'd be great if we could start winning some big races with him. I always said from the day he was born that he was going to be a star.'

Aidan laughed. 'There must be ten thousand girls every year who say the same thing each time they watch their mares foaling.'

'That's not fair,' Victoria protested. 'I don't think every foal we produce is perfect.'

'I know you don't. I'm just teasing. He's one of the best horses I've ever sat on.'

'Did you ever ride anything really good when you were in Ireland?'

'I did not, not in that class anyway. Where I lived, we were trying to make silk purses out of sows' ears.'

'Isn't it funny that you should have become so good with horses, even though you've been away for all that time.'

'Not really. I always did enjoy the horses from when I was a small lad, before you could even walk. I was straight into it when I got to Ireland. I've always felt happier riding a horse than doing anything else.'

'Anything?' Victoria said with a grin.

'I don't know what you mean, you coarse-minded little sister.'

'Not half so coarse as Lucy.'

'That wouldn't surprise me.'

'I heard her having a very graphic conversation about you with Emma on Sunday.'

'I don't want to hear about it, and I think it's a sin to earwig,' Aidan laughed but within himself, he felt a long way from laughter.

At half-past ten, Aidan drove back through the park gates, followed closely by Johnny. He dropped Victoria at her cottage and drove on down to the yard. Twenty minutes later, out in a paddock beneath a grey sky, and a long way from any prying ears, Aidan looked Johnny straight in the eyes and tried to read the truth.

'OK, what exactly happened when you went to Ivor's?'

'Basically, he told me that David was dead.'

This didn't produce the dramatic effect that Johnny had been expecting.

'Yes,' Aidan said. 'I know.'

'What? Who the hell told you?'

'Susan, yesterday. When they heard that the pathologist thought there was something fishy about the way Ivor was kicked, her mother broke down and said that Ivor had told her years ago that he'd found David's body at the bottom of the cliff after he'd taken a tumble on some young horse.'

'That's right,' Johnny said. 'That's just what he told me, and he thought he'd be blamed so he hid the body – Sue's mother didn't tell her where, I suppose?'

'No chance. He never let on – didn't want her to know.'

'Well, at least that means the chap in Fiji isn't anything to worry about, and with Ivor out of the way, our problems are over.'

'That's what's worrying me,' Aidan said coldly. 'It's a little too convenient; and who the hell else would want to kill Ivor?'

'For God's sake,' Johnny pleaded. 'I *swear* it wasn't anything to do with me. I didn't even touch the smelly little bugger.'

Aidan didn't say anything. He almost believed Johnny but, knowing him, his word wasn't enough to convince him entirely. He sighed. 'If only you weren't such a slippery devil. I wish to God I'd never got involved in this thing. You seem to have forgotten, someone tried to shoot me on Tuesday, and I don't think it was Ivor – why should he? He was relying on me to feather his nest for him. And if you didn't kill Ivor, someone else did.'

'Look,' Johnny said, 'the pathologist could have got it wrong, or Ivor might have been done in for some reason completely unconnected with you.'

'And what about the fella who dropped a sleeper on me?'

'That's just a possibility, for God's sake. Last week the police were happy to believe it was a genuine accident.'

'Well, they're not now. They think someone marked the roof of my car with fluorescent paint to identify it. This Sergeant King rang to say he's coming up to see me again.'

'He probably just wants a day off, a chance to look at the Devon countryside.'

'Who are you kidding, Johnny? Listen, we're in a mess here and we've got to sort it out – I don't mean just for me, but for my mother's sake, and for Sir Mark. I owe him that – he's been incredible to me. You've no idea what it's like to have a father when you've never had one before. It would really upset him if I'm found out and end up in jail. And the man's not well.'

Aidan immediately regretted telling Johnny that, especially when Sir Mark had told him in confidence. He tried to play it down.

'It's not much, but he's been suffering a bit from his back.'

'Oh, is that all?'

'That's not the point. I'm beginning to feel a real shit about taking them in, all of them. They've been so good to me; made me feel as if I've belonged here all my life.'

'Brilliant. That's just what we wanted. I told you you could do it.'

'Shut up, for Christ's sake. You may not have a conscience—'

'Yes, well it's a bit late for you to start developing one now.'

'Look,' Aidan went on more quietly, 'maybe they won't find this fella who dropped the sleepers, and maybe the

Ivor business will blow over. But I wouldn't count on it. I tell you, I couldn't stand it if anything else like this happens, or anyone else gets killed or hurt. Nothing could justify that. I don't have any choice. I can't go to the police, but I can't let go of this until I know what happened to that boy and where Ivor put his body. And, believe it or not, I would rather like to know who's trying to kill me,' he added.

Aidan didn't see any point in telling Johnny his plans in detail. He hadn't decided, anyway, exactly what his next move would be, but he was sure he wasn't the only person with an interest in finding David Tredington's last resting place.

Susan had gone home when he arrived back at the manor. He wanted to ring her, to let her know what he was planning in case anything went wrong, but he didn't want to risk using the phone in the house. He got into his Land Rover to drive down to the village to use the phone-box there.

He changed his mind before he reached the main gates. He wouldn't ring from the village. He might be seen, and he well knew country people's propensity for storing up instances of unusual or unlikely activity.

He turned left at the top of the drive and headed up the lane; he knew there was a public telephone two miles along the Porlock road. The phone-box was set on a muddy layby on the edge of a small wooded coomb. Aidan parked his car and went into the scarlet cubicle. He dialled Susan's number in Lynmouth and let it ring a dozen times before he accepted that it wasn't going to be answered.

Through the narrow belt of trees that lined the road, he could see the beginnings of the pasture fields that eventually joined up with the Barford cliff gallops. As he put the phone down, staring absently up towards the coast about a quarter of a mile away, he saw a brown-coated figure striding up towards the cliffs.

With adrenaline pumping through him as if he were at the start of a big race, he darted out of the phone-box back to his car. He pulled his OS map from the shelf under the dash and spread it on his lap. He soon found what he was looking for. A few yards from the phone-box, on the other side of the road, a red dotted line showed that there was a path which followed the edge of a field up towards the coast, where it joined the South-West Coast Path, just above Stanner Head.

The rain had stopped, and the wind was half the strength it had been in the early morning. Aidan pulled on his wellies and his long waxed coat and set off through the belt of trees to find the path.

He guessed that whoever he was following had a good fifteen-minute lead on him and had probably reached the cliff by now. But he kept close to the hedgerows where he could, well camouflaged in his khaki clothing.

At the east end of the bay, before Stanner Head jutted out into the sea, a small brook plunged over the cliff-edge and trickled messily down the almost sheer drop. At this point, the cliff dipped and a steep, crumbling path had been created to provide the only way down to the beach. Locals had used it for years, as well as the more adventurous walkers along the coast path. It wasn't for the faint-hearted or the clumsy.

Aidan stopped at the top of the cliff where he had watched Ivor on the previous Monday. Again he crouched, so as not to break the skyline visible from the beach below.

The tide was out, revealing a steep, sandy beach no more than seventy yards deep. From his viewpoint Aidan couldn't see anyone on it, but he waited, judging that the man he was following wouldn't have reached the bottom of the cliff path.

A few minutes later, the brown figure appeared on the sand below him and hurried across to the east end of the beach which was enclosed by the promontory. He went round some flat rocks which projected into the sand, and disappeared from sight.

Aidan got quickly to his feet and arrived at the top of the track down the cliff. A chamois would have found the going tricky. The surface was wet bracken, mud, and jagged, slippery rock. Though the drop from the top of the cliff was little more than three hundred feet, the track covered a third of a mile as it traversed the cliff-face, zig-zagging across the plunging brook.

Aidan was crossing the stream for the second time, below a waterfall where the rocks were worn smooth and coated with green slime. He slipped so smoothly and painlessly that it took him a moment to realise he had. He tumbled down a sixty-degree incline, bouncing from ledges of marram grass on to patches of bracken and bramble that clung to the cliff-face between naked rock and shale.

He had fallen fifty feet before he was caught by a wider ledge, a tussocky mattress half-way down the cliff. He heard the clatter of loose rocks that had accompanied him carrying on down to the beach below.

He glanced over the ledge towards the jutting rocks. While he waited to see if the noise of his fall had alerted his quarry, he checked himself for damage.

The whole thing had taken no more than ten seconds, but he felt as if he'd been put through a mangle. The scab on his arm from the gunshot graze had opened up. He could feel the warm seepage of blood into his shirt. There were scratches and cuts on his face and a painful throbbing in his hip. He groaned to release some of the pent-up pain, and stretched. At least nothing was broken.

He waited until he was certain that his fall hadn't alerted the man he was following, before he set off down the last leg of the track, taking more notice now of the tumbling brook.

When he reached the beach, Aidan could see the clear prints of a pair of Wellington boots on the damp brown sand. He followed the trail across the beach, and round the protruding flat rocks where they led straight to a cave which couldn't be seen from the cliff-top.

Beneath a narrow cleft, the mouth of the cave widened out to a width of twenty feet. Aidan kept close in to the cliff-face so that he couldn't be seen by anyone inside the cave. When he reached the edge of the entrance, he stopped and listened. But, against the whine of the wind and the surf breaking down at the low-tide mark, he couldn't be certain of what he heard from inside. He sidled round the edge, trying to avoid being silhouetted against the light. Further in, there was a secondary cleft into which he could tuck himself.

The sandy floor sloped steeply up towards the back of the cavernous tunnel, and there was a steady deluge of rainwater draining through cracks in the rocky ceiling.

He glanced out towards the sea which had lost most of the fury of the early morning, and wondered how long, once it had turned, it would take the tide to come back.

Slowly, he craned his neck round the buttress of rock that obscured his view, and peered into the depths of the cave. The sound of small stones clattering down to the sandy floor reached him, but it was too dark for him to see where they were coming from. He slipped out of his crack. Keeping his back to the wall, and his ears pricked for any sign that he'd been seen, he edged his way up the steeply sloping floor of the cave, along the creases of the rocky wall.

After twenty feet, the noise of the wind and surf were more muted and the trickle of escaping springs sounded more clearly. Above this he heard irregular movements, metal grinding on stone, and the occasional heavy thud of a larger rock bouncing down on to the sand.

Whatever the man was doing, Aidan guessed it was taking most of his concentration. He risked a moment's exposure to the direct light from the cave-mouth by stepping round a protruding buttress. As he darted back into the protective shadow beyond it, he heard a distinct grunt and a gasp of pain. With his eyes now attuned to the gloom, Aidan caught sight of a familiar brown coat and green Wellingtons.

The man wearing them was leaning face forward on a wall of rock which sloped back from the ground at an angle of about seventy degrees, and was worn smooth by a few million years' action of the incoming sea.

Standing on tiptoes, he was stretching to the end of his fingertips to grapple with some smaller boulders which had become lodged in a gap of no more than ten inches between the top of the rock slab and the roof of the cave. He had brought some kind of lever with him; it looked like an iron crowbar to Aidan. Evidently he had managed to dislodge a few of the stones which were scattered on the sand behind him, but he was having problems with the larger ones which were lodged fast beneath the roof of the cave.

Aidan held his breath. Abruptly, the distant sounds of the sea and dripping springs were shattered by a great, echoing shout.

Aidan looked sharply back towards the cave-mouth. Two people had come in and were experimenting with the resonant qualities of the rocky tube, laughing at the echoes they produced. Hastily the man at the back of the cave pushed himself away from the rock and spun round. Aware of the movement, Aidan turned his attention towards the cave's rear again. And in the fraction of a second before Aidan sank back to bury himself in the shadows, he saw a familiar, angry face.

George Tredington.

Aidan stifled a gasp, trembling with the relief of knowing at last who his enemy was.

The two visitors, coming further up the cave, saw George.

'Morning,' one said cheerily.

'Morning,' George answered uneasily. He had evidently realised that he was dealing with a couple of walkers who had strayed down from the coast path. 'Pretty bloody day for caving,' he said. 'But a friend of mine thought he'd got a surfboard washed up into the back here. I said I'd have a look for him.'

The walkers apparently accepted the explanation.

'Does much get washed up in here?' the other, a woman, asked.

'Can do,' George answered cagily, 'but not this time. Anyway, no luck with this chap's board.' He had walked down to join them, to lead them out of the cave with him. 'How far have you walked this morning?'

The walkers were glad to talk about their progress and turned with him. 'Not much so far, only about six miles from Lynmouth, aiming to be in Porlock for lunch.'

Their voices faded as they left the cave. Aidan stepped out of the cleft to watch them. He gave them a few moments, then ran down to the entrance. Keeping in the shadows, he glanced out. George and the walkers were heading for the foot of the cliff path which Aidan had come down earlier. He waited until they were well on their way up before he went up to the back of the cave where George had been scrabbling.

Aidan looked back down the steep gradient to the cave-mouth, sixty feet away, ten feet below the level at which he now stood. He turned and faced the rock and peered at the tantalising gap at the top. He was taller than George, and able to get a better look at what had to be moved if the gap was to be opened up. He also established that it was going to take more than his bare hands to clear it. He remembered that he hadn't seen George carrying the crowbar as he went to talk to the walkers. Aidan glanced down. It lay where it had been dropped, a little to his right

Rolling a couple of big stones up to the foot of the wall

to give himself more height, Aidan swung the heavy iron
bar above his head to plunge it down the side of one of
the larger boulders. He gritted his teeth and called up
all his strength.

He had been straining for a few minutes before he felt
any movement. With a grinding of rock on rock, the
boulder moved a few millimetres and then stuck fast
again.

After this small taste of success, Aidan renewed his
attack. This time he went the other way and tried to deal
with the large hunk of granite above his left shoulder.

He had no idea how long he had been heaving at the
immovable objects that George was so desperate to
shift. But he was sure that whatever he found behind
there would answer some of the questions that had been
taunting him for the past two weeks.

Determined to go on, first he went back down to the
cave-mouth to make sure that George, or anyone else,
wasn't coming back. Only the sea had approached, but
not enough to worry him yet.

He returned to the rock wall and the first boulder he
had tried to shift. After another session of straining,
Aidan suddenly loosened it. Triumphantly, he prepared
for one last enormous heave. He positioned himself so
that when it came down it would pass by him. He
inserted the crowbar once more to give himself maximum leverage, then pulled back on it with every fibre in
his body. He could feel it move infinitesimally, then,
abruptly, it was past the point of no return. It almost
sprang from its lodging between the roof and the
upright wall, and seemed to leap out and land with a
great thud on the damp, sandy floor.

Aidan could hardly believe he'd done it. He had opened up a gap like a child's missing front tooth. He used the fallen rock as a step and heaved himself up to the lip. He stared into black nothingness. Hardly a glimmer of light penetrated past him into whatever space lay beyond. He heaved his shoulders a little higher, wanting to go straight in. He guessed that there was enough of a gap for his long slim body to go through. But there was no point without any light. He wouldn't see anything of what was beyond. Reluctantly, seething with frustration, he slid back down to the ground.

The sound of the wind outside had risen in pitch, disguising the crashing progress of the incoming tide. A leading wave hit the cliff either side of the entrance with a thundering slap; a huge wet tongue was sent hissing up the sandy floor, to swirl for a moment around Aidan's legs, sloshing over the tops of his rubber boots. He turned, alarmed.

The wave ran back, and the sea settled for the next onslaught. The mouth of the cave was already full of water. With horror, Aidan judged it was already several feet deep.

Though it was obvious from the absence of marine animals and plants that the sea didn't reach the top of the wall he was leaning against, it clearly settled at a point around his feet – which would mean that the mouth itself became completely submerged at high tide.

He cursed himself for not checking the speed of the turning tide, though he'd had no plan to come to the cave when he'd left Barford that morning. He realised he must have been heaving away at the rocks for maybe several hours and, if he didn't move fast, he was going to be stuck there.

He glanced back at the gap he had made, hoping that by opening it up he hadn't given the sea a way to get in and disturb whatever lay behind the wall. Another resounding crash and the blocking out of the grey daylight announced the entrance of another mass of angry, hissing water into the cave. This time it soaked up to his thighs.

When it subsided, the sea level was within a few feet of the top of the cave-mouth.

If he was going to get out, he was going to have to do it now.

He waded back down the sandy floor, keeping pace with the retreating wave until, still twenty feet from the opening, he found he was out of his depth. Another wave surged more gently towards him. Barely hesitating, he pulled off his Wellington boots and mackintosh, filled his lungs, and plunged beneath its turbulence.

His open, stinging eyes could make out nothing through the sand-filled, churning water which gripped him with an icy clamminess. Desperately, he headed down to make contact with the safe, sandy bottom. He touched it with his fingers, found it with his feet and, fighting the extra buoyancy his clothes gave him, struggled to propel himself forward through the murky, heaving water. He didn't dare come up until he was through the arch. On the surface, the sea would crack his head like a ping-pong ball against the rocky roof.

He felt another surge push him back, but he dug his feet into the sand and faced the current as horizontally as he could, until finally he felt the water run back out. He pushed off and took the current, thrashing his legs and heaving through the water with his arms, going ever deeper to avoid the turbulence of the surface.

Another wave came to push him backwards, and then run out seawards with him. He couldn't guess how long it was since he'd taken a breath. His lungs were screaming and he hardly cared any more that they would fill with water if he opened his mouth.

Suddenly, the sea became lighter, a grey glitter appearing at the surface above him. With a last supreme effort, Aidan drove himself on, knowing that it wouldn't take much to drive him back towards the cliff.

Then he couldn't stand any more. Help me, God, he pleaded, and his head broke the foaming skin of the water above him.

He opened his mouth at last, emptied his lungs of spent air, and gasped to fill them again. Through his stinging eyes, he could just see a heaving mass of grey-white water – a wall of it six feet high surging towards him. Gasping again, he plunged into the midst of it, praying that it would pass him before it broke.

He felt nothing more than a slight tug as the crest passed over him. He bobbed up again, breathed again, and turned to see how far from danger he was.

The top of the cave-mouth gaped just fifteen feet away. He tried to remember the shape of the rocks around the foot of the cliff, turned and swam out as strongly as he could. All he could think about was getting away from the cliff.

It was five minutes before he dared turn back and look again. He had managed to put another thirty yards between himself and the visible rock-face. Gratefully, he turned parallel to the shore and swam westwards, until he reckoned he had cleared the bed of flat rock that protruded into the sand at the east end of the bay.

He turned landward and, exhausted, let the waves help him in towards the beach.

Ten minutes later, he lay on the sand; bruised, bleeding, completely spent, but safe. He crawled away from the sea until he was above the high-water line, where he lay shivering, trying to recover his strength.

It took Aidan twenty minutes to scramble barefoot back up the rocky cliff track to the soft pasture at the top. He looked both ways along the path that followed the coast. There was no one in sight. Sore, aching, but ultimately sound, he hurried as fast as his battered feet allowed back along the path to the road where he had left the Land Rover. There was no sign of George, or a car. He guessed that George must have hidden his BMW further up the road before he'd set off up the path.

Aidan's watch had stopped, but it showed half-past two. He guessed it was nearer three now. He had missed lunch, and people would be beginning to wonder where he was.

He drove to his cottage where he pulled off his sodden garments. He stood under a blissfully hot shower for five minutes, then did his best to patch up the more visible scratches he had received from the rocks and brambles. He rubbed liniment into his bruised feet, and winced as he inserted them into a pair of tight brogues. He was coming down the stairs when the telephone in his kitchen rang. It was Victoria from the house.

'Where have you been? We were expecting you for lunch,' she said, but didn't wait for an answer. 'Are you coming up for tea?'

'I'm just going down to the yard. I'll be up in half an hour.'

There had been no dramas or problems at the stables. Aidan checked each of his charges and gave the grooms a few last instructions. Feeling more able now to deal with the scrutiny of the family, he hobbled painfully up to the manor.

As he walked into the kitchen, he gritted his teeth and tried to smile.

Victoria looked at him with concern.

'What's happened to you? You look as though you've gone ten rounds with Tyson.'

Aidan tried to smile. 'The Land Rover ran out of diesel; I had to bleed the engine. I slipped into some brambles.'

'What a bore,' Sir Mark said sympathetically. 'Was there anything in the spare can?'

'There was, thank God, or I'd have had a long walk.'

'Anyway, I'm glad you're back. Sam Hunter just phoned. He's declared Letter Lad for tomorrow.'

'Great!' Aidan made himself sound enthusiastic.

'Sam's pretty confident this time,' Victoria grinned. 'And, though he won't admit it, so's Jason. George will be livid if he wins.'

'Do you think so?' Aidan asked, disguising his true state of mind. 'He seemed pretty relaxed about it all to me.'

'He may have been to you, but Jan told me he's

furious; he feels you've made a real fool of him. She says George thinks you did it deliberately.'

'Well, in a sense, he's right. When I rode that horse at Braycombe, I knew something was hurting him, but George wouldn't hear of it. Anyway, Johnny made sure George earned a bit of a profit on the animal so he'd not lose too much face.'

'You may have underestimated dear old George's sense of his own dignity. And after all, he hasn't got much to thank you for since you came back.'

Sir Mark intervened. 'That's not entirely true. Though he expected the court to grant him the right to inherit the title, on the presumption of David's death, I'd never given any firm indication about the future of this place.'

'Maybe not, Dad, but he and everyone else assumed most of it would go to him, didn't they?'

'I suppose so, but that's no justification for resenting David's success with this horse.'

This was the first time Aidan had been present at anything like a family discussion about George's attitude, although the substance of what was said had been implicit in other conversations about George. What came as more of a surprise to Aidan was the report of George's ill-feeling over the horse. The man was obviously a skilled actor when it suited him. But, though the Letter Lad incident had clearly added in a small way to George's dislike of him, this could have no bearing on his frantic scrabbling above the wall in Stanner Cave that morning.

Aidan was determined to get back down there as soon as possible, as soon as the tide would allow him back into the cave with lamps and climbing ropes. He told Sir

Mark and Victoria that he wanted to catch up on some paperwork, and went back to his cottage.

The first thing he did there was to ring George to establish where he was.

George was at home in Braycombe. He sounded exceptionally irritated when he answered the phone.

'What's the problem?' Aidan asked.

'It's nothing important.' He spoke as if Aidan were not his only audience. 'The police are here. They've come to talk about Ivor Butley.'

'But surely that's all cut and dried? He was kicked by a horse; he died. What's the mystery?'

'God knows, but someone saw Mike Harding's car at Bert Bacon's farm that morning. As it happened, I'd borrowed it, but I didn't go near the place.'

'Well, I hope you sort it out.'

'So do I. I must get back to them. What did you want?'

'It doesn't matter. I'll ring later. Will you be in?'

There was a pause. 'Yes, I should be. The vet's due round at six and I want to see him myself.'

'Fine. I'll call before then.'

Aidan judged that George couldn't be planning to have another go at the cave himself that day, not within the time he had, and especially not if the police were stuck into him. The likelihood that George had been down to see Ivor on Wednesday morning opened up a whole new set of possibilities.

Aidan put the phone down and went to gather up what he needed for his return visit to the cave. This time he made sure that he was fully waterproof, and properly equipped for scrambling over the rock wall into the unknown on the far side.

He parked his Land Rover where he had that morning, and retraced his steps back up to the coast path. It was nearly dark now, and he had to use his torch to negotiate the cliff path. He just had to hope that there was no one around to see him. On this remote stretch of coast at this time of day, it was unlikely. Wearing studded boots, he made better progress down the track, and arrived on the beach as the last wave lapped up to the mouth of the cave. That would give him all the time he needed to get in and search.

He entered the cave and walked up the steep slope of wet sand towards the wall of rock at the back.

The great boulder which he had loosened that afternoon hadn't been shifted by the waves which had swept in to block his exit. Aidan shone his torch at the smooth, six-foot wall. The upper lip showed no signs of dampness. It looked as though it was out of reach of the tongues of seawater which penetrated the cave at high tide.

He unwound the rope he was carrying round his waist, and tied one end of it firmly to the last boulder he had dislodged. He flung the other end up towards the gap and scrambled up after it, until he was able to put his head through the gap.

He played the beam of his torch into the space beyond.

On the face of it, it was a continuation of the cave, though how it had been hollowed out with this great bar of rock across it wasn't obvious. The floor of the cave beyond the bar was higher than on his side and, as far as he could see, consisted of fine, dusty, dry sand.

He pulled through a lamp he had tied to his waist,

fastened it to the end of the rope and lowered it to the floor.

Beside the lamp, clear in the light that it cast, lay a small but complete skeleton.

On its side, with legs crossed as if in deep, relaxed sleep, the bones were those of an immature human. Still clinging to the bones were a few tatters of clothing, and on the feet were a pair of shoes.

Aidan's heart almost stopped.

It was the picture that had haunted him since first he had found George desperately trying to get into this undisturbed resting place. He had no doubt at all that he was looking at the remains of the real David Tredington, and that the body had not been seen since the day the boy had disappeared.

He found himself trembling at this final meeting with the person whose life he had hijacked, and at the thought of whatever horrifying events had laid an innocent twelve-year-old boy to rest in this bizarre tomb.

Chapter Twelve

Aidan gazed at the skeleton. He felt that he'd always known the boy; now he was trying to cope with the finality that the bones represented. Not just the termination of David's existence, but also the end of Aidan's impersonation of him.

He wanted to touch the bones, to be sure they were real. He began to squeeze himself forward through the gap, which was no more than eighteen inches wide. He pushed his head and neck through and managed to insert one shoulder, but the other was blocked by the bulk of the rock which he had failed to budge. He had been sure he would be able to get through, and now he was desperate to, but, however he contorted himself, he couldn't get both shoulders into the gap. He yelled his frustration into the cavern beyond and winced as it echoed back at him.

Temporarily beaten, he slid back out and dropped down to the ground. He found the crowbar which he'd abandoned earlier, and thrust it in a crack between the stubborn boulder and the wall of the cave. He heaved and struggled until his hands were raw, growing more certain every minute that he wasn't going to do it.

Beginning to accept that he would never be able to break through into David Tredington's tomb on his own, he obstinately carried on while he tried to think about who to go to for help. And he had to make sure that George didn't get in first.

After an hour and several more attempts to squeeze himself over the ledge, he acknowledged defeat.

He pulled the lamp back from the inner cavern, and stowed it with the rope and crowbar on a shelf of rock beyond the reach of the waves.

Aidan saw no one on his way back to his car. He drove to Barford with a plan taking shape.

It was after seven. From his cottage, he dialled Susan's number at her mother's. Mrs Butley seemed strangely distraught at the death of a man she had rejected many years before, but managed to tell Aidan that Susan had gone back up to the manor to finish some work.

Aidan guessed that Susan was finding Shirley Butley's grief over Ivor hard to take; in fourteen years she'd never heard her mother say a good word about her estranged husband. He went to look for her in the house. She was still in the office, staring at the screen of her PC. Aidan had already checked that Sir Mark was safely out of the way in his own study.

'Susan.'

She turned and looked up at him. Her eyes widened. 'You look as though you've seen a ghost.'

Aidan nodded. 'I feel as if I have.'

She stood up. 'What? What is it?'

'I need to talk to you – not here. Could you tell

Sir Mark you're popping down to my cottage for something?'

'Sure.'

'Could you be there in ten minutes?'

She nodded.

Susan came in without knocking. Aidan was pacing up and down his small kitchen. He waved her into a chair and poured a cup of coffee without speaking.

'What the hell have you seen?' she asked.

'I've found David.'

Susan leapt to her feet and clutched Aidan's arm. 'What! Where?'

Aidan took a deep breath. 'In Stanner Cave.'

'But how did you find him?'

'When you told me about your father hiding the body, I was sure then there was some connection with the cave. I didn't tell you, but I saw your dad going there on Monday. There was someone else following him; I didn't know who – I didn't get near enough – but I saw Ivor clearly, climbing back up the cliff path. I spotted someone on their way there today, and followed him right into the cave. It was George.'

'George?' Susan gasped.

'Yes, George. And he went to see your father on Wednesday morning.'

'How do you know?'

'I phoned him this afternoon – I had to know where he was before I went back down to the cave. He was in a filthy mood; he said the police were there because Mike's car had been seen near Bert Bacon's farm – and George had borrowed it that morning.'

'But what's it got to do with George?'

'I'm not sure yet, but I've got a pretty good idea. I followed him up to the coast path this morning, then down to the beach by Stanner Head. He went into that big cave below it and I went in after him and saw him scrabbling about above the rocks at the back. He didn't see me, and after he'd gone I went back and had a look myself, then I got caught by the tide coming back in and had to swim for it.'

'Christ!' Susan said. 'No wonder you looked so rough when you got back here.'

Aidan nodded. 'But there was no real damage done, thank God. I've just been back down there with a couple of torches. I managed to lower a lamp the other side of the rock bar.' He paused, looking at Susan.

'What was there, for God's sake?' she asked, not wanting to hear it.

'Bones. A full human skeleton, lying just as it must have fallen, fifteen years ago.'

'David?' she whispered.

'I'm sure of it.'

'But how could he have got there?'

'He must have been put there.'

'But who by?'

Aidan looked at her horrified face. She already knew, but he spelt it out for her.

'Your father.'

Susan winced, closed her eyes and shook her head.

'He'd told your mother, hadn't he, that he'd hidden the body?' Aidan went on.

She nodded. 'He must have told George, too, when

George went to see him,' she blurted. 'Do you think George killed him?'

'I don't know. It makes no sense. With David's body finally found, George would be more certain of inheriting his share of Barford – and the title – but that's what it looks like. Listen, I'm going to need some help. As soon as I've found out exactly what happened to David, I'll tell Sir Mark.'

'It'll really break him up,' Susan said quickly. 'It'll be like losing two sons at once. And ... he's not well, you know.'

'I already knew that.'

'Maybe you should leave it until ... for a while,' Susan said quietly.

'I couldn't do that. I couldn't live with myself. And besides, I'm not sure that I'm safe until the whole mess is cleared up. I've opened a whole can of evil worms since I arrived here.'

'What do you want me to do?'

'Somehow, I want you to stick to George, keep tabs on him for every moment over the next couple of days. The chances are he'll come to the races tomorrow. It would look odd if he didn't. It'd look even stranger if I didn't. So we'll go out and win that race. Then we'll see what happens. There's another thing I want you to do for me. George borrowed the clay-trap from the house on Tuesday night. Could you get Jan to have a look around for it and bring it back up. Ask her to leave it in the store-room where it usually lives. And tell her to be sure George doesn't know she's done it.'

'What do you want it for?'

'I'm not sure, until I've had a look at it. But I saw George taking it, and there was something very shifty about the way he did it.'

Trying to behave as normally as possible, Aidan talked with Sir Mark that evening. He asked about his health – on which subject Sir Mark was non-committal – and, more animatedly, they discussed Letter Lad's chances the following day. All the time they were talking, Aidan was wondering how the man sitting opposite him would react when he learned the truth about his identity. Aidan knew that he had duped a man who, out of a longing for the return of his son, had fallen willingly into the trap he and Johnny had conceived.

Sir Mark had given him the father's love he had never had. And how had he repaid him?

Aidan doubted that, when the inevitable moment came to own up, he would have the courage to do it face to face. It would be easier simply to disappear and leave a note. But that, he reflected, would be the harshest blow of all.

He thought of the note David had sent. There was something about it that nagged at him for a few moments, until finally it came to him. Of course, David couldn't have sent the note. That was impossible; it had been posted three days after he had died. But Johnny had told Aidan that the handwriting was definitely David's; there had never been any question of that.

'What do you think?' Sir Mark was asking him, jerking him back into the present. He managed to bluff his way back into the conversation, but soon found an excuse to leave and go back to his cottage.

Aidan's night was disturbed by constant playbacks of the terrifying minutes he had spent fighting the thundering sea that morning. He was mentally and physically drained, but he scarcely slept.

At seven the next morning, he didn't feel much better, but he was determined to go out and make the most of the horse he had worked so hard on. He felt he wanted to justify George's resentment, increase it, perhaps, to provoke the maximum reaction.

But first he walked up to the house. He went round to the courtyard at the back and into the store-room with the green door.

The clay-trap had been left there as he had asked. Aidan knelt beside it, this time to examine it thoroughly. He didn't know what he was looking for, until, from the iron cup which held the clays to be ejected, he picked out three or four white hairs. He rolled them between his fingers to feel their texture, and nodded to himself. Satisfied, he put them carefully into an envelope which he tucked into a pocket in his Barbour, got up and went back to the stud.

Sam Hunter had been quietly concerned that Letter Lad might boil over before his second race-course appearance. The horse was so eager to race again that he had barely walked a stride since returning from Sandown – and that was despite being ridden by a lad specially chosen for his patience.

Over the years, Sam had trained dozens of horses who had behaved in a similar way after their first run.

Usually, a few days spent walking on their own away from the string settled them down, but in Letter Lad's case, it hadn't worked. The boy who looked after him was convinced that his next race at Chepstow would relax him, and had persuaded Sam that it wasn't a real problem. It turned out that he was right.

When Sam walked across from the weighing-room to saddle him, Letter Lad was walking around the parade ring as quietly as a child's first pony.

Rain was beginning to spit from a low, grey sky as Aidan legged Jason into the saddle and wished him luck. To his surprise, Jason looked back and thanked him. A pang of envy passed quickly as he watched his favourite horse leave the paddock ridden by someone else; Aidan knew he had no choice.

The soil at Chepstow was clay. When it was wet, it clung to the horses' feet as at no other course in Britain, hampering their natural action. Horses that could normally handle soft going were often completely lost. For Letter Lad, it was like coming home. He'd been raised on the clay in Connemara, played and galloped through it with the other youngsters in all kinds of foul weather. Now he was cantering happily to the start in what had become a heavy shower.

Aidan, watching through his binoculars, felt proud as his horse moved sure-footedly down the track while the horses around him slithered and slipped. Letter Lad looked as if his strength had doubled since his previous race; he seemed totally in control of every muscle in his body.

As Aidan surveyed the other runners, he had seldom felt so confident of winning. Even from a distance, he sensed Letter Lad's arrogance. The horse seemed to be looking at his rivals with disdain. It wasn't just that he was much bigger than them, he also knew he was much better.

All that was needed now was for Jason to do his bit.

Aidan had told his brother-in-law to sit in about fourth or fifth to make certain that the horse settled properly, but the big roan was having none of it. Jason held him until the first flight, but that was it. Letter Lad put in a leap that took him straight to the front, and there he stayed.

From then on, he jumped and galloped his rivals into the ground. He didn't put a foot wrong, barely broke into a sweat, and came home in a common canter with his ears pricked.

When the initial excitement of Letter Lad's first win had died down and people were starting to think about the next race, Aidan slipped out to the car-park to use his mobile phone.

He keyed the number at Barford Manor. Sir Mark answered himself.

'Hello. It's David.'

'Well done! The horse ran a brilliant race. Jason did a perfect job. A wise decision. Congratulations!'

Aidan winced at the depth of feeling in the baronet's voice. 'Thanks. He'd a bit of luck, but it went more or less as we planned. The horse jumped really great.'

'Thanks to your schooling. I imagine George is pretty fed up?'

Aidan sighed. 'He doesn't look too happy.'

Sir Mark chuckled. 'Serve him right.'

'Look ... I wanted to talk to you this evening. I've something important to tell you and I wanted to sort of ... prepare you.'

There was a moment's silence before Sir Mark answered. 'I hope it's something I'd like to hear. It would be a pity to spoil your win.'

'It's something we have to talk about, and I can't put it off any longer. That's why I'm ringing, to give myself no excuses.'

'All right,' Sir Mark said with reluctance. 'We'll talk when you get back. There'll only be the family here anyway.'

Back in the bar, there was still a large group of celebrators. Sam Hunter had joined the party. He made his way over to Aidan as soon as he came back in.

Over Sam's shoulder, Aidan spotted George looking at him. For an unguarded moment, a look of undiluted hatred flashed from George's deceptively placid eyes.

'David,' Sam was saying, 'I've got to congratulate you again. To tell the truth, I wasn't half as confident as you, but that horse has definitely got some ability.'

'Listen, Sam, it was you who trained him. I don't know what you think, but it's my guess he'd probably get a longer trip if we wanted him to, and jump a fence.'

Sam looked at Aidan with a hint of doubt. 'A few more runs over hurdles first, though.'

Aidan nodded with a smile. Sam didn't like to be hurried. It had been hard enough to persuade him to run Letter Lad as early as he had. 'I hope we get the same breaks in the Hennessy.'

'You've ridden the course a few times now, and you

294

know most of the other runners. Provided Mischief gets there in one piece, he should give a good account of himself.'

'The only thing is, there may be an upset in my training,' Aidan said slowly. 'But I'll let you know in good time if I can't ride him.'

Sam looked shocked. 'Why the hell shouldn't you? You're all right, aren't you? You look fine – a bit peaky maybe.'

'There could be something coming on, let's say. But you'll find someone to give him a good ride.'

'I don't like saying this to an amateur, but I'm not so sure I'd find anyone to give him as good a ride as you.'

'Flattery helps, of course,' Aidan grinned. 'But I'll let you know, probably tomorrow.'

Sam shrugged. 'Leave it till the day, if you like.'

'We'll see.'

Victoria drove Aidan back across the Severn Bridge and down the M5 to Devon. She was still bubbling over at the day's success, not least at the part her husband had played. Aidan reflected what a great sister she'd been to him; he was hating the idea of losing her. But he was committed now.

He hoped he'd be able to put his mother's mind at rest about finding the funds elsewhere to pay for the care she needed. While he'd been in England, Aidan had become far more confident of his own skills. He was sure that even without the backing of the Tredington family, he'd already made enough of a name for himself to go out and earn a good living on the open market. Whatever was discovered about David Tredington's death, and the inevitable change that would make to his own circumstances, he was determined to do everything he could to make his mother's life bearable as the disease took its final hold on her. The proceeds from selling Letter Lad would see them both over the first few months.

Aidan and Sir Mark found an excuse to be on their own in the library when they'd finished dinner with Victoria and Jason.

Somehow, Sir Mark seemed reluctant to let the conversation begin. He fussed about, pouring whisky for them both, and carried on talking about Letter Lad's race.

Eventually, when they were sitting in front of the fire as they so often had, he seemed to accept the inevitable. 'Well, what's this burning topic you have to discuss with me?'

Aidan took a big gulp of whisky, and stood up. He didn't want to look at Sir Mark.

He walked across the room and gazed at the silver Saint George. He took a deep breath. 'It's very hard for me to tell you this . . .' he began. He turned round. Sir Mark was sitting quite still, with his glass in his hand, watching him. Aidan closed his eyes. 'I am not your son,' he said, slowly and deliberately. 'I am not David Tredington. My name is Aidan Daly.' He let out a long breath and opened his eyes.

Sir Mark didn't move, nor did the expression on his face alter. He looked back at Aidan. Slowly, he put his glass down and leaned back in his chair. 'Why have you decided to tell me this now?'

'Because . . . I've found David.' Aidan put his head in

his hands. Then he peered over them at Sir Mark. 'What's left of him. He must have been dead since the day he disappeared.'

This time Sir Mark reacted. He sat up and his face suddenly showed a strange combination of great sadness and relief. 'Thank God!' he muttered to himself. 'How do you know it's him? Where is he?'

'In Stanner Cave, beyond a rock bar across the back. Believe me,' he said emphatically, 'it is David. He must have been pushed over, and then someone blocked up the gap with some boulders: they've stayed fast in place ever since. Yesterday I prised one out and saw inside. The skeleton's lying there; I'd say it was untouched since the day it was put there.'

Sir Mark sighed. 'All this time ... We even searched the far end of that cave, under the pot-hole.'

'What pot-hole?'

'It's not a true pot-hole; it's a kind of chimney fault in the rock, about a hundred yards back from the cliff. The top of it's all covered with brambles now, has been for years, it's so dangerous. And we've never talked about it – don't want to encourage any intrepid oafs to kill themselves down it. I sent two men down, thinking David might have fallen into it, but, as I say, they only searched the area immediately below the chimney. There wasn't any question of his being nearer the front, because of the bar. No one's ever got over it, as far as I know.' Sir Mark thought back over the events around his son's death. 'What made you look there?'

'George. I followed him there yesterday morning. Something happened to me that made me think he knew more about David than he's ever let on.'

'What happened to you?'

'Someone tried to kill me when we were shooting on Tuesday.'

'Good God!' Sir Mark stood up, shocked, and walked across to where Aidan still stood by the inlaid round table. 'Who? Do you know?'

'Not for certain, but ... I don't know why exactly – just from a change in his attitude – I had a sort of hunch that George was involved. I had thought it might be Jason, or Ivor, especially when he turned up out of the blue on Tuesday to beat. I'm sure George had something to do with that. Later that evening, I saw him go into that store-room and take out the clay-pigeon trap. I asked Jan to see if she could find it at his place, and she brought it back here last night. It was in the store-room this morning.'

'But what's that got to do with it?'

'I'm not sure yet, but I'm working on it. Anyway, I'm certain now it wasn't Jason who shot me and if it was Ivor, it was because George put him up to it. Or it was George himself.'

'But where were you when this happened, for God's sake? And why didn't you say anything about it then?'

'How could I? I hadn't made up my mind to tell you the truth about myself. It was while I was on that solitary peg on the third drive. People just thought I'd had a crack at a couple of birds myself.'

'But ... why did George go to the cave?'

Aidan lifted his shoulders. 'I imagine to see if David was still there.'

'Do you think George put him there, then?'

'No. I don't. I think Ivor Butley did.'

Sir Mark shook his head in astonishment. 'But Ivor didn't kill him?'

'No, no. Ivor thought he'd fallen from a horse and come down the cliff, near the path, and smashed his head on the rocks at the bottom. He thought it was all his fault because he'd let your son out on a young horse you'd forbidden him to ride. I guess he panicked.'

Sir Mark shook his head slowly. 'Yes, he would have done, but why should George be interested?'

'Maybe he wants to prove I'm a ringer?'

'Maybe,' Sir Mark said thoughtfully, 'but we'll have to make certain.'

Although the news of David's discovery had taken a lot out of Sir Mark, he stiffened up, determined to make some clear decisions about how to deal with what he'd just heard.

'How did you know about Ivor hiding David's body?'

'Susan told me.'

'She knows about this, then?'

'Some of it. Her mother told her after her father was killed what had happened. But they didn't know what he'd done with the body, just that he'd got rid of it.'

'Right. We'll have to let George tell us how he knew.'

'I don't think he'll tell you. He might tell me, if I set it up right, but we'll need some independent witnesses. How about the police who've been investigating Ivor's death?'

Sir Mark looked at Aidan and nodded. 'You're right...' He paused. 'Aidan,' he added with a faint smile. 'But just for the moment, I think you'd better continue to be David, don't you?'

Aidan could hardly believe the calmness with which

Sir Mark had taken the news. He looked at the man who had been his father for the past two months; his affection for him had not diminished at all. 'I'm truly sorry about that, about deceiving you, and all the others. I couldn't go on doing it, knowing that the real David was lying down there under the cliff.'

'I understand that. And I'm grateful – more than grateful – for your honesty.'

'I'll accept whatever happens once we've got at the truth about your son.'

'I've no doubt of that. Are you prepared to tell me who put you up to the whole thing?'

'I'd rather not say. There'd be no point involving other people unnecessarily. I'll take the rap on my own.'

'Very noble of you, but there's only one person, besides George and my daughters, who could have prepared you so well, and that's Johnny.'

Aidan said nothing.

Sir Mark shrugged with a faint smile. 'I understand.'

The telephone beside him chirruped. He answered it, then passed it to Aidan.

It was Susan. 'I thought you might still be there,' she said to Aidan when Sir Mark had handed him the phone. 'I'm at Jan and Mike's cottage at Braycombe. George seems to have settled in for the night. I don't think he's going to go out again now.'

Aidan glanced at Sir Mark before he replied. 'And he hasn't been anywhere near the cliffs today?'

'No. He came straight back here after the races and hasn't gone out since.'

'OK. Will Jan let you stay the night?'

'Yes, of course.'

'Then stay there so you can keep your eye on him tomorrow. I'm not going to take any chances, though; I'm going to keep a watch on the cave tonight. Tell Jan to give him a message from me in the morning. He's to meet me at the Anchor in Lynmouth at midday. Tell her to stress that it's vital I see him. I'll ring just before to check that he's coming.'

Aidan shivered and huddled himself more tightly into his sleeping bag. He had found a dry niche, a draughtless cleft inside the cave.

He didn't think that George would come back down here in the middle of the night, but it was possible, and if the boy's skeleton were destroyed, the truth about his death would be lost for ever.

He dozed but didn't completely fall asleep. As a dull light gradually lit the silver-grey sea, he shook himself and looked at his watch. It was just after seven. Aching and exhausted after two nights without real sleep, he heaved himself back up the cliff track and across the fields to the phone-box by the layby. He dialled the Hardings' number. Jan answered sleepily.

'Sorry to wake you so early on a Sunday morning,' Aidan said cheerfully, 'but I need to speak to Sue.'

'Hang on.'

A moment later he heard Susan's voice. 'Hello?'

'Is he still there?'

'Yes. Unless he's walked. No cars have gone.'

'Good. Make sure he doesn't go anywhere before you've got my message to him. I'll ring back every half-hour or so to check.'

Aidan walked down the coomb to where he had

hidden the Land Rover, climbed in and sleepily drove home.

In his cottage he lay on his bed, trying to prepare himself for the confrontation that would take place that day. It was going to take all his wits to get the right result, unequivocally and in front of witnesses. In his exhaustion, his mind wandered to Sir Mark and the lack of animosity he had shown on being told that the man he had accepted wholeheartedly as his son was not; to Susan and the strength in her passionate eyes. Whatever happened over the next few hours, even if it meant he had to spend months in jail, he had one aim he was now confident he would achieve.

Chapter Thirteen

At eleven-thirty, Aidan telephoned Jan's house to speak to Susan again.

'What's going on?'

'It seems to have worked. Jan delivered your message, and he's just left in the BMW, looking really pissed off. I'm sure he's gone to meet you.'

'Let's hope you're right. Come up later this afternoon. We may have got somewhere by then.'

'Best of luck.'

Aidan nervously fingered his beer glass. He wondered what all these people in the pub were going to think when they heard the truth about him. They would despise him, probably, for taking advantage of the Tredingtons and making fools of everyone else.

George walked into the bar.

He saw Aidan. For the benefit of anyone watching, he managed to produce a friendly grin.

'Morning, David. I got your message.'

'Have a drink, George,' Aidan said.

'I thought you wanted to talk,' George muttered impatiently.

'I do, but not here.'

George nodded. 'I don't think I'll have a drink, then.'

Aidan drained his glass. 'I'll walk back to your car with you.'

George didn't speak until they were outside and there was no one within hearing.

'Well,' he said, with no pretence at friendliness. 'What the hell's so urgent?' There was a barely controlled nervousness in his voice.

'What I have to say has to be said very privately, just between the two of us. Go back to Braycombe and I'll ring you in an hour or so and tell you where to meet me.'

George glanced at him. Guilt and fear flashed in his eyes. 'What the hell is all this cloak-and-dagger stuff about?' he said, not making any attempt to disguise his anger now. 'I've only just come from there.'

'I know,' Aidan said patiently. 'But I wanted to be sure you understood the importance of what we have to discuss.'

'Look, whatever it is, I haven't got time to hang about all day. Anyway, what's so important and what's it got to do with me?'

'Things that happened, fifteen years ago,' Aidan said quietly.

George opened his mouth to speak, but stopped himself.

They had reached his car. George, uncertain and surly, let himself into it. Aidan had parked his Land Rover a few yards further along the road. He walked to it and climbed in. He waited before he turned the ignition key; he heard George's starter whine for a few moments without any response from the motor. Aidan grinned to himself. He had estimated that it would take a good twenty minutes for George to identify the trouble and get it put right on a Sunday morning.

Sir Mark met Aidan by a clump of brambles that covered the top of the deep shaft in the granite, a few hundred yards from the edge of the cliff behind Stanner Head. There were two men with him, in jeans and anoraks – a sergeant and a constable from Devon CID.

The sergeant seemed irritated. 'Sir Mark's told me what you're trying to do,' he said to Aidan. 'I'm not too happy about it. Do you think it'll work?'

'He'll come. He'd have been up here before if he'd had the chance. Now he thinks he's got an hour, he won't be able to keep himself away.'

'How long till he gets here?'

'Fifteen minutes, no more.'

'I have to tell you, sir, we shouldn't be doing it like this.' The sergeant appealed to Sir Mark. 'If there are human remains down there, the place should be sealed off and left to forensic.'

'For God's sake,' Aidan said, 'the man's on his way. If he sees you lot, he'll run a mile. This will be the only chance you'll have of getting a confession out of him. I've the measure of the man now, believe me.'

The detective believed him only reluctantly, but he nodded. 'Right. Let's get on with it then.'

The policemen had already cut back the vegetation to reveal the little-known crevice. They efficiently secured a rope around Aidan's waist. He gave them a nervous grin, pulled on a helmet lamp, and eased himself into the damp black hole. The two detectives took the strain and lowered him down a two-hundred-foot shaft. He only knew he was at the bottom when his feet touched a soft, sandy floor.

He knew from the maps that Sir Mark had shown him that he was about a hundred yards from the rock bar across the back of Stanner Cave. He gave the rope a tug to tell the men above him that he was safely down, and untied the rope from his waist.

With the light from his helmet and a hand torch, he looked around the cavern into which he had descended. He shivered in the cold, damp air and at the knowledge that no other human had been down here for the past fifteen years. And he knew that now no obstacles lay between him and the remains of the twelve-year-old David Tredington.

He set off along the narrow cleft in the rock, sometimes having to drop to his hands and knees to get through. After a few minutes, he saw a needle-point of light from the opening he had made above the bar two days before.

The policemen helped Sir Mark Tredington down the cliff path. They would rather not have had him with them, but then, it was the murder of his son they were investigating now. Besides, Sir Mark could be a difficult man to say 'No' to.

At the bottom of the path, one of the policemen glanced at his watch.

'If George does decide to come straight here, we haven't got more than a five-minute lead on him. It took longer than we thought to lower Aidan down the hole.'

'I'm sorry,' Sir Mark said. 'Let's run for it.'

'We'll have to stick to the bottom of the cliff, or he'll see our footprints.'

They set off, scrambling along the rocks and dry sand at the top of the beach, checking every few yards that they hadn't left any tracks.

As they entered the cave itself, where the sand was still wet, the younger policeman went last, brushing over their prints behind him.

They quickly identified the dark cleft in the western wall of the cave. Aidan had been right. It was comfortably deep enough for the three of them to sink right back out of sight, and wait.

The sergeant carried on up to the rock wall that barred the way to the cavern beyond. It took him only a moment to find a secure hiding place for a sensitive radio-mike he had brought with him. He switched it on and ran back to join his colleague and Sir Mark.

They didn't hear George coming until he was inside the cave. He was panting heavily. He ran straight past them towards the bar, waving a lighted torch.

A moment later, they heard him exclaim, 'Oh, shit!'

The sergeant activated the tape-recorder in his pocket and gingerly leaned forward around the buttress of rock to watch George.

Aidan was standing beside the skeleton, looking through the gap down the long tunnel of rock that ran up from the beach, when he heard George coming into the cave. Every nerve in his body came alive and he ducked back into deep shadow as George's torch flashed nearer and picked out the spot where Aidan had removed the boulder.

He heard the other man swear.

'Hello, George,' he said.

George spun round to look behind him, sweeping the rocky walls with his light. At the same time, he pulled a nine-millimetre Browning from his jacket pocket.

Even where he was, hidden and protected by the wall of rock, Aidan felt a sudden surge of fear crawl up his spine and tighten his bowels.

'You got here a bit sooner than I planned,' Aidan said.

This time George worked out where the voice was coming from.

He pointed the beam of his torch directly into the cavern, where Aidan stood, out of reach of the probing beam.

'What the hell are you doing here?' George hissed nervously.

'What do you think? A bit of archaeology, you might say.'

'Where are you? How did you get in there?'

'I think you should come and have a look what's behind here.'

'Why should I?' George blustered. 'I don't give a damn what's behind there.'

'You were anxious enough to get at it on Friday morning,' Aidan said with a hint of surprise.

'Look, you fucking Irish con-man. Whatever's there, you can't do anything about it – not without landing yourself in jail.'

'And you with me. It could be worth it.'

'Nobody can pin anything on me,' George was shouting now.

'Ah, that's where you're wrong. You haven't seen

what's here yet. D'you want a look? If you chuck that gun back down towards the front of the cave, and pass me through your crowbar which I left on the ledge there, I'm pretty sure I can get this last boulder out from behind, then you can pop your head through and take a look.'

'Will you stop fucking about. What is it?'

'You know damn well what it is. Ivor told you he'd put it there, didn't he? And you just couldn't be sure he hadn't told someone else as well...'

George was leaning against the rock now. The torch beam filled the aperture. Aidan pressed his back hard against the wall, so that George wouldn't be able to see him unless he got his shoulders through the gap.

'You'll not get through,' Aidan said. 'I didn't, and I'm not carrying half as much fatty tissue as yourself. If you want, do as I say, chuck away the gun and pass me the bar.'

'Where the hell are you, you bastard?'

'Now stop getting excitable. Just calm down and let's talk about this like grown men. We're both after the same thing. You know about me, and I know about you. I'd say there was scope for a little horse-trading.'

'That's something you should know about, you bloody tinker. I know damn well that you set me up with that Letter Lad – you and Henderson. Is he in on your scam? I'll bet he put you up to the whole thing. I know – he was in Ireland during the summer, and he was seen with you. It was obvious. I don't know why my uncle was such a fool as to be taken in.'

'You had the advantage of knowing I couldn't possibly be David though, didn't you?'

George didn't answer.

'Didn't you?' Aidan insisted more harshly.

Still George didn't answer.

'Because you killed him, didn't you? And then you lost the body and you never knew what happened to it, until Ivor told you he'd found it. Poor old Ivor, he thought the boy had fallen from his horse and come down the cliff, and that it was all his fault. But that's not what happened, is it? I can see that from in here. If Ivor had looked a bit closer at the body, he'd have realised there was more to it than that.'

'What the fuck are you talking about?' George shouted nervously.

'I've told you, I can open up the gap enough for you to have a look for yourself – see what David was clutching in his hand when he died.'

Aidan heard his quiet words echo away towards the mouth of the cave, and George breathing heavily.

'Oh God,' George sighed, subdued suddenly. 'He is there.'

'Why did you kill him, George?'

'He was an arrogant little prick. He thought he had it all, and he was going to get it all. He was just a spoilt brat. And he pretended to be all cut up about his mother, just to get his father to pay a bit more attention to him. He'd have been unbearable if he'd ever inherited Barford.'

'You felt you were a more worthy candidate, did you, even then, at the age of sixteen?'

'Yes, I bloody did.' George's voice was rising again. 'And I still do, and I'm not having it taken away from me by some fucking ignorant Irish gypsy.'

310

'I've already told you, you needn't lose it all. I'll keep quiet about you, and you keep quiet about me. We put the rock back in the hole I made, and poor little David can stay in here for ever. Now Ivor's dead, there's no one besides you and me knows he's here.'

'I'll see you rot in hell before I do any deals with you. Do you think I'd let the title go to a bloody nobody who's got no right to it?'

'Well, we seem to have reached a bit of a stand-off. You can't kill me in here, and you missed when you tried on the shoot. And when I get out of here, I may just have to talk to a few interested parties – about David, lying here, about Ivor, and about the clay-pigeon trap you forgot to clean off – how did you use it exactly? I couldn't quite work it out.'

'You're a fucking idiot if you think I'll let you out of there alive,' George snarled.

'The only problem there is that, if I go missing, or I'm found dead, Mr Edwards, that nice lawyer in Lynmouth, will open up the little package I've left with him in case of such an event, and that'll tell him where to tell the police to look for David's body. And you're never going to get in here to get rid of it. And,' Aidan went on as he heard George starting to speak again, 'they shouldn't have too much trouble tracking down the fella you got to spray the roof of my car that day at Fontwell. And maybe you'll get done for pinching those sleepers, too. You could be charged with the manslaughter of poor little Mickey Thatcher, maybe even murder, who knows?'

There was a pause before George spoke again. 'How long have you known?'

'Not long, only since I saw you coming here on Friday morning. Up till then you had me completely fooled. It's funny, now I realise why you looked so relieved when you first saw me. Maybe you had an idea David had somehow survived, and really had run away. But you knew I wasn't him.' Aidan paused a moment before he went on thoughtfully. 'I've been wondering how. Maybe there should have been some kind of a scar on him which only you knew about; from something you did to him the day you killed him. Of course, it doesn't show on these bones in here.'

There was a moment's silence.

'How the hell do you know all this?' George almost whispered.

'I didn't know that last bit. I was busking. But you couldn't blow the whistle on me, could you, so you tried to kill me?'

George laughed. 'This time I'll do it. I'll starve you out in there if I have to.'

'We'll see, but in the meantime, just tell me how you killed David.'

'I didn't. The cliff did. I just helped him over. I'm an opportunist, always have been, that's how I've made money. The precocious little prick did most of the damage himself, thinking he could handle that colt. It threw him off – Ivor was right about that – but he was fifty yards from the cliff-top. It was just chance I was up there shooting seagulls with my four-ten. There was no one around and we were out of sight of the coastguard station. I ran across to him; he thought I was going to help him up.' George gave a short grunt of laughter. 'But I smacked him on the head with the butt of my gun. He

312

struggled a bit but it didn't take much to drag him across to the cliff-top, and he bounced all the way down to the beach. I went down after him and carried him up this end, tucked him under the rocks to deal with him later.'

'And when you came back, he'd gone.'

'I thought the sea had got him. I hoped it had; a corpse then would have suited me much better.'

'But now it's a bit of an embarrassment, isn't it?' Aidan laughed. 'Do you know what'll make it a bit more of an embarrassment? When he was struggling with you, he must have grabbed a handful of your hair. He's still got it, as a matter of fact, clutched in his bony little hand. Pity you can't get in here to retrieve it, really. They'd have no trouble making a DNA match these days.'

There was a scrabbling sound as George tried to climb the rock-face again. This time, with a grunt, the top of his head appeared. He pointed the torch through the gap, followed by the gun.

Aidan, still pressed hard against the rock, waited until both were a little further in, as far as he judged they were ever going to get. He raised his hand, holding his own heavy-duty torch, and smashed it down on the dull metal snout of the automatic.

The Browning rattled down the rock and thudded on to the sandy floor beside the undisturbed skeleton.

'Fuck you!' George hissed as his head and the torch abruptly retreated.

Aidan stepped round to give himself a view through the opening. George stood glowering back.

Behind him, three figures had detached themselves

from the shadows and were advancing up the steep sloping floor.

George suddenly heard them and spun round.

'George Tredington, I am a police officer and I'm arresting you for the murder of David Tredington, and others. Anything you say will be taken down and may be used in evidence against you. Do you understand?'

Aidan was in the bedroom of his cottage, packing his sparse collection of belongings into the suitcase and rucksack with which he had arrived ten weeks before. He was trying to get used to the idea that he was no longer going to live and work at Barford; that all his actions and motives would be scrutinised by the courts and the press; that all the fame he had earned in the last two months would backfire, splattering the story of his deception across the front pages of every tabloid newspaper.

He had agreed that he would present himself for questioning at Exeter police station the following morning. He hadn't rung Johnny; there was no point now. Anyway, he hadn't the heart.

Every so often, he paused in his packing to glance out of the window at the ancient trees and green pasture that surrounded the house. Despite the gloomy sky, there was a gentle warmth to the scene. He was surprised how much he felt as if he were leaving home. And he was dreading breaking the news to his mother. She would understand – after all, she hadn't objected to the plan in the first place. But he had wanted to be able to assure her that he could still make a good living in English racing, even without the Tredingtons.

Now that he was faced with the likely consequences of what he had done, he wasn't so sure.

He heard someone let themselves into the small hall below. He dropped the pile of clothes he was holding and went down. Sir Mark was standing at the bottom of the stairs.

'What are you doing, Aidan?'

'I'm packing. I've booked a room at the Anchor for tonight.'

'There's no need for that just yet. Come on over to the house. The girls and I would like to talk to you.'

In all the commotion since George had been arrested, Aidan hadn't been alone with Sir Mark. In fact he hadn't seen anyone since a police-car had driven off carrying George – limp, sweating and grey-faced – in the back.

Now that he had to face the family on their own, he dreaded it.

Sir Mark said nothing more as they walked the few hundred yards to the manor house. He led Aidan into the library, where a fire of large logs blazed, glitteringly reflected in the brass fire-irons.

Lucy was sitting in an armchair, lounging back with a leg over one arm. Victoria sat more awkwardly on the front edge of a sofa.

'I've told Lucy and Victoria what happened today.'

Aidan nodded and looked, first at Victoria, then at Lucy. 'I'm sorry,' he said simply. 'I know that's not enough, after all you've done for me.'

Lucy met his gaze with a blank stare. 'I can hardly believe it, though, God knows, I was never utterly convinced you were genuine. I even went to your cottage and had a snoop round. I didn't find anything much, but something odd happened while I was there. Someone rang in to get your messages. It couldn't have been you. It was the day of your first race at Wincanton, and you should have been on your way down to the start.'

Aidan nodded. 'It must have been George. He lent me that phone. He must have been monitoring all my messages.'

Lucy was looking at him sceptically. 'I still think the whole thing's incredible – George killing David, and you pretending to be him. It's like something out of a Gothic novel. How could you do it?'

'Do you think I'm proud of myself? Accepting your trust, then betraying it? There were lots of times when I wanted to own up, but the longer I was here, the harder it was.'

'But what made you do it?'

'Believe me, I didn't want to at all at first, but,' he sighed, 'it seemed like a way of helping my mother. She's dying; she's not got more than a few years. There was no way I could have given her any comfort from what we were making on the farm.' Aidan drew a deep breath and tried to grin. 'And then there was the chance to be with the kind of horses I'd only ever dreamt about at home. I didn't really believe I could do it, but Johnny was so sure . . .'

'Johnny Henderson?' Lucy said sharply.

Aidan glanced at Sir Mark, who shook his head ruefully. 'I hadn't told her that bit yet.'

'The rat!' Lucy was fuming. 'After all the friendship we've shown him! I suppose he told you to pull that stunt with the guillemot's egg when you turned up here. I remember, he was here the day Davy went.'

'Oh, Lucy,' Victoria protested, 'you've always known what Johnny's like. I've often heard you say you wouldn't trust him further than you could spit.'

'And you don't know what his motives were either,' Sir Mark added.

'No, but I can guess.' Lucy made a face.

'Well,' Aidan said, 'I let him talk me into it, and when I got here, hardly anyone seemed to doubt my story. To tell you the truth, I was amazed, but it made me bolder, and after I'd been here a while, I loved it – having a family, a father even ... I can't tell you how grateful I've been for that, and how much I'm going to miss it.'

Victoria was listening to Aidan with wide, glistening eyes. She stood up now and crossed to where he stood. 'It's been great for us, too. For me, anyway, having a brother,' she said. 'I can hardly believe you're not. I mean, you're so like the family – except for being Irish, of course.'

Aidan looked at her affectionate face with embarrassment. 'Well, you'll be able to come and visit me in jail when it all comes out.'

Victoria stared at him with amazement. 'What do you mean, jail? For God's sake, they can't send you to jail. Who would ride Mischief in the Hennessy?'

Aidan couldn't help laughing. 'I've already told Sam he'll have to get a substitute.'

'But no one will give him as good a ride as you.'

'Well, there it is. What I did was wrong, and I can't claim the purest of motives. Frankly, I'm relieved to be able to look you all in the face and know I'm not lying to you.'

'Aidan,' Sir Mark said, 'sit down. Let me get you a drink. Black Bush all right?'

Aidan nodded and sat on a sofa opposite Lucy. He was confused and disorientated. This conversation wasn't going at all as he had expected.

Sir Mark handed him a glassful of Irish whiskey. 'I can't claim this is the happiest day of my life but, thanks to you, I now know the truth about David's death, and he can be properly laid to rest at last. Whatever your motives may have been, you showed your true colours when you found out what had really happened to David and didn't try to hide it from me. Obviously George's part in it all makes it particularly unpleasant, but if it hadn't been for your ... deception, we'd never have known the truth. So you see, I'm rather grateful to you. And there's no question of your going to jail. The police can't proceed against you without my cooperation and, so far, you've taken nothing from me. Your pay and conditions have been exactly those of any stud manager – if anything, you've been somewhat underpaid. It would be very difficult for the prosecution to prove a specific fraud without my cooperation.'

Aidan could hardly believe what he was hearing. He didn't want to speak, in case he found he was dreaming.

'And, as Victoria says, who would we get to ride Deep Mischief?' Sir Mark was still standing in front of the fire. He looked at Aidan for a moment. There was the ghost of a smile on his face. 'I think we'd better leave things as they are, just for the moment. Quite honestly, I'm not sure that I could cope with two scandals at once. I've told those policemen that I won't be pressing any charges against you. You won't have to go down to

Exeter tomorrow; they're coming here, and so is that chap from the Hampshire police.'

'What have they done with George?' Lucy asked.

'They've taken him into custody. He'll be formally charged, and appear before the magistrates tomorrow.'

'Will he get bail?'

'Facing a charge of violent murder? I doubt it. In any event, I certainly won't be standing it.'

Lucy was looking at Aidan. She laughed. 'I suppose Dad's right. It's wonderfully ironic. If you hadn't turned up to con us, George would have got away with it himself. And at least you weren't a complete bastard; you could have kept quiet about it and done a deal with George, or bumped him off.'

Aidan couldn't help smiling at her capitulation. 'Maybe I would have done, if I'd thought I could get away with it.'

'No,' Lucy said thoughtfully, 'you wouldn't.' She turned to her father. 'When are we going to announce to the world that David Tredington isn't David Tredington?'

'I suppose it will have to come out when George comes up for trial. But that gives us plenty of time to think about the best way of dealing with it.'

Aidan was unpacking again, a few hours later, when he heard a knock on his cottage door. He stiffened. He still couldn't reconcile his conscience with the way the Tredingtons were treating him, and he was expecting something to reverse it all.

He went down and opened the door to Susan.

She was wet from the rain which had been pouring

steadily for the last two hours. Aidan had been hoping to see her all afternoon, but she hadn't come up to the house. 'Jesus, you look like an otter coming up for air,' he said, opening the door wider for her. The wet did nothing to diminish her attractions. Her eyes gleamed from her dripping face and her hair hung in shiny strands.

'I ran out of petrol at the gates, would you believe it, and I didn't have a mac or anything.' She walked in. 'I've been to the house. Vicky told me roughly what's been going on; I had to come straight here to see you myself.'

Aidan took her hand and led her into his tiny sitting-room, where the woodburning stove he had lit half an hour earlier was drawing well and blasting out heat. He filled a glass with whiskey for her. She took it, gulped and spluttered. Aidan laughed. 'Sip it. I'll get you a towel – a couple of towels – and some dry clothes.'

He went upstairs and collected two bath towels and a long-tailed white cotton shirt of his own. Back downstairs in the sitting-room, he drew all the curtains and closed the door. 'We'll try and keep the heat in until you're a bit drier.' He sat down in one of his two armchairs, poured himself a drink and looked at her with a grin.

'You're in a very subtle mood tonight,' Susan said, undoing her blouse, turning her back on Aidan a little to undo her bra, dropping them in a damp pile in front of the fire. She wrapped one of the towels around her, just below her armpits, unzipped her jeans and wriggled out of them.

'Jesus, I don't know about you, but I'm getting very warm,' Aidan said huskily.

'Yes, well ... keep cool. You're still here, which is something, but what the hell else has happened? Jan told me George has been arrested, but Sir Mark told me to come and ask you what happened; he said it was all down to you.'

'I don't think he realised that you were convinced I was a ringer, right from the start.'

'How's he taken it, you not being David?'

'He's been amazing. I can hardly believe it. He's told me I can stay here: he's not pressing charges.' Aidan shrugged. 'I don't know what I've done to deserve it, but I'm still going to ride Deep Mischief next week.'

'It's that irresistible charm of yours,' Susan laughed.

Aidan's eyes lit up. 'Irresistible, is it?'

Susan shook her head and wrapped the towel more tightly around her. 'Not that irresistible. Can I go upstairs and change?'

'Sure.'

'I'll put all my stuff to dry in front of the Rayburn in the kitchen.'

She gathered up her wet clothes. Aidan watched her as she left the room.

When she came back down, wearing his shirt like a model on a cat-walk, she was looking more serious.

'Right. Tell me exactly what happened.'

Aidan relived all his experiences of the last three days, stumbling over the naked terror he had felt being trapped in the cave, and then, that morning, being confronted with George's Browning. As accurately as he could, he related the admissions he had extracted from George.

Susan hung on to every word until he had finished.

'When you first told me,' she said, 'I could hardly believe that George might have killed Dad, but I suppose he must have done, knowing he was the one person who could say where David's body was. But how did George kill him?'

'I told the police, I think the weapon was a horse's hoof.'

'But the Home Office pathologist has already said he couldn't have been kicked by the horse – the angle was wrong, and it was the wrong hoof.'

'But I didn't say he was kicked by a horse.'

Susan looked puzzled.

'Look,' Aidan went on, 'I'm not going to tell you what I think until the police come up with something firm, but I'd take odds of ten-to-one-on that George killed him. I'm sorry. It looks as though your Dad suffered years of guilt about David; and it was never his fault.'

'Poor old Dad.' There were tears in the girl's eyes. 'We all gave him such a hard time. If only we'd known.'

'At least you know now,' Aidan said softly.

Chapter Fourteen

Detective Sergeant King arrived soon after nine, looking pleased with himself. It had, he said, been a beautiful drive across the country. He had set off at six and watched the sun come up through the mist over Sedgemoor.

'We've got a result,' he said cheerfully. He produced a police photograph of a thin, wiry face and hostile eyes. 'Recognise this bloke?'

Aidan stared at the angry individual and shook his head.

'Didn't really think you would, but Dennis Knight's his name. He was the villain who sprayed your car. He finally admitted that George paid him to do it.' The detective laughed. 'We'd told him he'd told us – he hadn't, of course, but I'm going down to interview George in Exeter, and I'll be able to tell him what this bloke Dennis told us.' He tapped the photo with his forefinger. 'But first I want to run through your statement again, from start to finish, so's we haven't missed anything. I mean, we'll probably get a confession out of him, but the court likes to see a bit of corroboration after all these recent cock-ups. And the local nick wants to tie it in with the two murders they've got up here. Of course, they've got George on tape, admitting to the whole thing. That should do the trick, even though it wasn't double taped. Ours isn't so easy.'

'But what about the sleepers?' Aidan asked. 'When you came up here last week you said you had a line on where they'd come from.'

'We do, sir, but we can't tie them in to George yet. I can tell you what probably happened, though. He bought half a dozen of them and a small trailer. He drove it over and left it just outside Boarhunt – a small village near Fareham. When he left the races, he picked it up and drove to the roundabout above the motorway and sat there until he saw you coming, with the fluorescent marker to identify you. He heaved one of the sleepers over, just missed, but almost did enough damage, dumped the rest, scarpered, and dumped the trailer back in Boarhunt. That's where it was found. Forensic confirmed that it carried the sleepers, but they can't prove George handled it or towed it with his car. We've got one unsatisfactory witness so far. But you never know, we could get lucky. In the meantime, at least we've got Dennis. Now, if you don't mind, we'll run through your version again, just in case you missed something last time.'

When Sergeant King had left, Aidan went down to the yard to see the horses. As long as he was at Barford, he had a job to do. But he hadn't been at the stables long when the sergeant who had arrested George turned up.

'I've left the forensic lads down at the cave. They've gone down the way you did. They'll photograph the remains of the victim, then bag him up and take him back to the lab. They may find something else to nail

Cousin George. Not, of course, that he is your cousin,' the policeman added with an ambivalent grin. 'But you're a lucky man. Sir Mark says you haven't nicked anything off him, so we can't do much about you. That's up to him, I suppose. But we'll still need you as a witness.'

'OK.' Aidan shrugged. He would have to deal with the publicity this would generate when the time came, but if Sir Mark stayed on his side, he should get through it. 'What do you want now?'

'Just to check a few more things, like what made you first suspect George.'

'Let me show you something. I didn't tell you about it before, because I couldn't see how it was relevant. It's up in the back courtyard.'

Aidan led the policeman to the house and through the arch that led to the back door. But they didn't go into the house. Instead, Aidan opened the battered green door to the store-room. They both went into the unlit gloom. Aidan pulled the tarpaulin off the clay-trap.

The detective looked at it. 'Well? What about it?'

'I think George killed Ivor with it.'

The policeman looked at it sceptically. 'How?'

'Take a look at the end, where the clays are released.'

The detective leaned down and played his torch on the arm of the trap. He pulled a pair of tweezers from his pocket and carefully lifted something from it. He stood up and walked out into the daylight.

'A white hair.'

Aidan nodded.

'But Ivor was killed by a blow with a horse's hoof, or at least something shaped like it.'

'That's not one of Ivor's hairs; and a horse's hoof fixed on the end of the launch aim would pack a hell of a punch.'

The policeman looked more closely. 'A horse hair?' He smiled. 'Right, I'll take this for forensic. We'll get the trap dusted. I'll need your fingerprints to eliminate them. And I suppose we'd better look out for a horse with one hoof missing.'

'I reckon you'll find it's already been processed in George's abattoir.'

The detective looked at him sharply, annoyed he hadn't been aware of that possibility. 'We'll check that out. By the way, talking of hair, when you were down in the cave with George, you told him there was some hair clutched in David's, er, hand. Our boys haven't found a trace of it and, anyway, they say there's no way it could have lasted that long.'

Aidan grinned. 'I was just trying it on. I didn't know if it was possible or not, and I didn't reckon George did either. Lucky really, wasn't it, because it was after that that he confessed.'

The sun was setting in a haze of bright orange mist by the time the local police left Barford Manor that afternoon. David's skeleton had been examined minutely and photographed where it lay, before it was carefully dismantled for removal to the police laboratories. The clay-trap had been bagged up and taken, too, along with the tapes of a two-hour interview with Aidan Daly.

Aidan went back to the stables to see the horses bedded down for the night. Conflicting rumours of the events of the past seventy-two hours were being aired among the staff on the estate. Aidan wanted to tell the grooms in the stud the truth, too, but Sir Mark had been adamant that they maintain the status quo for the time being. Nevertheless, everyone seemed to know that Aidan had been responsible for trapping George, and that was cause for general approval.

And though he wanted above all to tell them that a culprit had been found for Mickey Thatcher's death, he knew he had to wait until the police were able to confirm their case.

He tried to act as if everything were normal, as if he hadn't been packing his bags to leave the night before, and as if he were still Sir Mark Tredington's son.

He was about to leave and go back to his cottage when Victoria appeared.

'Hi. Dad wants to see you,' she said. 'Come and have dinner up at the house later.'

Aidan nodded.

As he showered and changed, he found that he was still nervous about his reception. Although even Lucy seemed to have overcome her scepticism about his motives, the fact remained that he was a stranger, an attempted usurper in the family, and there was no good reason why they should tolerate his presence longer than it would take Sir Mark to decide how to avert another unpleasant scandal.

When he arrived at the house, he found that Lucy had gone back to London. Victoria wasn't around. Sir Mark was, as usual at this time of the evening, in the library.

He stood up when Aidan came in, offering him a drink as he had done most evenings over the months since Aidan had arrived at Barford.

Aidan detected a nervousness in the baronet's manner, and his heart sank. It looked as though Sir Mark had decided he was going to have to give him some bad news.

First, though, Sir Mark asked a question. 'Tell me, Aidan, how are you feeling about what's happened over the last few days?'

'Relief, mostly. Of course, I realise it must be terribly hard on you, having to face up to what happened to your son.'

'In one way that's been a source of relief to me too,' Sir Mark said. 'Though I was always pretty sure he'd been killed.'

Aidan gulped on his whiskey. 'But ... but surely, you thought he'd run away. Johnny told me about a letter he'd sent a few days after he disappeared, saying how unhappy he was.'

'It wasn't exactly a letter. I've got it here, as a matter of fact.'

He picked up a school exercise book of lined paper, opened it and took out a single sheet that was loose. It looked like a leaf from the book, but the top of it had been torn off, neatly, with a ruler. He passed it to Aidan.

Aidan took it and saw a few lines of tidy, boyish writing.

'I'm still missing Mum, as much as ever. I wish Dad hadn't been away so much. I feel I've got no one to talk to. The girls are too little, and just cry. I'll just have to cope with it without anyone.'

Aidan read it again and glanced at Sir Mark. 'That was the letter he sent?'

328

'That's what arrived in the post two days after he'd disappeared, post-marked Bristol.'

'And it was definitely from him?'

'There's no doubt that he wrote those words. This book was a sort of diary he kept. Some builders found it when we were having all the fireplaces taken out of the bedrooms. It was stuffed a few feet up the flue. That page was taken from this book.' Sir Mark opened the book at a point where a page had been carefully torn out. He handed it to Aidan. At the top of the pages on either side of the missing one, was written the day of the week and a date. Aidan stared at it, leafed some pages further on. 'This was written a few weeks before he disappeared.'

Sir Mark nodded.

'So you knew someone else had torn out the page and sent it?'

'I couldn't be sure. David was a curious, rather devious boy. It was always possible that he'd done it himself to confuse us, except for the fact that the book was so well hidden it was unlikely we'd ever find it. All my instincts told me David wouldn't have run away, though. I also had a lot of searches made, but they came up with absolutely nothing, not a trace, so I became even more convinced that he was dead.'

'Until I turned up, fifteen years later, claiming to be him.'

'No,' Sir Mark said with a faint, apologetic smile. 'I knew you weren't David, but I also knew that, if David had been killed by the person I had begun to suspect most, your appearance would very likely flush him out.'

Aidan stared at him. 'Jesus!' he burst out with a

329

laugh. 'You mean all the time I thought I was taking you in, you were using me ... to trap George?'

'Once I'd met you, I formed the opinion that someone as resourceful as you would stand as good a chance as anyone of dealing with it. Yes, reluctantly, I admit that I used you.'

'So, all along you knew I wasn't your son?'

Sir Mark looked into his glass for a moment. 'I didn't say that. I said I knew you weren't David.'

Aidan leaned forward in his chair, staring at Sir Mark, trying to take in what he was saying. 'I don't understand. What do you mean?'

Sir Mark stood up and walked across the room to one of the library shelves. He pulled out a book and opened it. From between its pages, he plucked a photograph. He glanced at it for a moment, then looked at Aidan.

Slowly, with an air of submission, he walked back towards Aidan and held out the photo.

Aidan took it. It was a grainy shot, taken with an old-fashioned, cheap camera. It showed a young woman, standing in front of a neo-gothic, monastic sort of a building, holding a child of two or three.

Aidan stared at it for a long time before he looked up at Sir Mark.

'How long have you had this?'

'Since shortly after it was taken.'

Aidan's heart almost stopped for a moment. He tried to speak but his throat was suddenly dry. 'Why?' he croaked.

Sir Mark sat down opposite Aidan and leaned back in his chair, gazing at his whisky as he swilled it around his glass.

'I met your mother just before I was married, in 1965. My brother, Perry, had organised a rather extravagant sort of stag party for me. He took a fishing lodge up on the Dee and asked the ten friends he thought I'd most like to see for four days' fishing and drinking. And when I say drinking, that's putting it mildly.'

Aidan gazed intently at the old man.

Sir Mark glanced at him, then looked away at the fire.

'There was an old Scots woman at the lodge, who did the cooking and so on. And there was a young Irish maid.'

'My mother?' Aidan whispered.

Sir Mark closed his eyes and nodded his head. 'She was a very pretty girl. My friends bet me.' He shrugged. 'I'd probably had a little too much to drink, but if she'd made it clear she didn't want me, I wouldn't have touched her, I can promise you that, on my word of honour.' He sighed. 'It was a wonderful night, but she knew, and I knew, I was getting married at the weekend; I was never going to see her again. But I never forgot her.'

He looked up at Aidan. 'It's extraordinary, isn't it, the huge ripples in our lives the smallest pebble can make. I often thought about Mary after that, though I loved Henrietta and respected her enormously. After a couple of years – I don't know why, on some whim, a rough patch in my marriage, a sense of guilt or something – I hired an agency to track her down. They brought me back this photo; they'd bought it from one of the other domestic staff there. I knew at once the child was mine.'

Now the words were out, Aidan got to his feet, almost trembling with excitement. He wanted to show Sir Mark what he felt in some dramatic way, but he couldn't yet. He walked around the room, shaking his head in amazement. 'Jesus! You mean ... God, I can hardly take it in.' He took a deep breath to force the words out. 'You're my natural father?'

Sir Mark nodded slowly, and a smile spread across his face. 'I knew it the moment I saw you. And, of course, I was expecting you.'

Aidan was mystified. 'Why?' he asked.

'Johnny had told me he'd found you.'

'Good God! You mean he told you about me, when he first saw me in Westport?'

'I mean, I told him about you when I asked him to try and track you down in Mayo.'

'I can't believe it. There I've been, racked with guilt about what I was doing to you, and all the time, you'd set the whole thing up, right from the start.'

Sir Mark nodded with a grin. 'Don't feel too guilty about it. I may as well tell you that you'd never have got away with it. Though I admit Johnny prepared you very well, and of course my acceptance of you removed most of the doubts anyone else round here might have had.'

'Jesus!' Aidan was laughing now at the bizarre irony of what had happened, and out of sheer happiness at knowing that this man really was his father. 'It's just incredible.'

His father was laughing, too. He stood and walked towards Aidan. When he reached him, he put his arms around him and hugged him tightly. After a moment he asked, 'Did you tell your mother where you were going when you came here?'

Aidan nodded. 'Now I know why she didn't mind. She knew.'

'I thought she might.' Sir Mark took his arm from around his son and stood back to look at him with pride and affection.

'But, Dad – thank God, I can say it without lying now – what about this fella who was supposed to have been shipwrecked somewhere in the South Pacific?'

'Johnny told me you'd found out about that. When I first heard about it, it worried me for a bit, but I was pretty confident there was nothing in it, and there's no doubt the chap had assumed the name deliberately before the yacht went missing. I think we'll find that George was behind all that. It just so happened he was getting impatient that we hadn't applied to the court for presumption of David's death, clearing the way to his inheriting the title, at least.'

'You think he set up the fella and rigged the boat being lost?'

'Yes, probably. I don't know for sure. By the way,' he said, looking oddly contrite, 'before we tell the girls about all this, I owe you an apology – not least for the fact that you nearly lost your life twice. I almost had to put a stop to it all after that crash, but at that stage the police seemed fairly sure it was an accident. When you told me George had shot you, I realised it had gone far enough, but we were nearly there, and you seemed determined to see it through. I also admit that I had set out to test you, in a way. And I couldn't be more proud of the result. Now,' he went on before Aidan could answer, 'go and find Victoria. We must tell her right away, she'll be absolutely delighted to hear you really are her brother. And pick up a bottle of champagne on your way back.'

The day the Hennessy Gold Cup was due to be run dawned grey and overcast. Aidan woke an hour before the light began to seep through the windows of his cottage. Since riding Deep Mischief on the gallops the day before, he had found it hard to control his excitement; the horse had been at the top of his considerable form. Aidan and his father had studied every performance of every other runner in the race. There were three who might have improved beyond Deep Mischief's rating, but Aidan's faith was undiminished. He had spent hours watching videos of steeplechases round the Newbury course to make up for his relative lack of experience of it. He felt he knew every yard of the running now, and he would ride as if his life depended on it.

The traffic making its way to Newbury race-course tailed back in long, trickling streams which converged on the large iron gates at the entrance. The first major steeplechase of the season always attracted a large, enthusiastic crowd.

Almost two inches of rain had fallen on the Berkshire course in the preceding week. The going on the chase course was distinctly soft. Aidan wanted to be absolutely certain he knew where to find the good ground. As he left the car-park, he turned up his coat-collar against the fierce wind which buffeted the marquees by the entrance, tugging the guy-ropes tight on their metal stakes. Whatever route Aidan planned for Deep Mischief, it would be as well to keep him protected from the gale. Three-and-a-quarter miles of racing into the wind could waste a lot of vital energy. He looked up at the sponsor's flag flying horizontally at the far end of the course. The wind would be blowing directly into the runners' faces as they headed up the straight. He would have to be sure that whichever horse he used as a shield was a safe jumper.

The Hennessy would be Aidan's first ride in a Grade One race. As he pushed his way through the crowd to the changing-room an hour before the first race, he was surprised by all the excitement around him.

Up until then, he had managed to keep fairly relaxed, not letting himself think about what the race meant or the sense of occasion with which it was held. But people he had never seen before reached out to wish him well as he approached the new weighing-room, and the adrenaline began to seep into his veins and his muscles began to tingle. His stomach felt empty. The pressure on him to succeed was almost all his own. As far as the punters were concerned, Deep Mischief had a good each-way chance at best; they wouldn't be looking for blood if he didn't win. But for his father's sake, he wanted to succeed as never before. He knew, too, that Sam Hunter would be very disappointed if he didn't do well, and Aidan didn't want to disappoint Sam: he had developed a great respect for him. The trainer had an aura about him that brought out the best in people, made them raise their game.

He dropped off his kit-bag and went to walk the

course. By the time he had completed the whole circuit, he had come to the conclusion that the faster ground was close to the inside. With no running rails on the far side, except on the bends, it would be possible to jump a fence and then pull slightly to the left so that Deep Mischief would be racing marginally off the course until he came back in for the next. That meant that he would only be sheltered from the wind on one side of the course, but Aidan calculated it was worth risking that for the sake of the better ground.

Sam's instructions were simple enough. 'You go out and enjoy yourselves.'

Aidan told him about his plans for dealing with the wind, but Sam didn't seem unduly worried about keeping the horse covered up.

'He's got no weight, so don't be afraid to let him bowl along in front if he's happy. It's harder to make ground in the wind than it is to gallop in it.'

Of the twenty other runners, Sam was concerned about only one, a strongly built mare called Kirsten who had finished third in the previous season's Gold Cup. She was big and only seven years old, so entitled to some improvement. On the strength of that, and despite carrying top weight, she had emerged as four-to-one favourite. Jason Dolton was riding a hardened old campaigner who had been made an each-way chance more out of nostalgia than form-book logic.

With three committed front runners in the race, the pace was bound to be furious, and as they set off from the start at the beginning of the back straight, Aidan found Deep Mischief struggling to hold a position. Aidan didn't want a repeat of the uncharacteristic sulking of his last race. He niggled away quietly at the horse, just doing enough to keep him in the running, but not letting him race so fast that it affected his jumping.

They had covered more than two miles before the murderous gallop of the leaders began to ease, and Aidan at last had a moment to catch a breather. Deep Mischief seemed to sense that he was getting on top of the others, and the boost this gave him renewed his enthusiasm.

The early pace had already wiped out any chances of winning for half the field. Three had fallen at the first ditch on the straight; another two had gone at the second fence on the final circuit. Others just couldn't keep up.

Aidan had stuck with his plan to use the good ground on the margin whenever he could. He had just moved off the course after jumping the penultimate fence on the far side when Jason moved up quickly to take his position. For a moment, Aidan was sure his brother-in-law wasn't going to let him back inside the next wing. Jason looked across at him like a chess-player holding a checkmate position. After a few strides, to Aidan's relief, he gave a half-smile and moved fractionally to his right to let Deep Mischief squeeze in.

Four more leaps put Deep Mischief where he wanted to be, without another horse in sight. His backers in the crowd may have been in the minority, but they were a very vocal minority. Deep Mischief heard them through pricked ears, and seemed to sense they were on his side. Aidan took a quick glance behind and grinned. He wouldn't even have to raise his stick.

It wasn't only the speed of Deep Mischief's finish that

blurred Aidan's sight of the winning post as it flashed by.

Once the first euphoria of victory had diminished, and Aidan's back was sore from the congratulations, he found a chance to walk down to the rails with Johnny, partly to watch the runners in the second last race take the water jump in front of the stands, but mainly because they wanted some privacy.

It was the first opportunity they had had of talking alone together since George had been arrested, and since all the revelations that had followed.

'Christ, you had me fooled,' Aidan grinned. 'I was beginning to hate you. It didn't occur to me once that you weren't a genuine chancer. It was a brilliant performance.'

'You didn't do such a bad job yourself.'

'That's rubbish. Dad said I'd never have got away with it if he hadn't accepted me.'

'Your sisters did. All the locals did.'

Aidan shrugged. 'I'm not so sure. Still, I'm bloody glad it's over. I hope I never have to live through another two weeks like the last two. But Dad's been brilliant about it.'

'So I hear. I hope I can continue to count on your custom.'

'I dare say I'll need the odd old knacker from the west of Ireland,' Aidan laughed. 'By the way, he never told me what kind of arrangement he had with you.'

'I only really did it for the crack,' Johnny grinned. 'I had a long talk with Mark over Goodwood. We were staying in the same house-party. When he told me he was worried about his health and he wanted to sort things out in case he got worse, he also told me about your existence. Actually, bringing you over was partly my idea. He gave me all the back-up I needed and, as it happens, he's shown his appreciation in a way that could only be described as generous. And Lucy's promised to help in my pursuit of Emma, now I gather your interests lie elsewhere.'

Aiden's face rippled into a grin. 'That's for sure.'

Aidan drove straight from Newbury to Heathrow, to catch an Aer Lingus flight to Shannon.

When he had landed in Ireland, he hired a car and took the road through Ennis towards Galway. As he drove through the soft misty drizzle that drifted in off the Atlantic, he contemplated the extraordinary changes that had taken place in his life in ten short weeks.

He was the same man, in the same body, but he had undergone a complete metamorphosis, as if he had finally burst out of a chrysalis shell.

And though he was happy to see the soft brown-green hills and lush, lake-strewn pastures of his homeland, he knew that his future belonged to England.

His mother had almost sounded relieved when he had told her, somewhat obtusely over the phone, what had happened. He had thought that in some way she would feel betrayed, but she had protested little, only asking him to come and see her as often as he could manage it. He had arranged at once to fly back to Ireland.

When he saw her, he was worried by the decline in her since he'd last seen her ten days before. It was clear that every movement she took caused her pain. But mentally, spiritually, she was as strong as ever.

Her neighbour's daughter had moved in full-time to help her, until a more professional arrangement could be made. The girl, Maeve O'Keane, in her twenties, was gentle and kind, and censorious of a son who could have gone off and left his mother like this. But when they were eventually left on their own in the house, Mary made it clear to Aidan that she didn't support this view.

'Aidan, if you knew how I've enjoyed reading about you in the papers,' she said, 'even though I couldn't tell anyone around here that it was you.'

For a moment, Aidan didn't answer.

'You knew,' he said, 'as soon as you heard the name Tredington.'

'Of course. And I trusted in God that the truth would be revealed to you, if it was . Iis will.'

'It's funny really,' Aidan mused, 'I made a complete fool of myself, thinking I'd taken Dad in. He's a canny old fella.'

'He was a fine young man. I stayed in love with him for years. Somehow, I found the strength to cope with the shame, and the hardship, at first for him, then for you.'

'I understand why you couldn't ever tell me. You weren't to know that he would want to find me again.'

'I always thought he might, though.'

'He's an honourable man,' Aidan nodded. 'He told me he'd never forgotten you. I think when he realised that he might not have too long to live himself, he wanted to put the record straight, before it was too late. You know, he offered a house for you, back in Devon, but I told him you wouldn't want to leave here.'

'I would not, and besides, there'd be no purpose in trying to put the clock back that far. It's better that we never see each other again. Both of us on the way out – it would be too miserable. No, I shall be happy staying here, just so long as you come and see me every now and then.'

Aidan looked into her brave eyes. Now that he knew the secret she'd been keeping for so long, his regard for her was limitless.

'Well, your trust paid off,' he admitted. 'The result of my mission couldn't have been more different than I planned with Johnny Henderson. I feel terrible, though, that it led to the death of a young lad – a real keen young horseman – and poor old Ivor Butley.'

'Was he something to do with this Susan you've been telling me about?'

Aidan nodded. 'You'll like her. She's a real strong girl, no side to her, and the loveliest thing you ever set eyes on.'

His mother smiled. She'd almost lost hope of her son setting his eyes on a girl long enough to become committed.

'You bring her out here to see me now.'

Aidan accepted that his mother could never move far from home again. 'I will,' he said, then, more briskly, 'I'm into Galway tomorrow to sort out the nurse and everything for you. We'll let the ground to Eamon O'Keane. You'll not want the bother of the animals. And everything else you need will be taken care of by the lawyer in Galway. You're not to worry about a thing, now.'

Mary smiled. 'That's all fine, but the best thing is

knowing you've found yourself at last. You're a changed man, Aidan Daly.'

'David Aidan Tredington, I'll be, at the end of the month.'

'And so you should. That'll keep the wagging tongues busy around here. Old Sean MacClancy from Westport was telling some tale he'd heard from his brother Emmot. You remember Emmot? He was the odd-job man at the convent. It seems he realised who you were from something he'd read in the papers.'

'Yes,' Aidan nodded with a rueful smile. 'I remember Emmot MacClancy.'

Over the following week, Aidan made arrangements for his mother's care. He and his father had agreed that she would know nothing of the trust that was to be settled on her, of which Aidan was sole trustee.

But all the time he was there, among the soft hills he had known most of his life, part of him longed to be back in England.

Mary showed no signs of trying to keep him as he said goodbye to her and promised to be back soon. He flew to England the next Saturday with an easy conscience, and drove back to Barford feeling that he was finally entering his new world, rightfully and for good.

He parked his car outside the front door and let himself in. In the hall, all he could hear was the deep ticking of an ancient long-case clock that had stood there for two hundred years.

A slit of light showed beneath the library door. His heels clicked across the oak boards as he walked towards it.

He pushed the door open.

'Welcome home!'

Lucy, Victoria and Sir Mark were standing expectantly as they shouted their greeting. Susan and Jason stood in the background. Even Jason was smiling.

Aidan stopped and grinned. 'Hello, Dad, sisters.'

Later, after a celebration dinner that had left his face aching with too much laughter, he let himself into his cottage and went upstairs to change. He had removed his final sock when he heard a rapid knock at the door. Tired but cheerful, he wrapped a towel robe around his naked body and went down to see who it was.

Susan was standing outside, soaked again.

'D'you know,' Aidan said. 'I think it's about time you bought yourself a brolly.'

Susan grinned and slipped past him into the hall.

'I'm afraid there's no fire going this time for you to dry your clothes,' Aidan said.

'You get that Rayburn going. They'll be dry in the morning.'

'You're a wicked temptress.'

Susan reached forward and took hold of the tie around his robe. Slowly she unknotted it. The robe fell open. She slipped her arms inside it, wrapped them around him, and squeezed herself to him.

'Now it's my turn to welcome you home,' she whispered.

More Crime Fiction from Headline

JOHN FRANCOME

BREAK NECK

'Francome writes an odds-on racing cert'
Daily Express

When apprentice jockey Rory Gillespie abandons his fiancée Laura Brickhill, in favour of trainer's daughter Pam Fanshaw, it's a decision made from ambition not love. And Rory has to wait ten years before Laura will forgive him.

Now one of England's leading trainers, and married to property tycoon Luke Mundy, Laura asks Rory to ride her best horse, Midnight Express, in Cheltenham's Two Mile Champion Chase. Shortly afterwards, Luke is killed on one of Laura's horses and she is arrested for manslaughter. Rory won't desert her this time and, setting out to prove Laura's innocence, he discovers that there is more than one person who will benefit from Luke's death.

Packed with intrigue and excitement, the plot unravels at breakneck speed, revealing bribery, blackmail and corruption as ingredients in this highly accomplished racing thriller.

FICTION / CRIME 0 7472 4704 8

JOHN FRANCOME

OUTSIDER

'Francome writes an odds-on racing cert' *Daily Express*

'Spirited stuff' *OK magazine*

'Pacy racing and racy pacing – John Francome has found
his stride as a solo novelist' *Horse and Hound*

Already a leading jockey in his home country, Jake
Felton comes to England to further his career and
avoid confrontation with New York's racing mafia.
But his plans to combine the life of an English squire
with that of a top-flight jockey look like coming to
a sticky end when he falls victim to a series of
accidents that begin to seem all too deliberate.

Aided and abetted by typical English rose Camilla
Fielding, Jake discovers that he's been targeted by a
ruthless and professional killer. And now he urgently
needs to find out why . . .

With an intricate and thrilling plot and all the drama
and excitement of Derby Day, *Outsider* shows John
Francome at the top of his form in this new novel of
danger and skulduggery on the race track.

'A thoroughly convincing and entertaining tale' *Daily Mail*

'The racing feel is authentic and it's a pacy, entertaining
read' *The Times*

FICTION / CRIME 0 7472 4375 1

Now you can buy any of these other bestselling books by **John Francome** from your bookshop or *direct from his publisher*.

FREE P&P AND UK DELIVERY
(Overseas and Ireland £3.50 per book)

Safe Bet	£6.99
Tip Off	£6.99
Stud Poker	£6.99
Outsider	£6.99
Stone Cold	£6.99
Rough Ride	£6.99
High Flyer	£6.99
False Start	£6.99
Dead Ringer	£6.99
Break Neck	£6.99
Blood Stock (with James MacGregor)	£6.99
Declared Dead (with James MacGregor)	£6.99
Eavesdropper (with James MacGregor)	£6.99
Riding High (with James MacGregor)	£6.99

TO ORDER SIMPLY CALL THIS NUMBER

01235 400 414

or e-mail <u>orders@bookpoint.co.uk</u>

Prices and availability subject to change without notice.